the
Granddaughter

the

Granddaughter

A NOVEL

Bernhard
Schlink

TRANSLATED FROM THE GERMAN
BY CHARLOTTE COLLINS

HARPERVIA
An Imprint of HarperCollins*Publishers*

"The Moon is Risen" by Matthias Claudius.

English translation © 1916 Margarete Münsterberg

"Autumn" by Friedrich Hebbel.

English translation © 2022 Sean Thompson

HarperCollins books may be purchased for educational, business, or sales promotional
use. For information, please email the Special Markets Department at
SPsales@harpercollins.com.

Originally published as *Die Enkelin* in Germany in 2021 by Diogenes Verlag AG.

FIRST EDITION

Designed by Input Data Services Ltd, Bridgwater, Somerset

Library of Congress Cataloging-in-Publication Data has been applied for.

ISBN 978-0-06-329523-0

24 25 26 27 28 LBC 5 4 3 2 1

the
Granddaughter

Part One

I

He came home. It was ten o'clock: he didn't close the book-shop until nine on Thursdays, and at half past, after lowering the grilles in front of the shop windows and door, he had taken the half-hour route through the park, which was longer than walking along the street, but refreshing at the end of a long day. The park was overgrown, the rose borders covered in ivy, the privet hedges untrimmed. But it smelled nice, of rhodo-dendron, lilac, lime blossom, of mown grass or wet earth. He took this route in summer and winter, in good weather and bad. By the time he got home, the irritation and worries of the day would have fallen away.

He lived with his wife in an art nouveau building several storeys high; they had the grand main-floor apartment, bought cheaply decades ago and now worth a lot of money – provision for their old age. The wide staircase, the curved banister, the stucco, the plaster relief of a nude whose long hair wound its way up the walls of the staircase – he liked to step inside the building, to climb the stairs to his apartment and unlock the door with its stained-glass panel of flowers. Even though he knew what would await him.

Birgit's coat lay on the floor in the hall, with two shopping bags of food that had toppled over. The living room door stood

3

open. Birgit's computer had slipped from the sofa to the floor, along with the woollen blanket she liked to put over herself. Next to the wine bottle, the glass had been knocked over and had spilled red wine onto the rug. A shoe lay in the doorway, the other by the tiled stove; presumably Birgit had simply pulled off her shoes and flung them aside, as she often did.

He hung his coat in the wardrobe, placed his shoes by the chest of drawers and went into the living room. Now he saw that the vase of tulips had fallen over as well; the broken shards and wilted flowers lay in a pool of water beside the grand piano. He went from the living room to the kitchen. An empty packet of chicken rice lay next to the microwave, and Birgit's half-finished plate sat in the sink with the plates from the breakfast they had shared. He would have to mop and wash and tidy everything up.

He stood there, feeling the anger in his belly and in his hands. But it was a weary anger. He had felt it rise and subside too many times. What was he meant do? If he confronted Birgit angrily the next morning, she would give him a look, embarrassed and defiant, then look away and tell him to leave her alone, she'd only had a little drink, wasn't she even allowed a little drink, how much she drank was her own business, if it bothered him that she drank, he could leave. Or she would burst into tears and humiliate and excoriate herself until he comforted her, said that he loved her, that she was OK, that everything was OK.

He wasn't hungry. Birgit's leftover chicken rice was enough for him. He heated it in the microwave and ate it at the kitchen table. Then he unpacked the shopping and put it away in the fridge, carried the wine bottle and glass, shards and wilted flowers from the living room to the kitchen, mopped up the water, squeezed lemon juice onto the red wine stains in the rug, closed the laptop, folded the woollen blanket and washed the dishes. A small room, once the pantry, now the laundry room, led off the kitchen; he transferred the contents of the washing machine to the dryer and the contents of the laundry basket to the washing machine. He boiled water, made tea, and sat down with his tea glass at the kitchen table.

It was an evening like many others. On some evenings, when Birgit had started drinking early, there would be more than just two bags and a wine glass on the floor, and more than just a vase in pieces. On other evenings, when she had drunk her first glass not long before he got home, she would be cheerful, talkative, affectionate; and if it was not wine but champagne, she was vivacious in a way that made him both happy and melancholy, like all good things that you know are not right. On these evenings they would go to bed together. Otherwise, when he got home she would often already be lying in bed; or she was lying on the sofa, or on the floor, and he would carry her to bed.

Then he would sit on the stool by her dressing table, looking at her. The wrinkled face, the withered skin, the hairs in her nostrils, the saliva in the corners of her mouth, the cracked lips. Sometimes her eyelids would twitch, her hands fidget; she would say nonsensical words, or groan or sigh. She snored, not so loudly that when he lay down beside her later on he couldn't sleep, but loud enough that he had difficulty falling asleep.

He also had difficulty with her smell. She smelled of alcohol and acid reflux, and sometimes it was acrid in a way that reminded him of the mothballs his grandmother used to put in her wardrobes. When she threw up in bed, which fortunately didn't happen very often, he would open the windows wide and hold his breath while he cleaned her and the bed and the floor beside the bed, taking deep breaths at the window in between.

But he never skipped that moment on the stool. He would look at her and see in her ravaged face the unblemished one of her good days, which could look so different in different moods that it sometimes bewildered him, but which always, even when sleepy, exhausted or bad-tempered, was full of life. How lifeless her expression was when she had been drinking! Sometimes, her earlier faces appeared in the present one: the determined face of the blue-shirted student; the face of the young bookseller, careful, subdued, often – to him – both mysterious and enchanting; her face after she had started writing, concentrated, as if she was always thinking about her novel or could never get it out of her head; her rosy face when she, who had taken up cycling late in life and liked to go off on her bike for an hour or more, came home.

She had an old face. But hers was the face he loved. The face he wanted to talk to, that he wanted to talk to him, whose warm brown eyes warmed his heart, whose laughter made him laugh; the face he liked to take in his hands and kiss, the face that moved him. She moved him. Her search to find her place in life, the secret she made of her writing, her dream of late success, her suffering with alcohol, her delight in children and dogs – in all this there was much that was unfulfilled, could not be fulfilled, that moved him. Was compassion a lesser form of love? Perhaps, if that was all there was. It wasn't all there was for him.

When he rose from the stool, he was never reconciled. He never stopped wishing things were different. But he was calm. This was just how it was. He went into the living room, sat down on the sofa, and read newly published books: the inexhaustible stream of new books was the reason he had become a bookseller.

2

On this particular evening, though, when he went to the bedroom to sit with her, she was not in bed. He went into the hall and up the stairs to the maid's room over the kitchen. It was narrow and low-ceilinged, the window was small and opened onto the courtyard at the back, but Birgit liked the low narrowness of it; she liked the two doors, one at the bottom and one at the top of the stairs, and had made this little room her study. He knocked; Birgit didn't like to be disturbed, certainly not surprised, by him. She didn't answer, and he opened the door. The desk was tidy: a pile of paper on the left, the fountain pen he had given her as a present years ago on the right. A note in her handwriting was pinned next to the window. He knew he shouldn't read it. 'You have . . .' He didn't read on.

He found Birgit in the bathroom. She was lying in the bath, her head beneath the surface of the water, her dark hair clinging to the sides of the tub. He lifted her head; the water was cold; she must have been lying in the bath for hours. He pulled her up far enough to be able to rest her head on the edge of the bathtub. In a modern tub she wouldn't have been able to slip below the surface of the water. Why didn't they have a modern tub! They had both cherished the luxury of the long, deep art nouveau bath, had enjoyed bathing in it together, and had had it restored at some expense.

He stood and looked down at Birgit. At her breasts, the left a little bigger than the right, at her stomach, with its scar, at her outstretched arms and legs, at her hands, which seemed to be hovering, palms down, above the floor of the tub. He remembered her wish, often expressed and never realized, to have her left breast reduced; his fear when her appendix became inflamed and was removed; her piano-playing, which her long fingers should not have given up. He looked down at her and knew that she was dead. Yet at the same time it was as if he would be able to tell her, later, that he had found her dead in the bath, and talk about it with her. As if she were only dead right now; not for long, not for ever.

He had to call the emergency services. But it wasn't an emergency; there was nothing to be done. And he dreaded the commotion; the ambulance driving up with blue lights and siren and stopping outside the house; the stretcher bearers; the police, who would secure evidence and question him; the inquisitive caretaker in the basement apartment. He sat down on the edge of the bath. He was glad Birgit had closed her eyes. Had they been open, Birgit staring at him with a fixed, empty gaze – the thought horrified him. They would have been open if Birgit had been surprised by a heart attack or stroke. No: she had fallen asleep. Just like that? Had she simply drunk too much? Or had she taken something as well? He stood up, went to the medicine cupboard, and couldn't find the Valium that was kept there. He flipped up the lid of the little waste bin with his foot. There was the box, and the empty blister pack. How many pills had there been in the pack; how many might Birgit have taken? Did she just want to make sure she fell asleep? Or did she not want to wake up? He sat down again on the edge of the bath. What did you want, Birgit?

He had known about her depression for years. Again and again he had tried to get her to go to a therapist or psychiatrist; he had friends who had alleviated their depression with therapies, or suppressed it with pills. But she hadn't wanted to. She didn't have depression; there was no such thing as depression. There were melancholy people, there always had been, and she was one of them. She didn't want medications that would turn her into a different person. The idea that everyone had to be balanced and optimistic was just modern foolishness. And it was true that, even when she wasn't depressed, she was more thoughtful, more serious, more heavy-hearted than others. Not that she couldn't laugh at an amusing incident or comment. But the playful lightness, the ironic superiority with which people in their circle of friends and colleagues discussed books and films, society and politics, was alien to her; still more alien was the way politicians and artists failed to take themselves and what they did seriously, but were content for it just to attract attention – astonishment, laughter, displeasure, attention of any kind. If a thing was serious, she took it seriously. Only later, after the Wall came down, when he became better acquainted with booksellers from East Berlin and Brandenburg, did he understand that in this Birgit was a child of East Germany, of the GDR, of the proletarian world that, with Prussian socialist fervor, yearned to be bourgeois and took culture and politics seriously, as the bourgeoisie had once done and had forgotten how to do. Since then, he had looked at her with new eyes: with admiration, and sorrow for what his world had forgotten, what it had lost.

No: her melancholy had not driven her to suicide. It, and the red wine, one glass after another, had made her tired. And then she had not wanted to wait for sleep to arrive; she had wanted to make it come to her. And she had made it come, and it had made her succumb. Why couldn't you wait, Birgit? But he knew that she was impatient. It was why she had no time for the taking off of shoes and the unpacking of shopping and the washing-up and the laundry. Death by impatience.

He laughed, swallowing his tears. He stood up and called the ambulance. Then he called the police. Why wait for the ambulance staff to do it? He wanted to get it over with.

3

It all took two hours. The ambulance came and went. The policemen, two in plain clothes and two in uniform, secured the scene and collected evidence. He described to the detectives how he had found Birgit, explained why he had washed up the glass she had drunk from, showed them the box and the blister pack in the little waste bin, and watched as they searched in vain for a suicide note. They called an undertaker, who packed Birgit into a body bag and took her to forensics. They asked him what time he had found Birgit, and what he had been doing that afternoon and evening. When he answered that he had been in the bookshop until nine o'clock, as his colleagues and customers could testify, they grew friendlier. Would he please come by police headquarters the following day?

He escorted them out of the apartment, closed the door and slid the chain across. He didn't know what to do. He couldn't sleep, couldn't read, couldn't listen to music. He wished he could cry. He went into the laundry room, transferred the dry laundry to the kitchen table and loaded the wet into the dryer. When he found himself holding a T-shirt of Birgit's, one she had liked and often worn, he couldn't face it any more and left everything where it was.

He went upstairs to Birgit's study, entered and sat down at the desk. This time he read the whole sentence. 'You have what a harsh God has given you.' Who had said that? Why had Birgit written it down? Why had she pinned it up? What was it supposed to remind her of? He drew the pile of paper towards him. It was a manuscript; he recognized the author's name as that of a woman who had been in Birgit's writing group. But he didn't want to read something by some woman he didn't know; he wanted to read something of Birgit's. He opened the desk drawers one after another. The top one held blank paper, all sorts of pens, rubbers and pencil sharpeners, paper clips and rolls of sticky tape. In the bottom two he found folders with typed pages, some only a few lines long, some with long paragraphs; notes in Birgit's handwriting, letters, newspaper cuttings, photocopies, photographs, brochures. The folders were not labelled, and their contents seemed not to be in any particular order. But he knew Birgit; the disarray must be deceptive, the different folders must represent different concepts or aspects or chapters of her novel for which their contents were relevant. But he couldn't concentrate, and he couldn't see what the order might be.

In among the folders was a postcard. It was of *The Chocolate Girl* by Jean-Étienne Liotard, in the Old Masters Picture Gallery in Dresden. He turned it over. The card had a GDR stamp and no return address. 'Dear Birgit, I saw her the other day: a happy girl. She looks like you. Paula.' He turned the postcard over again and examined the chocolate girl more closely. He couldn't see any resemblance. Watchful, yes; Birgit could look watchful, too, but she didn't have this sharp nose or this sharp mouth. And happy – no, the chocolate girl didn't actually look happy.

It occurred to him that there were no pictures of Birgit in the apartment, or on his desk in the bookshop. Some of his friends had photo galleries on their apartment walls, framed in silver and black and hung above chests of drawers: pictures of their wedding, of holidays and trips, of their parents, their children. He and Birgit had no children. And there were no pictures of their wedding in 1969; they had been a bit embarrassed about it, because in their friends' eyes it was an outdated ritual, so they had avoided making a fuss. They didn't take photos. He slipped his wallet out of his trouser pocket and checked that Birgit's passport photo, which he had carried around for years, was still in there, with his vehicle registration document and driving licence. He would arrange to get it copied and enlarged.

He didn't find what he was looking for in Birgit's desk. There was no manuscript in any of the drawers. In the bottom one was a bottle of vodka, and he drank from it as he went on searching in the bookcase on the narrow wall of the study. He fell asleep on the floor as day began to break, and was woken soon afterwards by birdsong. For a moment he didn't know where he was. For a moment he didn't remember what had happened the previous day. Then memory returned, flooding first his head, then the whole of his body. Finally he was able to cry.

4

It was weeks before he went into Birgit's study again. He couldn't clear out her things: not the coats and dresses from the wardrobes, not the underwear from the chest of drawers, not the hairbrush and bottles and jars from the dressing table and the cosmetics cabinet over the basin, not her toothbrush from the beaker. He didn't open anything that contained her belongings, not even the study. It was inconceivable to him that a man might bury his face in his dead wife's clothes and inhale her smell, as he had once seen someone do in a film. Seeing or touching or smelling her things – it was more than he could bear. His surroundings, where Birgit ought to have been and was not, already made him suffer enough. He suffered in the apartment and he suffered in the bookshop and was thinking of giving both of them up. But because he also suffered when walking around, he couldn't really believe in a new start in a new place. Birgit would accompany him wherever he went. Wherever he was, she would be all around him and she would not be there.

Then a letter arrived from the Baden publishing house. The publishing director, Klaus Ettling, introduced himself as a friend of Birgit who had been corresponding with her for a long time and had taken an interest in her work. He hadn't read much of her writing, but he admired the few texts he had seen, and had often spoken to her about other texts, and about her novel. He expressed his sorrow and condolences. And he enquired after Birgit's manuscript, finished or unfinished. Unfinished books, like unfinished symphonies, could still reveal consummate mastery and delight the public.

He knew the Baden publishing house. A small publisher with a good list, and attractive books that he enjoyed displaying and selling in the bookshop, while also wondering whether they actually made a profit. He had never met the publishing director. How had he and Birgit got to know each other?

He looked at Birgit's photograph. She looked back, with an indeterminate gaze; the photograph, enlarged, was still a passport photo. But her dark, curly hair was pinned up, which he liked; her face was fuller than in recent years, more feminine, more inviting; the corners of her mouth were turned up in the hint of a smile, and her brown eyes had a startled expression, blinded, perhaps, by the flash, not alarmed but pleased, as if she had just had a nice surprise. What texts did you send him? What were the other texts you told him about?

The letter had arrived on a Tuesday. That weekend, he went into Birgit's study, sat down at the desk, took the folders out of the drawers, piled them up neatly and opened the one on top. On the first page, in Birgit's handwriting, it said: 'How does she learn to be herself? If she can't be by herself, if she can't be alone with herself? Always, everywhere, voices, whispering, stammering, screaming, wailing, night and day. The noise, the smell, the light.' Then a new paragraph: 'Blinded. Out of warm darkness into harsh light. Birth is blinding. If the children did not behave, the children's homes left the light on at night. Or they switched it on and off, on and off, on, off, on, off, on. The sun is blinding. The snow is blinding. The ceiling light is blinding. The torch is blinding. The torch, shined on the face, to see if it is asleep; the torch, shined on genitals, to see if they scream. Blinded face. Blinded genitals. Blinded into blindness.' This was followed by newspaper cuttings, photocopies and brochures about orphans in the GDR, about adoptions, forced adoptions, how children were raised within the family and how they were raised in residential children's homes, homes for difficult children, workhouses, re-education camps, labor camps; the organization and procedures of East German youth welfare services.

The next folder contained material about neglect and about individual and group violence among juveniles; on xenophobia and right-wing extremism, skinheads and neo-Nazi groups in the GDR and in Germany's new federal states; more newspaper cuttings, photocopies and brochures, as well as letters to journalists and research centers, together with their replies. Again, Birgit had handwritten a few lines on a piece of notepaper: 'At last / punch, hit, stab / free. / At last / drink like the boys / equal. / At last / sweat, blood, tears / brothers.' Another folder contained snapshots of streets, houses, gardens, landscapes. He didn't know the places, and couldn't see what made them worth photographing or why they had been photographed; sometimes there was a date on the back from the 1950s, but no other indication.

He opened another folder and found copies of articles from the *Sächsische Zeitung* of 1964. A man named Leo Weise at the official opening of the wastewater pumping station, Leo Weise at the official opening of the agricultural production co-operative's open cattle barn, Leo Weise visiting the publicly owned enterprise Niesky Wagon Construction, Leo Weise welcoming the group of university students sent to work in its factory. Leo Weise is tall, with an open face, and alongside the other, stiff state and party functionaries at the official events he looks relaxed. He is smiling as he welcomes the Student Brigade, and the students in the picture with him are smiling, too. One of them is Birgit. She is dressed in a warehouse coat and head-scarf, and the grainy reproduction and faded photocopy rob her face of its freshness. But it's her. He found a scrap of paper on which she had noted the stages of Leo Weise's career: Workers' and Farmers' College; Free German Youth (FDJ) instructor in Weisswasser; FDJ High School; First Secretary of the Görlitz FDJ district committee; FDJ Central Council; Party Academy; PhD in Social Sciences; Second Secretary in the Görlitz district committee of the Socialist Unity Party (SED); First Secretary of the Niesky SED district committee.

The last folder contained a longer, typewritten text by an unnamed author, presumably Birgit. 'In the forty years of its existence, the GDR locked up 120,000 juveniles in state-run homes: ordinary children's homes, homes for difficult children, special homes, reformatories, re-education and labor camps, transition homes. On admission their bodies were searched, their body cavities inspected, their heads shaved. The young person was initially locked up in a solitary cell with a stool, a plank bed and a bucket. Then they were put in a communal cell. The recalcitrant were put with thugs, the culturally or politically rebellious with criminals, victims of violence with violent perpetrators, victims of sexual violence with sexual offenders. They were put where they would be broken. The others broke them because they were different, because they could break them, because they were broken. If they didn't make their bed properly, if they put their toothbrush back the wrong way in the toothbrush holder, or spoke when they were supposed to be quiet, or were quiet when they were supposed to speak, the management punished the collective, and the collective punished the individual. Some tried to escape. When that failed, they tried to fight. When that failed, they seized up. They froze. Even after their release, they didn't thaw; they suffered from amnesia, claustrophobia, agoraphobia; they suffered mentally or physically; they became impotent or frigid or miscarried; they became alcoholics. Young people were raised and broken in the children's homes of the GDR as they had been raised and broken in German children's homes before 1945, and continued to be so long after 1945, in . . .' The text continued in this vein, generalizing at first, then detailing the different homes and the methods of treatment and mistreatment in each. Whatever this was, a transcript, or a summary of the material in the first folder, for her own use or for publication, it wasn't what he was looking for.

He opened the little window. The chestnut tree in the courtyard was still bare, but the air that blew into the room was already suffused with spring. He heard the antiphonal song of a pair of blackbirds, searched for them, spotted the closer, louder one on the roof ridge of the rear apartment building, and behind it the other, quieter, on top of the church spire. He remembered how one morning, years ago, Birgit had woken him because the first blackbird of the new year was singing. He had only started to hear the blackbirds when Birgit taught him to listen for their song.

How long ago was it that she had started work on her novel? One day she simply stopped working in the bookshop, and, after months on a retreat in India, the pause became a departure. Birgit completed an apprenticeship as a goldsmith, and another as a chef, but worked only briefly in each profession; then she became active in nature and climate protection, organizing events, campaigns, demonstrations. She liked to talk about this. She did not talk about the novel; not why she was writing it, not what it was about, only that she was working on it. For how long? Six, seven, maybe even ten years? What did you do when you retreated to your study? Did you write in your head? Did you write on paper, and screw the paper up again and again and throw it away? Did you gaze out of the window, listening – to the blackbirds, to the sparrows that make such a racket in the chestnut tree in summer, to the children playing in the courtyard or practicing piano or violin in the neighboring apartments, to the rain rustling in the chestnut tree and pattering on the metal windowsill? Did you daydream the years away?

In his grief, he missed Birgit all the time, in all places, as if she had always been right there, all around him. He had forgotten how often she was absent, and how remote she had been.

5

He didn't want to expose Birgit, so he wrote to the publisher saying that he was still in the process of sorting through her estate and putting things in order. 'You enquired after the manuscript of Birgit's novel. It would help me with the sorting and ordering if you could let me know the novel's subject, if you are aware of it. Birgit was extremely secretive about her writing; I respected this, and did not ask about her novel or any of her other texts. Now, in dealing with her estate, it would be helpful to have knowledge of her projects.'

The reply came swiftly. The publisher wrote that he and Birgit had met five years earlier at a yoga week on the Baltic coast. When he went for walks, he kept passing a dune where she would sit and write, until eventually he sat down beside her and asked her what it was she was writing. Without hesitation, she had read out the poem she was working on, and had shown him the other poems in her notebook as well, without embarrassment. He remembered the notebook: the leather cover, and the leather ribbon that could be wrapped around the book to fasten it. She had never sent him her poems, although he had often asked her to. But he remembered them clearly: their idiosyncratic, moving tone, simultaneously lyrical and austere; their confusing imagery; their sometimes shocking

20

conclusions. When he told her he wanted to publish a volume of her collected poems, she laughed. She wasn't a poet, she said. She was a novelist. When he asked her about the novel, she said it was about life as flight – her life as flight, all life as fleeing. This had interested him, and whenever he and Birgit spoke at length on the phone, which they did once or twice a year, he asked about the novel and heard that it was coming along. 'Send me the manuscript, finished or not, and I will publish the novel. And if you find the notebook with the leather cover and the leather ribbon, I will be delighted to collect the poems of Birgit Wettner in a single volume and publish them at last.'

He had never seen a leather notebook, had not known that Birgit wrote poetry, had not known that she was making progress with the novel. He was hurt. Birgit had written poems and shown them to a stranger without hesitation or embarrassment – but not to him? She had discussed her writing with a stranger – but not with him? She had written about life as flight, about her life as flight – when he was the one who had helped her not just to flee, but to arrive, to settle here?

He missed Birgit no less than before. Her presence; her body, which he could no longer cuddle up to at night; her expressions, cheerful, serious, defiant, sad; her laughter; conversations, about everyday things, or a campaign she was planning, or a new book he was reading; gazing at her in bed from his seat on the stool. Now, though, a touch of resentment crept in with his love and his grief.

He took Birgit's computer to the IT specialist who had set up and managed the bookshop's computer system. Could he bring the dark screen back to life? The IT specialist plugged in a different screen, and it lit up with a request for the password. He didn't know it. The IT specialist asked where and when he and Birgit had met, where and when Birgit was born, what her birth name had been, the names of her parents and siblings, what other dates and places and names had been important to her, what secrets she might have had. Berlin, May 17, 1964; Berlin, April 6, 1943; Hager, Eberhard and Gerda, Gisela and Helga. He also thought of January 16, 1965, the day Birgit had landed in Berlin, but none of these provided the password; nor did his name, Kaspar Wettner, nor did his birthday, July 2, 1944. The IT specialist didn't know how he might get into the computer, but he kept hold of it and promised he would think of something.

Yes: Birgit had landed at Tempelhof on January 16, 1965 – had arrived in West Berlin, had settled with him. That was when their life together had begun, and he had felt as if his whole life began then – his adult life, after childhood and adolescence and the break-up with his childhood sweetheart and a false start at university. Or had it in fact begun earlier, on May 17, 1964?

6

Kaspar had studied in his home town for two semesters, but in the spring of 1964 he transferred to Berlin. He was fleeing his childhood sweetheart, who had left him for someone else; he was seeking the excitement of the big city; he wanted to go to the university that had been founded by students; he hoped that life and his studies would be more exciting here, at the heart of the East–West conflict. And he wanted to experience Germany – all of Germany, not just the West, where he had lived up until then, in the stolid, Catholic Rhineland. His father was a Protestant minister; Kaspar had been raised on Luther and Bach, and in the holidays, at his grandparents', he had read patriotic history books, which said Germany owed its unification in 1871 to Prussia. Berlin, both East and West, Brandenburg, Saxony, Thuringia – all the land east of the Elbe was part of his Germany, as much as that in the west and south.

The doors on the train to West Berlin were locked on the long stretch through East Germany. Kaspar arrived on a Saturday, and took a room in a shared student apartment in Dahlem. The next day he got up early and walked for two and a half hours through the Sunday-morning quiet to the Brandenburg Gate to cast an eye over the Wall. Then he took an S-Bahn train to Friedrichstrasse, where he was checked by border guards in green uniforms, changed West German to East German money, stepped out into the street and set off to make himself at home in the whole of Berlin, the whole of Germany.

He walked until nightfall. He had no plan and no objective, just went wherever the fancy took him. He boarded a U-Bahn subway train and found himself in the east of the city; he walked the length of Karl-Marx-Allee from east to west, from the 1950s apartment blocks with their sections, colonnades and ornamentation to the plain, prefabricated buildings of the 1960s; he saw Alexanderplatz, the cathedral, and the university on Unter den Linden, found his way across the Museum Island to Prenzlauer Berg, to the wide, cobbled roads, the once-splendid, now-shabby town houses, the occasional parks. The city was greyer in the East than in the West; there were more vacant lots, there was less traffic, the cars smelled different. But his morning walk to the Brandenburg Gate had taken him along enough empty streets with grey buildings for the differences to seem small to him. In any case, he had come to the East to find not differences but things in common. To him, the big advertising hoardings were something they had in common: in the East they announced the state- and party-organized Pentecost Meeting of German Youth, a GDR propaganda event, while in the West they extolled the virtues of Persil or Zuban cigarettes or Elbeo stockings.

In the afternoon, the city came to life. After twelve o'clock, the cool, misty morning turned into a warm, sunny spring day. On the edge of Friedrichshain public park he found a stall selling bockwurst with potato salad and lemonade. He took his food, sat down on a concrete bench at a concrete table, and watched the children playing and the mothers talking. A man greeted him, sat down opposite him, waited until Kaspar had finished eating and drinking, then asked if he could ask him something. Kaspar nodded, and learned that the man wanted the ballpoint pen sticking out of his shirt pocket. He worked in a ministry, the man said, writing important documents, and the ballpoint refills they had here smudged.

Kaspar looked at him more closely. Middle-aged, thin hair, an officious, irritated expression, beige windbreaker over a beige shirt. How strange, thought Kaspar, that in order to better serve his state and his class, this man was begging a favor of the class enemy from the enemy state. The zeal of the socialist official. But officious souls like his existed in the West, as well. Kaspar had set out to find things in common, and had found them in his first encounter with a citizen of the GDR. He smiled at the man sitting opposite him, and gave him the pen.

In a cinema on Friedrichshain he watched *Black Velvet*, a crime thriller with a convoluted plot about East and West German agents and a perfect loading crane. This had been developed by the GDR, which planned to present it at the Leipzig Trade Fair, and the Western agents were trying to destroy it to make the GDR look bad. Here, too, Kaspar found things in common: the East German agent was essentially James Bond, but staid, simply dressed, humorless, technologically undemanding, and not fussy about what he drank.

Kaspar returned to East Berlin the very next day, to Humboldt University, and at reception he was so insistent about wanting to speak to the dean of the Faculty of Philosophy that a student was fetched to take him there. Kaspar explained that he was studying German and History – could he be enrolled as a student for one semester? The dean cited a whole host of reasons why this was impossible, from matriculation and administrative problems to the status of Berlin and the absence of peaceful coexistence between the two German states. At least the student who had accompanied Kaspar took him to the canteen before bringing him back to reception. He rhapsodized about the present day as the start of the future predicted by Marx and Engels, and lectured Kaspar about freedom as the consciousness of necessity, and the end of exploitation, and the equal rights of men and women in the GDR. Kaspar tried to discuss personal matters: the student workload, career perspectives, holiday travel destinations. His interlocutor stuck with Marx, Engels and the GDR.

Kaspar was discouraged. How was he supposed to make himself at home in the whole of Berlin, the whole of Germany? Over the following weeks he confined himself to occasional theatre trips to the Berliner Ensemble. At lectures and seminars at the Free University he met students who, like him, were looking forward to the Pentecost Meeting of the German Youth as an opportunity to meet their peers in the East. It started on May 16.

7

Kaspar soon got bored of the parades and processions of banners on Marx-Engels Square, and wandered around instead. He was too shy to speak to any of the girls or boys in blue shirts, the uniform of the FDJ. They went about in groups, sitting in squares and parks, listening to music, watching plays, dancing. Many of them were around his age. But they seemed to him like a closed community, in their shirts and in their groups, and he felt that if he attempted to join them, they would stare at him in surprise.

He did, however, consider who might be the best person for him to approach. Some of them didn't care that their blue shirts were too big or too small and didn't fit properly. They wore them like an unloved uniform. Others wore them proudly, as if they wished they had a military jacket on instead. Some girls stretched the blue shirts tight across their breasts and undid the top buttons; they looked seductive, but the seductiveness was completely different to that of girls in the West. A few had donned a thin pullover or a brightly colored scarf, as if trying to hide the blue shirt. Would they be open to meeting a student from the West?

That first evening he came home dissatisfied: dissatisfied with the day, dissatisfied with himself. The next day would have to be different. He would cross over again. He would overcome his shyness. He would speak to someone. If at first he didn't succeed, he would try a second time, and a third.

On Bebelplatz he saw some students he recognized from his classes chatting to some blueshirts, and he went to join them. West challenged East, East challenged West, a well-rehearsed, dogged war of words to which Kaspar only listened because of a girl in a blue shirt who said the same things as the others, but with charm. She was stunning, too, with loose, curly brown hair, brown eyes, strong cheekbones and a wide, curved mouth. They happened to bump into each other again on Alexanderplatz, started talking, took a liking to each other, and spent the rest of the meeting together; they watched, listened, talked, laughed and danced together, and got to know other students from both East and West. They all became friends, and met frequently.

Whenever Kaspar spoke of how he had met and fallen in love with Birgit, it was always love at first sight. The moment he saw her on Bebelplatz, vivacious, sparkling, quick-witted, not ideologically blinkered like the others but relishing the debate, he was swept off his feet. He had not found an opportunity to speak to her, had walked off, reproached himself for not finding an opportunity, wanted to go back but didn't dare. Meeting her again on Alexanderplatz felt like divine intervention. As if the God Kaspar did not believe in were blessing that first sight of Birgit on Bebelplatz that had swept him off his feet.

Kaspar was not generally a fast mover. He had been slow to fall in love with his childhood sweetheart, who was as ill suited to him as he was to her, and had she not left him he would have been slow to break up with her; he was slow to decide on a course of study, and found it terribly difficult to make a decision when buying a new item of clothing or a coffee machine or a bicycle. Now, though, everything moved fast. When he and Birgit said goodbye at the end of the semester – he to go back to his home town to do an internship in a publishing house, she to work with a Student Brigade at a holiday resort on the Baltic coast – it was clear that they would stay together. She immediately rejected his suggestion that he emigrate to the GDR. So he would bring her from the GDR to the West. He didn't yet know how, but he would find a way.

At the start of the winter semester, he found students who helped organize escapes and knew people who sold forged papers. He made contact with them, and was told to come to a café in Neukölln. They drove up in a black Mercedes coupé with whitewall tires, like the one made famous by the notorious call girl Rosemarie Nitribitt; they wore camelhair coats and clunky, jewelled rings. Birgit could flee on January 15. She would escape via Prague to Vienna. She should apply to go on a weekend trip to Prague, and Kaspar should get hold of passport photos and five thousand deutschmarks: the photos right away, the money by the beginning of January. The conversation was brief, the business sealed with a handshake.

When Kaspar got home, he was trembling, and felt feverish. Suddenly the escape was no longer just an idea: it was actually happening. He had given his word, and had a duty to follow through. He must carry papers over the border, and they must not find them on him. If they found the papers, he and Birgit would go to prison. Birgit would be at risk of imprisonment until she had crossed Czechoslovakia and entered Austria. The dangers were no longer imaginary. They were real. Kaspar was afraid.

And utterly exhausted. He lay down on his bed, trembling, and woke two hours later, drenched in sweat. To his astonishment, he realized that the fear had gone. Sometimes, years later, he would wake at night with a pounding heart because he had dreamed he was at a checkpoint with something to hide, or was being interrogated and trying to withhold information. The fear did not return in the weeks leading up to Birgit's escape, not even in his dreams. Kaspar was completely calm about all that needed to be done.

8

At the same time, he experienced everything with the utmost intensity. He went to East Berlin at noon the next day to get the passport photos. Birgit had no phone; he couldn't call her, couldn't let her know he was coming, he could only hope to find her at home. He had been to her house once before, had met her grandmother, mother and sisters – Helga, who, like Birgit, still lived at home, and Gisela, who happened to be visiting; he had been invited into the living room for coffee and cake, sat on the sofa Birgit slept on at night, was inspected, and was relieved when he and Birgit left to go to the theatre. He remembered the way: out of the S-Bahn, under the tracks, across a big road and down a little one, past a brick-built school with arches and columns, around a corner where the trams also turned on screeching wheels, across a street and past a small bakery. He found the house, rang the bell, waited in vain for the buzzer, and pushed at the door anyway. The door remained shut.

It was three o'clock. Kaspar walked around the block, and when he returned he saw a woman on the first floor leaning out of a window, arms propped on a cushion. What ought he to say if the bell went unanswered again, and she asked him who he was looking for? She would be able to tell by looking at him that he was from the West. His friends from the East had once listed for him all the things that marked him out as a Westerner, and told him what to wear when he went to Potsdam and visited Sanssouci Palace, which, as a Westerner, he wasn't allowed to do. He should have dressed like that again. What would the woman make of a Westerner coming to the door again and again? What sort of woman was she? Suspicious? Kind? Would she sense a threat from the class enemy? Would she think of youthful love? Kaspar would have liked to look for suspicion or kindness in her face, but for that he would have needed to get closer than felt safe. He turned and did a circuit of two blocks this time; then, as the woman was still leaning out of the window, three blocks, which brought him to the banks of the Spree.

The December fog lay thick and grey over the city, muffling sounds and obscuring the view. But for Kaspar everything was oddly clear and close: the houses, the streets, the river. As if the perilousness of his plan had sharpened his vision so things took on a more solid form. And it wasn't just his vision; all of his senses were sharpened. The saw in the joinery sounded so loud, the rubbish in the bin smelled so acrid, he felt the gentle wind on his cheek so clearly, that it was as if nothing stood between him and the world any more.

He sat on the riverbank and stared at the water. Birgit had told him about the boring Sundays of her childhood, the hated walks along the Spree, come rain or shine, always the same views, of water, cargo boats and warehouses, and, where the houses came right down to the Spree and the path switched from riverbank to road, houses with and without front gardens, until they reached the park at Köllnische Heide, went in, came out, and headed home again. He, too, remembered Sundays from his childhood when he had been bored. When nothing interested him and nothing could hold his attention; no game, no book could distract him; he would look in on his sister in her room, take an apple from the kitchen, go into the garden, lie down on the grass, only to get up again, kick a ball against a wall and walk off, leaving it there. They were happy memories of a state of pleasurable, drowsy blankness. Now, too, there was nothing for Kaspar to do, or even anything for him to think. He could have blanked out his mind and left it blank and enjoyed it, in a pleasurable, drowsy way. Instead he was excited, tense, fidgety.

All at once he was freezing. The day was mild, and the wind that blew along the river was gentle. But the ground was cold. He got to his feet, feeling stiff, and walked back. The woman was no longer leaning out, but the window was open, and when he rang again and no one answered, he heard a voice from above: 'Who are you looking for, young man?' Without looking up, he gave an exaggerated shrug indicative of futility and regret, and left.

Now he did the walk to Köllnische Heide and back that Birgit had described. There was nothing to see, and he could understand the boredom she had suffered. Boredom can only be enjoyed alone, when you can allow yourself to be distracted by it, not when your mother or big sister is holding your hand and tugging you this way and that.

Then it got dark. When Kaspar came back and stood in front of the house again, the window the woman had been leaning out of was closed and he could see a bright lamp behind the thin curtain. The windows of what he assumed was Birgit's apartment were dark, and again no one answered the door when he rang. He began to worry. There were many reasons for Birgit and Helga not to be at home. But the grandmother had difficulty walking, and if even she was not at home, perhaps it meant there had been an accident and the whole family was at the patient's bedside in hospital. They might be ages. He had to be back at Friedrichstrasse by midnight.

He bought two bread rolls at the bakery and put them in his coat pocket. Then he stood on the pavement, hesitating. The school opposite lay in darkness. He crossed the road, and at the entrance he found an alcove behind one of the columns where he could just about sit on the base of the column and keep an eye on the front door of the house. He ate the two rolls.

There was not much activity on the street. The occasional car drove past, engine rattling, exhaust stinking. Every ten minutes a full tram approached from one direction, then two minutes later an almost empty tram came from the other. People also came around the corner by the school every ten minutes: the S-Bahn was bringing them home from their work in the city's factories and offices. Kaspar saw them in the light of the streetlamps, in coats, jackets, scarves, overalls, with hats, kerchiefs, briefcases, swinging their arms or with hands buried in their pockets, their footsteps weary, or brisk, or quiet. Some disappeared through the front doors of houses on the other side of the street, and shortly afterwards a light would go on in one of the apartments. As evening drew closer, the train brought fewer and fewer people.

Never before had Kaspar watched people passing by. There had, of course, been occasions when he had stood or sat somewhere and people had passed by, and he had seen them. But he had been talking to someone, or had opened a book, or had been following a train of thought. Now he was doing nothing but watch people, and he realized how many lives passed him by, lives that had their work and their apartment, their family or their loneliness, their happiness and their worries, that were resigned to their fate or not reconciled with it. He had been living his life, and these other lives had surrounded him in much the same way as the houses and streets and trees. Unless, that is, he had some connection with them, and they with him: then he had a sense of who they were, and what they were to him. Now, for the first time, he had a sense of what they were to themselves: each individual life a whole world, entire, complete. Yes, he loved Birgit, and she loved him; she didn't want him to come to her in the East, she wanted to come to him in the West. But she had her own life, and this, too, was entire and complete in its way; it was just that he wasn't familiar with it, and he didn't know what was good and what was bad about it. She had introduced him into her life. Yet suddenly he felt like an intruder, and it shocked him.

It grew quiet. There were hardly any pedestrians rounding the corner now, or cars driving past; Kaspar could hear them coming from a long way off. There was a church not far from the school; Kaspar had seen it on the way from the S–Bahn. He would have been glad of its chimes to keep him company as the hours went by, but he waited in vain; the clock was broken, or else the chiming of a church clock was not tolerated under socialism. The tram reliably kept on coming, every twenty minutes now instead of every ten, two brightly lit glass compartments with just a few passengers, and sometimes none at all. The lights in most of the house windows had turned blue. What were people watching?

Kaspar stepped out from behind the column and paced a little, aimlessly. The movement did him good. But a suspicious look from a purposeful passer-by drove him back into his alcove. He thought of how, on train journeys, when he reached his destination, he often felt he would like just to remain in his seat, not because he was keen to travel far away, but because he felt at home on the train. The alcove behind the column, the darkness of night, the feeble light from the sporadic streetlamps, the few street noises, the screech of tram wheels – he liked it. If he had not been worried that Birgit wouldn't come home in time, that he wouldn't make it back in time to Friedrichstrasse, he could have felt at home in his alcove.

Then a young woman rounded the corner. It wasn't Birgit, but she reminded him of Birgit, and she walked up to the front door of the house and started fumbling with the lock. Kaspar ran across the street: it was Helga. They glanced at each other in the darkness; she said nothing, and neither did he. She unlocked the door, and he followed her up the dimly lit stairs. When she had opened the door of the apartment and switched on the light in the hall, she turned to face him. How beautiful she is, he thought; how beautiful, mysterious, attractive. Why didn't I notice that before?

'I need passport photos of Birgit,' he stammered, confused.

Helga nodded, gestured to him to wait in the hall, and walked off. Somewhere, a clock struck: the eight notes with which Big Ben announced the half-hour. Half past ten. Kaspar was happy to wait in the warm apartment; he realized how cold he had been, and that he craved warmth. Helga soon returned with an envelope. He put it in his pocket.

'Thank you.'

'She's one metre seventy-four, and has brown eyes.' She hugged him, and he was about to hug her back, but she had already said, 'Take care of her,' let go of him, and opened the apartment door.

9

There was something else that left a deep impression on Kaspar when they were preparing the escape. The woman with the yellow scarf.

Birgit and Kaspar would have liked to stay in Berlin and spend Christmas together. Birgit's friend Ingrid was going away, to the Harz Mountains, and was lending Birgit her apartment. Kaspar would have to go back and forth across the border each day, but even so – they would have an apartment to themselves for a whole week! But he needed to go home and borrow from his friends, to put together the money for the escape. He managed it: one could give five hundred, another three hundred – nobody refused. By the beginning of January, Kaspar was able to give the two men in camelhair coats the envelope with five thousand marks.

Two weeks later, they gave him the papers for Birgit. And not only for her. Someone else would also be escaping in two days' time; he had to take the other woman's papers across as well. She would meet him tomorrow at two o'clock on the steps of the Staatsoper; he would recognize her by her yellow scarf, and by the fact that, when he spoke to her, she would ask him if he had just returned from Venice.

Every now and then, the guards at the Friedrichstrasse border crossing had not just checked Kaspar's papers, but had ordered him to accompany them into a back room and strip to his underpants. He told himself that, if this happened again, it would make no difference whether he was carrying false papers for one woman or for two, and this helped him to pass calmly through border control.

He didn't see the woman in the yellow scarf until he was standing right in front of the opera house. She had squeezed herself into the corner at the bottom of the steps, as if trying to vanish into it.

'Have you just returned from Venice?' She was tall and strong, with a pretty, lively face, and she spoke firmly. Why, Kaspar wondered, does the firmness sound so forced? He nodded, and she pulled him into the corner with her.

'I don't want the things. I'm not going to do it. It's not possible.'

'I don't understand. It's all ready. The money's been paid, the men wouldn't have given me the papers otherwise; the guy who paid . . .'

'My fiancé.'

Kaspar waited a moment, but she didn't go on. 'Why is it not possible?'

She stared past him. 'The party didn't happen on Wednesday, as we planned. It's tomorrow.'

'What party?'

'We've been preparing for it for weeks. The children are looking forward to it. I've been practicing a piece with them, and without me, they . . .' Her voice faltered; she took out a handkerchief and turned away.

Kaspar stood there, not knowing what to do. Was she crying? Should he stroke her shoulder, put his arm around her? 'A children's party . . .'

She turned to him and continued, with the same counterfeit firmness. 'I'm the head of the kindergarten. I can't sabotage the party. I won't hold it against you if you can't understand that, and I won't hold it against my fiancé, either.'

'Do you want to stay here?'

'Stay, flee . . . Just leave me alone. I can't go tomorrow, that's all there is to it. I can't.' She gave him an unfriendly look, like an unrepentant child. 'I'm going now.' Without another word, she walked past him and crossed Unter den Linden. Kaspar watched her go until she disappeared between the Neue Wache memorial and the Zeughaus museum.

When you decided to escape, he thought, you knew you would be leaving everything here behind – the kindergarten and the children and the parties, all of it. So how can this one party scupper your decision? Kaspar would have liked to ask her. Can some people not get past what lies immediately before them? Can they engage with what lies beyond while it is still a long way off: in summer, when the escape is planned for winter and still abstract? And then, when it gets closer and demands to be realized, it remains powerless against that which is already real and close at hand? Was that why the aristocrats failed to escape during the French Revolution, despite the threat of the guillotine? And it wasn't the guillotine the kindergarten teacher was facing, only the loss of her life with her fiancé in the West, which to her perhaps had only ever been an abstraction.

Kaspar had plenty of time; he wasn't due to meet Birgit until five o'clock. They had arranged to meet at St Mary's Church, not far from the building where Birgit was studying economics. She was still going to university, as if nothing had changed, as if she intended to stay. Kaspar couldn't imagine that she, too, might decide not to escape. But for her, too, the impending escape was not a reason to miss an upcoming lecture or seminar.

What would I do if I had to give up my old life overnight and start a new one? Plant a tree the day before I die, as Luther said, and then go on living as if nothing has changed – Kaspar couldn't think of a better alternative, either. As long as you didn't miss out on the new life in doing so.

He wandered aimlessly through the streets. He knew East Berlin well enough by now that, wherever he ended up at half past four, he could find his way to St Mary's by five. The sky over the city was low and grey again; there was an occasional sprinkling of rain. Kaspar thought he could already sense the coming of spring in the unseasonably mild air. Since his first visit to East Berlin he had begun to feel at home among the cobbled streets, the shabby old townhouses, the many vacant lots, the small, barren parks, the few, stinking cars. This would be his last visit to East Berlin for a long time. After Birgit's escape, her social circle would be interrogated, their relationship revealed, and he would be suspected of helping her to flee.

He had never walked around Dorotheenstadt Cemetery; now was his last chance. He found the philosophers and writers, the theatre people, the politicians and officials. Although they came from different, often mutually hostile worlds, here they lay side by side. They must find it a bit close for comfort. Kaspar thought of the books that stood beside each other on shelves in libraries and bookshops and must also find it a bit close for comfort: Hegel next to Kant, Marx next to Feuerbach, Heine next to Platen. The booksellers and librarians couldn't help them. Bookseller . . . for the first time, he thought of becoming one.

Then he met Birgit, gave her the papers, a travel bag, a scarf, a packet of Marlboros, and explained to her what she had to do. They were both a little awkward. Ever since that evening when he had waited outside her house, he had been unable to shake the idea that he had intruded on her life. He could tell that she

40

was frightened of what might go wrong, and was trying not to show it. They hugged each other, unable to let go, partly because they didn't know what to say. Then they heard someone whistle, and others laugh, and Kaspar and Birgit moved apart and watched as the young lads walked away.

'I love you, Birgit.'

'I love you, too.'

'Until Saturday, at Tempelhof.'

She nodded, gave him a kiss, and went to the S-Bahn. He would have liked them to go for another walk together, or for a coffee, or a beer. But if she wanted to go, she should go. On Saturday, at the airport, he would take her in his arms.

IO

And so it came to pass. On January 16, 1965, Birgit landed at Tempelhof, and it was the start of more than just their life together. Until then, Kaspar had taken life as it came. Bringing Birgit from the East to the West was also something that just came into his life and had to be done, because they loved each other. But looking for, finding and renting their little apartment, dropping out of university and becoming a bookseller's apprentice, taking over and expanding the bookshop, buying the big apartment – that wasn't taking life as it came, it was shaping it. This was his life, and it began on January 16, 1965. 1611965 – if he could have placed a bet on these numbers, he would have, and he would have won.

But 1611965 didn't unlock Birgit's computer. What did, in the end, was the password kbaisrpgairt, Kaspar and Birgit combined, which pleased him. The screen was damaged; you could write on the computer, but you couldn't read what you had written. Hadn't this bothered Birgit? Had she gone on writing nonetheless?

Kaspar asked the IT analyst to print everything out for him. Everything? Yes, Kaspar wanted everything, no matter how much, how short, or how banal. He wanted to know what Birgit had collected, saved, written, thought, what had been in her brain and on her computer. He wanted to see inside her brain.

But after receiving the big pile of printed pages, putting it on the desk in Birgit's study and sitting in the office chair, he balked at starting to read. As if, in order to see inside her brain, he were about to saw her head open and remove the top of her skull; as if he were about to violate and destroy her brain's protective shield. He thought of when he had needed her passport photos and had waited for her in the alcove at the entrance to the school; of how he had felt like an intruder, even though he had been invited and let into her life. Now he wanted to read what she had saved on her computer and secured with a password. He appeared in the password – but that did not give him the right to intrude. Nothing gave him the right to intrude. Certainly not the resentment that flared up when he thought of the poems and the progress of the novel that she had kept secret from him.

Then his gaze fell on the first page, the printout of an email from six months ago in which Birgit confirmed receipt of a watch she had sent off for repairs, and he settled down to read. The emails held no secrets; instead, the daily life of the last few years passed before him, Birgit's daily life and their life together. Invitations, responses accepting and declining, birthday and get-well wishes, ticket reservations for concerts, the opera and theatre, emails in which he wished her good night, if he was at the Frankfurt or Leipzig Book Fair and couldn't reach her on the phone, emails in which they reminded each other over the course of the day of things that needed doing. They had also sent each other suggestions and brochures for their next holiday: South Tyrol, a vineyard estate and guesthouse in the hills above Bolzano, where they planned to relax and use it as a base to go hiking; the last few days would be spent in Venice and Trieste. He loved holidays with Birgit; she drank little, had a clear head and a warm, light heart, and they would walk and swim and read to each other in bed.

He wouldn't go on the holiday without her. He wouldn't go on holiday ever again. He wouldn't go to concerts, the opera, the theatre any more. Without her, he could take no pleasure in daily life, either; the back-and-forth between apartment and bookshop, his morning and evening walks, the old routines and the new books had given him a sense of security. He knew how to function: Birgit's death had not caused him to forget this, and he would not forget. It was all that was left to him.

He stared at the night, and the darkness was not just outside, it was inside him. He thought of Orpheus. He was able to enter the realm of the dead and find Eurydice because there was light inside him. His light was so bright that his lyre-playing and singing sparkled, bewitching Charon the ferryman into rowing him across to the realm of the dead, and the hellhound Cerberus into granting him admission. Would I find her, Kaspar thought, if the light in me shone as brightly as it did in Orpheus, if my love for Birgit sparkled like Orpheus's songs? For a moment he dreamed of himself and Birgit, face to face in the light of his love. Would she follow me, and the light? Would my faith be strong enough not to turn to look at her on the path back to life? Or would I lack faith and need to assure myself of her presence? Or would I resent her for her secretiveness, and take her to task then and there?

Suddenly he was seized with fear that, in spite of his longing for her, in spite of his mourning, Birgit might slip away from him as Eurydice had slipped away from Orpheus on the path back to life. Although Birgit was dead, she was still with him; but if he stopped believing in her, if he began to resent her, she would die all over again, and stay dead.

II

Over the days that followed, Kaspar read Birgit's emails. He found in them not just the daily life of the last few years, but also Birgit's friendships within the writing group, her activism for nature and the climate, her involvement in protests. She had been planning a sit-in in a treehouse, in a wood that was to be cleared to build a railway – she hadn't told him about that, either.

The emails were followed by pieces of text that he recognized; these were the printouts in the folders. There was one long text he didn't recognize. Unlike the others, it had a title, 'A Harsh God', and it started with the question of who Birgit would have become if she had stayed in the GDR. It must be a fragment of the novel, or notes she had made of her recollections, or a personal essay. In any case, this text was not an ordinary one he could casually go ahead and read. If he read on now, he would be intruding, against Birgit's will, on her innermost thoughts, abandoning the loving reticence with which he had accepted her decisions to steer her life in this or that direction, and also the secret of her writing.

Because, in the realm of the dead, Eurydice was a shadow, Orpheus could not hear her footsteps behind him on the path back to life. Whether or not she was following him was a secret

Orpheus had to endure. Kaspar knew that, in snatching the secret of Birgit's text away from her, he was turning to look at her. However much he learned by reading it, however well he got to know Birgit, she would slip even further away.

He didn't read on. More weeks went by, during which Kaspar did not enter Birgit's study. He waited for time to heal the wound of Birgit's death, but it didn't. He walked from the apartment to the bookshop in the morning and from the bookshop to the apartment in the evening; usually ate the same microwave meal – chicken rice – or, if he had forgotten to go shopping, a pizza at the Italian restaurant on the corner; forced himself to go for a walk on Sundays, or to the cinema if it was raining; let his colleague, who was concerned about him, invite him over a couple of times for dinner with her family; and while reading newly published books in the evening, he drank more than he used to. Summer had arrived, a summer of thunderstorms. Looking out of the bookshop, seeing the wind whirl up dust and leaves and scraps of paper beneath a canopy of black clouds, running home in the pouring rain amid thunder and lightning, getting soaked to the skin, freezing a little outdoors and warming up again at home under a hot shower – all of this did him good. Afterwards, when he had dried himself and put on his dressing gown and was wandering around the apartment, he would tell himself there was life in the old dog yet.

One evening, he found he no longer cared what happened to Eurydice. He had had a lot to drink, and felt a seething anger at Birgit, the anger that is born of grief when it can no longer abide its own impotence. Birgit's selfishness, lack of consideration, obstinacy, self-pity! Why was he always the one who had to please her, put up with her departures and outbursts, clear up her vomit? He went upstairs to Birgit's study, one unsteady step after the other, holding on to the wall with his hands; he made it to the desk and onto the chair, and started to read. But he was drunk, the text was complicated, and he couldn't keep his eyes open. As he was taking it downstairs, he slipped on the steps; he managed to save himself but not the text, and the pages scattered all down the stairs and across the hall.

The next morning, he gathered up the pages. He had lost Eurydice that evening. Now it didn't matter any more. He took the text back up to Birgit's study, sat down at the desk again, and read.

A Harsh God

Who would I have become if I had stayed? If I hadn't met Kaspar, if I hadn't fallen in love with him, if I hadn't decided to be with him? If I'd never even thought of leaving, if staying was all I had ever known?

The father's photograph, skull on the collar, stood on the chest of drawers in a silver frame with a black mourning ribbon across the bottom right-hand corner. The little girl gazed up at the photograph and saw a good, strong face and good, warm eyes, and she yearned for her father, who had not come back from the war. Not come back? Every day he demanded self-discipline, striving and endurance. That was what her mother said. Her mother also said that he had been a hero, it was just that you weren't allowed to say so any more, and a good man and a good father. He loomed over the little girl; he loomed over the big girl as well. Wherever she stood, he stood behind her; wherever she went, he followed; he cast his shadow over her. His shadow of death.

The girl turned the photograph face down. But her father righted himself again, stepped behind her again, cast his shadow over her again. The shadow of the old, bad era. The girl wanted to be part of the new, good era. In which those who had fought against her father and liberated the country and its people were creating a new country and a new kind of person. Did the shadow girl deserve to be a new person in a new country? Perhaps if she tried hard, if she proved herself, if she was willing and compliant.

I did try hard. If I had stayed, would I have gone on trying harder? If the effort had proved fruitless, would I have blamed myself? Because I was the shadow girl? Because the new era could not be the reason? Because the new era was the good era?

If, one day, it had become impossible to ignore the fact that the circumstances were not OK, the assignments we were given perverse, the efforts we were making pointless, would I still have believed in the new era, even then? Would the new era still have been the good era? Would I, too, have helped embroider the pacifying tapestry of false hope? The new country's economy is stagnating – at least it has thrown off the yoke of private ownership, takes care of everyone, employs everyone and exploits no one. The new country's culture is stiff and lifeless – the old comrades were in the resistance, they did not yield, and what does not yield inevitably stiffens. The new country's politicians don't trust their citizens – when they were in the resistance, the old comrades had to learn not to trust, and, having learned it, they could no longer set their lack of trust aside. They may not be leading the country as quickly and directly into the new, good era as we might wish, but we still owe them respect and patience. We do not have the right to wrest the torch from their hands. It is our duty to help them carry it, until they can carry it no longer and pass it on to us. Then it is up to us to continue along the path, to reach the goal, to complete their work.

The guilt I felt from growing up in the shadow of death prevented me from rebelling; would it have prevented me from being ambitious, as well? Would I have made do? Would a job as a librarian or administrative assistant have been enough for me? And if the library or administrative office or factory had continued to exist after reunification, would I have adapted to the new laws, new technology and new bosses, while also mourning the loss of my former hopes? The loss of my old, small country that had wanted to be a new country for new people? The loss of all that could have been, if only . . . I would not have known what, just that there must have been something, that somehow it should have turned out differently, and better.

No: it wouldn't have been like that. I wasn't that small and stupid and dutiful. I didn't go on being the shadow girl. I turned the photograph face down and left my father's shadow and my mother's words behind. I believed in the new era that was creating a new country and a new kind of person, and in my right to be a new person in the new country. I worked hard to make the new era a good era. I was always willing. But I was not always compliant.

If I had understood that the economy was stagnating, that the culture was stifling imagination and creativity, that the politicians were infantilizing the people, that the circumstances were not OK, the assignments we were given perverse and our efforts pointless, I would not have turned against the new era. But I would have hoped that the torches would be wrested from the hands of the old comrades, and passed on to the young. I would still have believed in the goal, but I would have sought to reach it by a different route. In Prague, in the spring of 1968, I would have believed it almost within reach; in 1985–86, with Gorbachev in Moscow. Finally, November 1989 would have been for me a Berlin Spring, a German hope of glasnost and perestroika.

How would I have lived all through this time? Would I have started out by pursuing a career, at a publishing house, a school, a cultural or academic institution? Would I then have made trouble, and got into trouble, and been sent to work in a factory for two, three years? Would I eventually have found a niche for myself, as many people did? I liked foreign languages; when I was young, I had a Kazakh penfriend. I could have learned Kazakh, translated Kazakh literature, and written poems in my spare time. A good life? I can imagine that I would have been increasingly sad and quiet in my niche – and happy in November 1989.

But by 1990, spring, glasnost and perestroika were over in Germany. My niche would have disappeared in 1990, as well. No one would have needed German translations of Kazakh literature any more; the little publisher that published my poems would have gone bankrupt, and the building in Prenzlauer Berg, where I would have had a cheap apartment, would have been bought by an investor and divided up into private apartments. Would I have moved out to Marzahn and lived on benefits?

Or would I, in 1990, have been in demand as an interpreter for German companies investing in Kazakhstan? Would I have earned good money – good enough to take out a loan, take advantage of my option to buy my rented apartment? Would I have found my way from poetry to writing hit songs or advertising slogans, and had success with that? Would I have been one of the winners who did well after reunification?

Or would it all have been very different? After my love for Leo, Leo's deceit and the birth of our child, would I have become a totally different person? Disillusioned, careworn, bitter? In those days, an illegitimate child was not a problem if the mother was reconciled with herself and with the child. Would I have been reconciled with myself and with the child? Or would I have seen the duplicity of the system in Leo's duplicity, and the cold way the system used people in the cold way he tried to use me? Would I have rejected the system, kept myself and my child separate from the world in which we lived? Would I have understood my mother – not her love for the father with the skull on his collar, but her life without and in opposition to the world? Would I and my daughter have stayed with her and Grandmother?

I wouldn't have cared what I did to earn money, in an era and a country I did not love. I would have found something. I would have done something.

I would have gotten by, expecting nothing and disappointed by nothing, not even by my daughter. Nothing would have changed with reunification. What would there have been to change? I would have gone on living without and in opposition to the world, would have trudged on, would have grumbled. Would I have enjoyed the fact that we had better alcohol? Or would I not even have noticed by then?

I'm glad I didn't stay. I'm glad I left. I don't want any of these unlived lives. But I cannot shrug them off. My unlived lives are mine, as much as the lived one. They are sad, and I bear the sadness of the life of guilt in the shadow of death, the sadness of life in my niche, the sadness of life without and in opposition to the world.

The GDR makes me sad. The enthusiasm for the new era, the hope of a new country and a new kind of person, the readiness, in the early years, to take action and make sacrifices – even if there is nothing left of that beginning, it was still a beginning. Even if there is nothing left of the attempts to move the country forward – despite the system, against the system – and nothing of the insistence that socialism and freedom belong together and the future belongs to both: it did exist, once upon a time, and it was real, and it was good, unlike the bad reality of actual socialism. Its disappearance makes me sad, even though I know that the good reality could only exist as a contrast to the bad, and was bound to disappear with it.

When you live in a country with a bad regime, you hope for change. One day it actually comes: a good regime takes the place of the bad. Those who were against can now be for. Those who had to go into exile can return. For those who stayed and for those who left, the country becomes theirs again, the country of which they dreamed. But the GDR will never be the country of which we dreamed. It no longer exists. Those who stayed cannot enjoy it again. Those who left cannot return; our exile never ends. Hence the emptiness. The country and the dream are irretrievably lost.

The irretrievable loss doesn't make me sad. But the emptiness makes me sad.

The outing to Quitzdorf Dam. It was January; the day had started out mild, but it turned cold, and we made a fire. When Leo came over, we thought: We're in for it now. But he laughed. We should get a permit next time, he said, and told us to clear away the campfire before we went home. He hadn't come to check up on us. He just wanted to know if we were all right. We were his first Student Brigade. He had only been made district secretary a year ago. Then he sat down and joined us at the fire. He ate and drank and sang along.

Was it intentional, as he told me later? Or was it really a coincidence? That he decided to stretch his legs just as I had sat down a little way from the others, at the water's edge? First he stopped and stood beside me, then he squatted next to me, offered me a cigarette, took one himself and lit them both. I remember he shook the packet until two cigarettes were sticking out, let me take mine with my fingers and took his with his mouth.

We had been talking about dogs around the campfire, and he continued the conversation. 'My brother had a dog, half sheepdog, half fox terrier, a sweet, ugly, loyal animal. He was a companion. Companions are equals, aren't they? Sometimes Cato was, too; we would turn left in the wood instead of right because Cato wanted to turn left, and we would let him swim in the marshy pool, even though we had to wash him afterwards. Ultimately, though, Cato was in our power. If he wanted to go out and we wanted to stay in, he stayed in; if he was sniffing around a tree and we wanted to walk on, he'd be pulled along on the lead; we decided what he ate, and my brother decided when he would be put to sleep. I couldn't bear to have a dog. To have him as a companion, and have power over him at the same time.'

'Isn't that what a district secretary does? The citizens and comrades are his companions, in a way, but he has power over them.'

He laughed, and I liked his laugh. It came from his belly, not his throat. He lowered himself from a squat to the ground. 'I hope I carry them with me. I talk to them. I convince them.'

'And what if they can't be convinced?'

'Then it's not me that has power over them, it's the Party.'

'And the citizens and comrades are the dogs.'

'When I get impatient and pull the dog along on the lead, it's myself I'm thinking of. The Party isn't thinking of itself. It's thinking of us.'

He said it as if he believed it, earnest and cheerful. I was a little cold; I was shivering, and he put his arm around me. Not pushy, not forward; and soon afterwards he said, 'We should go back to the fire.' But I stayed sitting, and leaned against him. This was how I wanted to be loved. As a companion; as an equal.

That was when I fell in love with him.

I knew that you can't escape yourself, that you always take yourself with you everywhere. But I didn't know that you always take others with you everywhere as well.

Grandmother. She sits in my head as she sat in our living room. In an armchair, eyes open, hands folded, blanket over stomach and legs, no book, doesn't listen to the radio, doesn't watch television, always ready with a nasty remark. Mother: repressed, fearful, trying hard to bring up her three daughters as strictly as their father would have done, admonishing, threatening, criticizing, nothing too minor for a telling-off. Gisela, who did everything right, chose the right profession, married the right man, had the right children, one boy and one girl; whose whole world fell apart with the divorce, who could never warn me often enough that nothing and no one could be trusted. Helga, who withdrew from everyone: Grandmother, Mother, Gisela, me; who showed me that if you want to protect yourself, you must shut yourself off.

They didn't stay over there, like the apartment we shared and the photograph of Father on the chest of drawers. They came with me, and they torment me: Grandmother's nasty remarks, Mother's scolding, Gisela's bitterness, Helga's example. They're here, even though Grandmother died soon after my escape and Mother, too, has been dead for years. If I had become bitter, Gisela's bitterness would have been absorbed in mine. But I am not bitter; I am sad. I shut myself off and protected myself more than was good for me.

How do you escape others? By resolutely living your own life. Did I not live my life with enough resolution?

Because Grandmother and Mother, the GDR and the FDJ taught me to please others? Because I didn't learn to please myself, to seek my own happiness? But I liberated myself from what I learned. I sought my own happiness. At my daughter's expense, at Kaspar's expense. I betrayed and abandoned her, I left him to run the bookshop on his own, I did whatever I felt like doing: travelled to India, took up goldsmithing and cooking, then writing.

With writing, it is not about others. It's just for me. You can't write for readers or critics or a publisher, for your grandmother or mother, only for yourself. Is that why I'm not making progress with the novel? Because the others have come with me and are tormenting me? Because I haven't actually liberated myself from what they taught me? Because I still haven't learned: for myself?

That's why I have to write the novel. Because I have to learn it: for myself. And I have to stop drinking. When I drink, it's as if I'm drinking for myself, and am fully myself already. As if immediately afterwards, first thing in the morning, I could easily start writing – or that I would no longer need to, because I am fully myself already.

Could I have found someone to get rid of the baby? Or could I have gotten rid of it myself? While I might still have been able to, the idea didn't occur to me.

No – it did occur to me, but Leo wouldn't hear of it. He wanted me, he wanted the baby; we just had to wait. He and his wife had been estranged for years. They both wanted a divorce. His position meant he was exposed, so the divorce had to be handled in the right way; there couldn't be any washing of dirty laundry, he couldn't be accused of irresponsible behavior. If he were to leave his wife now and move in with me, the Party and the court would consider that irresponsible, and it would go against the workers' moral views regarding marriage. He took my face in his hands. 'They don't know how serious we are.' He kissed me and smiled. 'I myself didn't know that a love like ours was possible.'

Which is better: a weak Leo, who couldn't stand up for our love, or a deceitful Leo, who toyed with me? When he told me he couldn't get divorced – not now his wife was ill with breast cancer, and he would be accused of thoughtlessly abandoning her – he looked so despondent that I consoled him. He was in Berlin for a conference; we had met in the Mokka Milch Eisbar for an ice cream and were sitting on a bench in Monbijou Park when he came out with this. In the ice cream parlor and on the way to the park he had been in a good mood, and only turned sombre on the bench, which was another reason I didn't take it too much to heart. I thought his wife would either have an operation to cure the cancer, or she would die of it. I thought we would just have to wait a bit longer, which was not nice, but not terrible, either.

He came back to Berlin a week later. He came just to see me; I was delighted, and persuaded Ingrid to let me have her apartment for the afternoon. I met him at the Ostbahnhof; we took the U-Bahn to Alexanderplatz, walked to the Rotes Rathaus and had lunch in the Ratskeller restaurant. I didn't like to ask how things stood with us, and he was so cheerful that I didn't actually think I needed to; I thought there was good news, and that at some point he would tell me of his own accord. We went to Ingrid's apartment, we slept together, we lay there side by side, and it wasn't until he said I shouldn't smoke, seeing as I was pregnant, that I asked him where we would go from here.

'You don't need to worry.'

'Worry?'

'It's too late for an abortion; you won't find a doctor who'll do it now, and home remedies won't work now, either. You'll have the baby, and as a last resort, I'll take it.'

'You?' I didn't understand. I didn't understand what he was saying, or his tone of voice, or his body language. He was sitting like a stranger beside me in the bed and talking to me like a stranger.

'I don't know how to say this, Birgit . . . What we dreamed of is not going to happen. The Party wouldn't understand, and it wouldn't forgive, and Irma – we've grown apart, but she's always been a good wife to me; she would have been happy to have children and be a mother, and I can't abandon her to be happy and have a child with you, I can't do that to her. It would be as if I were taking the baby she wanted so badly away from her.'

'Are you talking about my baby?' As he spoke, I felt everything I had believed in and looked forward to collapse. But I didn't understand how it had collapsed, or what exactly lay in ruins. Was he talking about my baby? Who was taking it away from whom? What was going on with him and his wife? What did he want from me? Did he want to go on seeing me? Did he not want to see me any more?

'I won't desert you. You can't abort the baby any more; you have to have it. But you want to study and get a job and be successful; a baby is not what you need right now. We'll take it, Irma and I. We'll be good parents to the child. I've spoken to Irma, and she's agreed.'

'You want to give my baby to your wife?'

'I'm sure I can persuade Irma to let you visit now and then. I don't want to ask her now; she's too hurt and too jealous, you have to understand that. But once she's got the baby, things will be different.'

I shook my head, and then my whole body started shaking, with outrage, revulsion, disgust. I was disgusted by Leo, his suaveness, his scheming. I was disgusted by his proposition and by his wife and by the thought of my child growing up with them. I was disgusted by myself. I had been intimate with this person. This was a person I had loved.

I didn't even have the strength to tell him to get out of the apartment. I got dressed in silence, while he got dressed and nagged me: what was wrong and why was I behaving like this and I shouldn't behave like this and his proposition was only fair. I was quicker than him, and by the time he got out of the apartment I had already run down the stairs and hidden in the courtyard. I heard him on the stairs, calling me, and I heard the front door slam, and when I went out into the street a while later he was nowhere to be seen.

He couldn't call me, because we didn't have a phone. He wrote to me, saying we had misunderstood each other, he had only wanted to help me, we needed to see each other again and talk things through, he loved me, we couldn't live out our love as we had dreamed of doing, but we could live it as we had up till now; he wanted to try to get me an apartment of my own. I didn't answer any of his letters, and once, when he waited for me outside the university, I walked straight past him, and was proud to have been so aloof and unapproachable that, after walking alongside me for a few paces and saying a couple of things, he gave up.

He was right: it was too late for an abortion. Friends gave me the names of doctors, all of whom turned me away. Jumping off the table and drinking infusions of juniper, feverfew and ragwort didn't help, either. I couldn't poke about inside myself with knitting needles. They were already talking about the reform that would make abortions easier to obtain, but that didn't happen until years later.

For a while I was in despair, not least because I was struggling with nausea and vomiting, more than I had seen in my girlfriends who had children. I even considered agreeing to the terrible proposition after all. Leo would ensure that I was well cared for during the pregnancy, would guarantee a safe birth and smooth adoption.

Then, one weekend, it was suddenly spring. That Monday, riding the S-Bahn under a blue sky to Friedrichstrasse station and walking to the university under the new green of the limes, all my despair fell away. It was a bright, sunny day; instead of the brown coal smell that had clung to the city all winter, I smelled the freshness of the morning, and the sun was so warm that I took off my jacket and slung it over my bag. I would manage. Pregnancy, birth, keeping the baby or giving it away, studying, working – I would manage. And if I gave the baby away, I would make sure Leo didn't get it. And I would let him know that I had brought it into the world, but had not given it to him.

Do pregnant women often fall in love? At first, I felt guilty. Didn't I owe these feelings to the child that was growing inside me? Was I depriving it of something?

But how womanly I felt! I had always been happy with my body, insofar as any woman is happy with her body: my body as something that belonged to me. Now I was my body. My outline was softer, my breasts larger, my hair shone, my face glowed. I liked looking at myself, and I liked it when men looked at me. And they did look at me; they couldn't take their eyes off me. They desired me. I was life.

In May, people couldn't tell that I was pregnant. They couldn't tell that I was pregnant for a long while after that, not just because of how I dressed, but because my belly stayed small. I had always played a lot of sport, my stomach muscles were strong, my connective tissue firm, and I ate no more than usual. Perhaps it was also partly because I was repressing the pregnancy. By the time the belly could no longer be overlooked, the holidays had begun; I went to the Baltic with Paula, and returned only after it was all over.

But I don't want to write about that here. I want to write about how I fell in love. I was pregnant, and after my love for Leo and the disgust I felt for him, I was drained. I couldn't imagine that any man would ever find me attractive again, or that I would ever love anyone again. I enjoyed the fact that men desired me. But it was a cold pleasure. Had I let any of them near me, it would only have been to hurt them.

The Pentecost meeting of the German Youth was in May. There was propaganda, marching in step, parades with flags, gymnastics and dance displays, public declarations and pledges and salutes for one delegation after another. But there was also the new youth radio station, DT64, broadcasting beat music and, for the first time in the GDR, the Beatles, and there was dancing in the streets and on the squares. Hundreds of students came from West Berlin, curious about us, as we were curious about them. Some came to discuss politics with us, the Wall, reunification, free travel and free elections, and as Free German Youth we demonstrated ideological steadfastness. Others wanted to know how we lived, what we were interested in, how we got on with each other, what we did in our holidays, how we dealt with the political situation, what we wanted to be. They asked us the things we asked ourselves, and that brought us together. Our answers were also more exciting to them than they were to us, which made us feel more exciting than usual. When we met up we went for walks together, sat together on Bebelplatz and in Monbijou Park and beside the Spree, talked and danced with each other and found each other exhilarating. It felt good to be admired and desired, in my blue FDJ shirt, by a student from the West.

I met Kaspar on the second day. Helmut, my FDJ secretary, had assigned me to debate on Bebelplatz; he assumed, correctly, that the Association of Christian Democratic Students would seek an exchange of views with FDJ students there, outside the Humboldt University. And so I defended the necessity of the anti-fascist barrier to protect us against enticement, subversion, espionage, sabotage and infiltration by the West, the establishment of peaceful coexistence between the two German states as a precondition for the reunification of Germany, and the freedom of elections in the GDR. Kaspar stood and listened before interrupting, aghast. 'Why are you even talking to each other? You know everything already. You know what you're going to say next, and what the others will say next. And if one is not as quick-witted as' – here he looked at me – 'the other, what does that prove?' For a moment the others stared at him in astonishment, but then the discussion continued as if he hadn't spoken. Kaspar stayed a little longer, as if he didn't want to turn away abruptly, then he detached himself from the group and walked on. I watched him go. He was wearing jeans and a shirt, and a jersey draped around his shoulders, sleeves knotted over his chest. He strolled along, upright, relaxed – I liked the way he walked, and the way he looked at me, and that he had admired my quick-wittedness.

I saw him again on Alexanderplatz. I had a token for the meal they were doling out at the field kitchen; he hadn't realized that you needed a token, had gone to the back and stood patiently in line, and when he got to the front and was turned away, he looked so disappointed that I asked the woman with the ladle to give him a bowl of stew, even though he didn't have a token. He thanked me, thanked her, too, and followed me to the square by the Haus des Lehrers, where many others were already sitting eating. I sat down with them. He stood there, not knowing whether to sit next to me, and I could see that he wasn't looking for more interesting people to eat with, he just didn't want to impose. Then he sat down beside me, and when others came and sat next to him, he shuffled closer and smiled at me, as if this was where he belonged. That was what he was like. He didn't want to impose on anyone, but once he made a connection with you, he was instantly trusting and affectionate.

'Are you just on a break, or have you done enough work for today?'

'You mean the discussion on Bebelplatz?'

'Yes. It's work, for the Christian Democratic Students and for the FDJ. All that talking that doesn't go anywhere . . . But you're good; I enjoyed listening to you.'

'I meant what I said. I wasn't just talking.'

'Oh,' he said, putting his bowl down on the ground and raising his hands apologetically, 'I didn't mean to offend you. Of course you mean what you say; the others mean what they say as well. But I don't think there's any point to the discussion if people don't talk about why they mean what they say. What they hope to gain, what they're afraid of, who they are with this opinion, and who they would be without it. Do you get what I'm trying to say?'

'You mean people's dreams?'

'That, too; not their political dreams, their personal ones.'

I wondered whether it was possible to separate them, thought of the fiasco with Leo, and ate my stew. He picked up his bowl again and went on eating, until I asked, 'What are your personal dreams?'

He laughed. 'Something like this, right now. Where socialism and capitalism aren't an issue, we just sit and eat and chat with one another.'

'What are you studying? And is it important to you that we use the formal form of address? Over here, students address each other as *Du* rather than *Sie*.'

It wasn't important to him. When he told me his first name, Kaspar, I thought perhaps he was embarrassed by it and that was why he preferred to keep things formal. But he talked about the Three Wise Men, and how Kaspar was the black king of the three, and that he had learned as a child to defend his name, and to like it. He was studying German and history. 'I love the books from the eighteenth and nineteenth centuries that no one reads nowadays, like Karl

Philipp Moritz and Friedrich Theodor Vischer. I'm a bit of an anachronism.'

'That's why you dream as if there were no such thing as politics. We can't just sit here together while you reject peaceful coexistence.'

He smiled at me, and I could see what he was thinking: but we are just sitting here together. Then he said: 'We belong together. We speak the same language, and if you don't like Moritz and Vischer, who perhaps are interesting rather than likeable, I bet you like Fontane or Döblin or Frank. What are you studying?'

I had wanted to study German, too, but I was assigned to economics, and by this time, after two semesters of Marxism–Leninism, I was in my third semester, studying accountancy and bookkeeping for publicly owned enterprises. I read a lot: contemporary literature, but Kaspar was right, I liked Frank and Döblin and Fontane.

'What about poems? Do you like poems?' He looked at me, saw that I liked poems, beamed with delight, and recited:

> *Spring sends its blue ribbon*
> *Fluttering through the air once more;*
> *Sweet, familiar scents*
> *Drift, full of promise, o'er the land.*
> *Already the violets lie dreaming,*
> *Soon they will burst forth.*
> *Hark – the soft note*
> *Of a harp in the distance!*
> *Spring – yes, it is you!*
> *I hear you coming!*

The astonished, amused looks of people sitting nearby didn't bother him; he was completely immersed in the poem – and completely with me. He didn't take his eyes off me, recited to me and me alone; he gave me the poem as a gift, along with himself. When he stood to walk away, he took my hand, and I let him do it.

We spent the whole of the Pentecost meeting together, from noon on the second day. I didn't report to Helmut again or let him put me down for any more discussions. Kaspar and I wandered around, listened to bands and watched performances and danced a lot. If we came across a group of students from East and West, some in blue shirts, others in jeans, we joined them, and by the end of the meeting we had a list of students we found interesting, and had agreed a date to meet up at Ingrid's one evening.

That first evening was followed by many more. We usually met at Ingrid's; sometimes we went to the theatre or cinema and afterwards to a bar. There were ten of us, sometimes more, sometimes fewer; four were in couples, the rest of us single. We talked about everything from love to politics; about books from the West that they brought with them, and ones from the East that we gave them; we recited our favorite poems and listened to our favorite music. I was introduced to jazz by the records Stephan brought along; on Matthias's poetry-and-jazz albums I first encountered Gottfried Benn, who wasn't published in the East, and heard Gert Westphal's recitations of Heine's poems that made my heart leap to my mouth.

After our friends from the West read Hermann Kant's *A Bit of the South Sea*, Erik Neutsch's *Trace of Stones* and Karl-Heinz Jakobs's *It Happened One Summer*, they wanted to know whether we knew any comrades like those in the books: loyal to the Party, staunch believers without being narrow-minded; honorable, sincere, tough on others and on themselves, but always alert to others' needs; capable of doling out harsh criticism, but also of showing understanding and offering advice and help; not avid for status or career opportunities, devoid of vanity. Could we bring along some such comrades to join our circle? We gave it a lot of thought. We hadn't met any in the factories where we'd worked; most of the workers we had met were hard-working and reliable, but this was to do with money and their honor as workers, not the Party, whose interventions they scoffed at, either genially or in irritation. We considered our teachers, but they were either staunch believers and narrow-minded, or open-minded and cautiously distanced from the Party. Some of our circle had mothers and fathers who were members of the SED, and although they respected their parents politically, they saw all too clearly how conflicted they were, between loyalty to the Party, loyalty to their profession, and loyalty to relationships with friends and family, for these parents to constitute ideal comrades. We couldn't come up with anyone.

But it wasn't this experience, or Robert Havemann's *Dialectics Without Dogmatism*, or his fate, or the persecution of Wolf Biermann that made me lose faith in the new era. I didn't repudiate my faith. I wasn't even aware that I had lost it. It came to an end, as winter comes to an end when summer arrives, or as hunger does when you eat. There were too many things that were more important: conversations with friends, the new literature and the new music, the developing relationship between Kaspar and me. And I no longer needed faith in the new era as a refuge from my home with my dead father, with my grandmother, mother and sisters. I found refuge elsewhere. Life was elsewhere.

When I went to the first meeting at Ingrid's, I dreaded entering the apartment. I hadn't been back there since that afternoon with Leo. As if he knew how I was feeling, Kaspar took my hand, squeezed it and smiled at me. I had met him at Friedrichstrasse station, and we greeted each other with a hug. We had already held hands a few times at the Pentecost meeting, while walking around, and had hugged each other goodbye at the end of the evening. We hadn't kissed, only hugged. There was a closeness between us; we knew that what we had together was good, though we didn't yet know what it was. When he took my hand outside Ingrid's apartment and squeezed it, I knew he would hold on to me.

We didn't only meet with the others; we met alone, as well, the two of us. We became girl- and boyfriend, but we didn't admit it to ourselves, and certainly not to anyone else, until the end of the summer semester. I had wanted Leo and me to be a couple, and that had been stupid and wrong; I no longer wanted to want to be or to see myself as half of a couple. For Kaspar, it was more a fear of being pushy; not only did he not allow himself to be pushy, he didn't even allow himself to hope for more from the other than they gave of their own accord. But we were in love. For me, it began when he laid that poem at my feet, oblivious to the world and all around him, amid the crowds at the Pentecost meeting. He said he had fallen in love with me on Bebelplatz.

'Why there?'

'Because when you talked about politics, you spoke casually, instead of being grimly determined, like the others. As if it was all a game.' He blushed. 'And because you were gorgeous. I mean, you are gorgeous, but that day I saw you for the first time.' He lowered his eyes, embarrassed, then looked up at me again and said, 'You're the most beautiful woman I've ever seen.'

I laughed.

'You can laugh, but it's true.' We were lying on his second-hand American army jacket in Treptower Park, beside the Spree. He propped himself up on his forearms and gazed around. 'Not that beauty matters. Plenty of things in Berlin are not beautiful, on your side and on ours, but Berlin is still a great city.'

I was hurt that he had immediately qualified his compliment about my beauty, but I didn't show it. 'So what does matter?'

'Wanting to do something again and again. To walk down a street again and again. Read a book again and again. Listen to a piece of music again and again.' He sat down and turned to me. 'Look at a face again and again.'

'And what is it that makes us want to do something again and again?'

He shook his head thoughtfully. 'I don't know. Or rather, sometimes I know, and sometimes I don't. The look in your eyes – sometimes it's dreamy, lost in thought, then it's suddenly focused, like the look in the eyes of a flautist or a violinist when the camera zooms in on them during a concert. The way, when you laugh, your eyes laugh, too. The way your lips go thin when you're outraged by something. The way your cheeks burn when you've been running, or when you get excited.' He laughed. 'When we ran for the S-Bahn at Alexanderplatz, even as we were running I was looking forward to seeing your face afterwards.'

I was happy with that. I was also happy with what we had together in the two months between mid-May and mid-July. He always had to be back in West Berlin by midnight; we didn't have a single night together, he couldn't show me his world, we couldn't go on any trips together. But we enjoyed what the theatres had to offer, we had afternoons in Monbijou Park or Treptower Park, lay beside the Spree on a blanket I brought with me, smoked the cigarettes he brought with him, and read and talked and cuddled.

I was happy with what we had, because I didn't want to

think beyond it. Not about what would happen next, with the baby, with me, with Kaspar.

No book provoked such intense discussion at our meetings as Christa Wolf's *Divided Heaven*. Who was right – Rita, who stayed in the GDR, or Manfred, who left? Rita's most fervent champion was Volker, whom I had sat next to at extended secondary school; he had fled right after the Wall was built, but came back a few days later. Some people can't be ripped from their soil, he said; whether it's good or bad, it's where their roots are, and they can't grow without it. People argued that Rita had not been rooted in that way; she moved from the village to the city, left her office life and decided to study and become a teacher. Matthias and Stephan understood why Rita continued to believe in the socialist ideal, in spite of the deficiencies in the socialist reality: Christians believed in God's justice, after all, even though reality was far from just. The East German students found Rita's unquestioning belief too ideal-ized, too romanticized, while for the West German students Manfred's resignation came across as too self-pitying. What connected Rita and Manfred? What made them lose each other? The political contrast of East and West? The irrecon-cilability of socialist and capitalist lifestyles? The differences in background, age and status, the differences in their characters? Or had they just drifted apart, as people do? Was their heaven already divided before the Wall was built, or did it divide only afterwards? Was the division an inevitable result of politics, or was it up to us whether we saw the heaven above us as divided, or as one?

On July 2, we lay beside the Spree and Kaspar poured the champagne he had brought into paper cups.

'What are we celebrating?'

'My birthday. And the coming year.'

We raised our cups in a toast. I wished him luck, and gave him a kiss and a questioning look. What was there in the coming year to celebrate?

'I don't see heaven as divided. It's God's heaven that's around me, here as there – you know the Heine poem. I'll move here.'

I shook my head.

'If you want me.'

I put my arms around his neck. 'Have you forgotten how the poem continues? With the stars hanging over him at night like death-lanterns? God's heaven was only around him here as there when he was dead. The poem is inscribed on his tomb.'

'I've been making enquiries. People from the West do often go to the East. They end up in a camp, and as long as they're not spies or criminals or crazy, they're let out after a few weeks and go off and live their lives. I won't become a good socialist, or have a great career, but I don't need one. I'll find something. We'll find something.'

I was appalled. I was appalled by the prospect of staying in the GDR. In the weeks since the Pentecost meeting, something had been taking shape in me without my realizing, and it was suddenly crystal clear. I didn't want anything more to do with the GDR. I didn't want to work hard and prove myself there any more. I didn't want to study economics, I didn't want to waste my time with the FDJ and the Student Brigade and harvest work, I didn't want to be careful what I said, and to whom, and what I thought. I didn't want to wait for a new era or a new country or a new kind of person. I didn't want to wait; I wanted to live. I didn't want this little piece of land between the Ore Mountains and the Baltic. I wanted the world.

I hadn't really been listening to Kaspar any more. He had been talking about jobs and towns, where we might go and what we might do together. He held me, and said, 'I want to be with you, Birgit. Every day. I want to fall asleep with

70

you at night and wake up with you in the morning. Do you want me?'

What is he talking about? I thought. Moving here, us living together; he's barely twenty, truly in love for the first time, how can he know what he wants? Falling asleep and waking up together, every day, that's easy to say, but we've never fallen asleep together, never woken up together. He's asking if I want him. Do I want him? I like looking at him, I like listening to his voice, I like touching him, I like how attached he is to me, I know he's reliable, but is that love? Or will it become love if I decide to be with him? I can't decide to be with him if it means living here with him, I know that, I don't want to live here, with or without him, and deciding to be with him, loving him, wanting him, none of that was on the table, what is he talking about, naïve, trusting, attached, what is he talking about.

'I don't want you to move here. You don't know what you're talking about. You wouldn't cope here. You might if you wanted to help establish socialism. But you don't. And I don't want to establish anything here any more, either. I want the world.'

He didn't let go of me, didn't scrutinize me, didn't contradict me. He went on holding me, his arms around my back, his head against mine. After a while he said quietly, 'Fine. Then I'll get you out of here.'

I know that at this point I should have told him about my condition. I didn't know what concealment does. That I would always maintain a certain caution, a certain reserve towards Kaspar that inhibits both me and him. Not that I'm afraid I'll suddenly give myself away. But whenever I want to confide in him, there is always a moment's hesitation. Should I really say that? Or should I put it in the chamber of concealment, whose door I keep locked and whose contents I would like to forget?

71

Even when we make love, I'm never free of that caution and reserve. We still enjoy sleeping together. But we have never truly lost ourselves in one another.

Later, because I hadn't told him I was pregnant, I had to conceal that I had given birth to a daughter, and what I had done with her. I can't tell him that I want to look for her, either. When I jerk awake at night, when I can't sleep and he asks me what's wrong, I shrug it off. He enjoys watching me play with children, but he doesn't understand what I am feeling. He can't understand why I keep my writing secret, either; he is hurt by it, and it hurts me that I'm hurting him. But I can't tell him what I'm writing about: myself, my daughter, and my longing for her.

I didn't know what concealment does, long-term. If I had known, if I had thought long-term, would it have changed anything? He wanted to move in with me and live together, if not there, then here: he wanted to get me out. Me, not me and a child. How could that ever have worked? I had heard of people who had fled, hidden in cars, trains or boats, through tunnels, across the Baltic, or across the Czech or Hungarian border, none of which were any good for children, who can't keep still when they're hidden and can't keep quiet and suddenly find they can't walk any further. Would he still want me at all if he knew I was expecting someone else's child? Or that I was betraying and abandoning my child because I wanted to get out and couldn't get out any other way? What sort of woman, what sort of mother, does that?

I knew that Kaspar wasn't just saying it as if it were taken for granted, he really did take it for granted – he would get me out of there. He wanted me, and he took the fact that I didn't pull away when he said 'fine' as confirmation that I wanted him, too. I didn't want to risk losing that. I thought, too, that our love would carry me past every difficulty. Kaspar's clarity, certainty and decisiveness were so convincing, so overwhelming, that I decided, too. It was a leap: I left doubt behind like clothes on a riverbank and leapt into love for Kaspar.

Since July 2, 1964, since his twentieth birthday, I have loved him. I knew he was going back to his home town at the end of the semester to do an internship with a publisher. I had told him that I was being assigned to a holiday resort hotel on the Baltic with a Student Brigade. We weren't going to write to each other, because we didn't want to write with the censor looking over our shoulders. But although the long separation made me sad, I wasn't afraid. I was certain I would see him again, and that he would get me out of there. I was certain. In the certainty of his love, I was also certain of mine.

We lay beside the Spree until it got dark. We told each other about our parents and siblings, what the Church meant to him and what the Party had meant to me, what we found exciting and who we'd had a crush on, our first flirtation and first kiss. We were jealous of kisses given to others, and laughed about it. I wanted to tell him about Leo – not what it was like with him, only that he existed – but I didn't.

We saw each other again once or twice before the end of the semester. For me, though, the evening of July 2 was both welcome and farewell. Soon we would have to bid each other farewell, but we were welcoming each other for life. The day had been warm, and it would stay warm into the night. The water of the Spree slapped on the shore; children called and laughed in the distance; a blackbird sang. It grew quiet. Kaspar said, softly:

> *How still the world reposes,*
> *While twilight round it closes,*
> *So peaceful and so fair!*
> *A quiet room for sleeping,*

Into oblivion steeping
The day's distress and sober care.

I looked forward to the poems he would know for me for the rest of my life. I closed my eyes. I would have liked to fall asleep and wake up the next morning in his arms.

Paula had a dacha near the Baltic. Her grandfather had built a shed before the war for his boat and fishing gear, and she had added a second room, a small bathroom and a small kitchen. I wonder if the dacha is still there? Or if they were forced to demolish it? Paula didn't follow building regulations when she extended the shed, and the authorities at the time turned a blind eye, because they wanted to avoid getting into disputes about all the many dachas whose construction was similarly questionable.

The dacha was on a lagoon some distance from the sea and the beaches and the holiday hotels. Unless we went shopping, or came across someone while walking or cycling, we didn't see anyone at all. That was fine by me. When my belly got bigger, Paula went shopping without me. I didn't want people to see me pregnant and ask me about my baby after it was born.

Paula and I had known each other since kindergarten. We had bonded because we were both teased, me about the two long plaits my mother made me wear, she about the red birthmark that covered her right cheek and half her forehead. We sat next to each other at the polytechnic secondary school, and remained friends when she went to Erfurt to become a nurse, while I stayed in Berlin and went to the extended secondary school. She had the summer off before starting her first job in October, and had invited me to the dacha, knowing nothing about Leo and the pregnancy and Kaspar. Later, she told me she could tell I was pregnant as soon as I arrived, but she didn't ask any questions. She waited until I felt able to talk, in the second week I was there.

I knew I could count on her friendship and loyalty, but I was afraid of how she would react to what I had to tell her, and what I wanted to do. We sat on the jetty that stretched out from the meadow in front of the dacha into the reeds, and dangled our feet in the water. She always wanted me to sit on her left, even though I had not only got used to her birthmark long ago but actually liked it; framed by her red hair, and with her many, many freckles, it lit up her face. I imagined that an Irish Carmen would look like this. Sitting there beside me, she was so beautiful, so calm, and so self-assured that I was a little in awe of her. How hasty I had been; how quickly I had entered into relationships, how sudden were my decisions.

I told her everything: about Leo, the pregnancy, Kaspar, that I didn't want to stay in the GDR, that Kaspar would get me out. Why I didn't want to keep the baby, and also why I couldn't give it to Leo.

'So what will you do?'

'Leave it on the doorstep of a hospital, or an orphanage or parsonage.'

She glanced at me, as if to make sure it was really me sitting beside her, that it was really me who had said that. 'And what'll happen to your child? It'll be adopted by goodness knows who, or fostered by goodness knows who, or it'll be put in a home and then, if it doesn't behave, in another one – one home after another, each worse than the last. Doesn't that bother you?'

'I haven't thought about it yet.'

'Then think about it. I don't know Leo, I don't like what you've told me about him, I understand that you don't want to give him the baby. But is this about you, or is it about the baby?'

'Any adoptive father, any foster father, any home, is better than Leo. Leo is a pig.'

'Oh, Birgit.' She shook her head. 'How do you see this working? You don't want the baby; you don't even want to see it and take it in your arms and breastfeed it. Do you want to get on your bike straight after giving birth and take the baby to the next-best pastor? You can't do that; only I can do that. You want me to help you with the birth, then take the baby somewhere out of sight and out of mind?'

'I told you, I haven't thought about it all yet. There's still plenty of time.'

She looked at my belly. 'Three months?'

'Two or three.'

She gazed out over the lake, narrowing her eyes as if she were inspecting the swans or the boat with the angler or the cormorant on the rotten mooring post. 'There's nothing to think about; there's just a decision to be made. But you need me, and you can't decide without me. I don't like any of this: not abandoning it on the doorstep, not leaving it to grow up with random adoptive or foster parents, certainly not growing up in a home. If you don't want the baby, it belongs to the father. He wants it. Why wouldn't he be a good father? He was good enough for you to fall in love and sleep with him.'

Paula kept on at me for several days. However much I disapproved of my own father, wouldn't it have been better if he had been there and had not been killed in the war? Leo had used me: didn't that show how much he longed for a child, and how lovingly and caringly he would look after it? I wanted to flee: didn't I want to bring things here to a good conclusion, and be reconciled with myself before I fled? Leo the villain, me the victim – was that really how it was? Hadn't I seduced him just as much as he me? Why hadn't I used contraception – had I wanted to bind him to me by getting pregnant?

What could I say? I knew that Leo must not have the baby, I knew it with my head and with my body, I knew it the way one simply knows. I still know it. I am not a birthing machine, and my child is not an object to be pulled out of the machine after putting in a bad penny. I know that there are bad adoptive and foster parents, and that there are terrible homes. But there are others, too: adoptive and foster parents brimming with love for their children, homes led by dedicated educators. And if someone is unlucky enough to grow up in a terrible home, it can also make them a resilient character.

I'm sure my daughter didn't suffer any damage. That, when I find her, she will be a strong, vivacious, happy young woman. When I find her . . . Why does the search have to be so hard that I can scarcely even bring myself to start? I mustn't find my daughter too soon, either. I mustn't find her when she's still too young. Her age has to be right; so do her personal circumstances, family and work, and she has to have dealt with some minor difficulties in life, as well. How could she understand me otherwise?

Eventually Paula gave up. 'If you can't, then you can't. I'll take the baby elsewhere. When the time comes, we'll hire a car.'

I have happy memories of that summer on the lagoon. I would wake early, make coffee, take the cup outside and sit on the jetty. I often watched the sun rise. It didn't just color the mist over the water and reeds in the east, it also tinged the sky in the west pink. It rose up red out of the mist, and when it stood gold in the clear sky I would stretch out on the jetty and gaze up at the blue, find the morning star, wait for the sea eagle, and listen to the birds and frogs. Sometimes I would fall asleep again.

I spent hours on the jetty during the day, as well. I read *War and Peace*, which I liked, but I didn't really make much headway, and didn't finish it, either. I would daydream for hours, and if I did pull myself together and read on, it wasn't long before some hope of Natasha's or Sonya's modesty, or

Pierre's awkwardness, made me think of my own concerns and I would start daydreaming again. I dreamed of bidding farewell to my grandmother, mother and sisters; of my revenge on Leo; of how my professor, whom I liked and who liked me, would react to my escape; of a discussion with Volker about escaping and staying abroad or coming back again; of life in the West with Kaspar, and a life in the West without him, too. I dreamed of my childhood, playing hopscotch in the street, raspberry sweets in a tall glass at the co-operative store, the raisin buns at the baker's next door, the carousel at the Christmas market, the chestnut trees in the schoolyard, joining the Young Pioneers, my pride in the blue kerchief. I dreamed of the excruciating boredom of Sunday afternoons. Back then, I had been impatient that life was standing still; now, it made me happy. I was happy not to have to do anything but wait. I didn't even wait; waiting is an activity, and it wasn't me that was active, it was time. It passed.

When it rained, I daydreamed the days away on the sofa in the dacha. Paula sat at the table, studying; she wanted to be a district nurse, and was preparing for the additional training – and for the birth, which was one of a district nurse's responsibilities; she would get to practice with me. I listened to the rain on the roof, the initial drops, the furious pelting of a rainstorm, the soft rustle of steady rain, the last drops falling from the branches above the dacha. Sometimes Paula and I just slipped on dresses and walked through the warm rain till the wet dresses stuck to us and we laughed as we helped each other take them off again and jumped off the jetty into the water.

I learned to love the forest. My mother never took her daughters to the forest. When we went on trips into the forest with the Young Pioneers and the FDJ, there were instructions to be followed and assignments to be completed, and we did everything busily and noisily. The forest around the lagoon was quiet. I heard the wind in the trees, the birds, twigs snapping when trodden on by a deer or a wild boar, my own footsteps. I smelled the forest, the dry pine needles on the ground, the musty smell of rotting wood, the resinous smell of felled trees, the heavy, pungent, sensuous smell of mushrooms. When Paula and I walked together, she found the mushrooms I could only smell, and she knew which tasted good and which tasted bad and which were poisonous. I collected wild strawberries and little sour raspberries and blackberries. Unlike the forests around Berlin, this had undergrowth and beeches and oaks, not just Scots pines. Sun and wind conjured a play of light and shade in the leaves that I never tired of watching. It changes constantly, and yet remains the same – like a fire, like a lake, like the sea.

Early one morning, coming out of the dacha, I saw a fox. It emerged from the forest, where the dacha stood beneath the last few trees, and walked across the meadow. It turned its head towards me and looked at me. It acknowledged me, the way a house owner acknowledges the soldiers who are billeted in his house, whom he does not permit to disturb him in his room, and who will soon move on. It disappeared into the reeds, as if it planned to go swimming. I would have liked to talk to it.

Later, when I told Kaspar about the landscape, he wanted to go there with me as soon as it was possible again. I didn't say yes and I didn't say no. When it became possible again, when the signing of the Basic Treaty meant we no longer had anything to fear as a consequence of my escape from the GDR, he pressed me, and I had to tell him that I didn't want to. That summer, back then, had been so magical, the pictures in my head were so fresh and so clear – I didn't want to overlay them with new pictures and new memories. Kaspar didn't understand it: all the beautiful things he had experienced without me he wanted to experience again with me.

Above all, he didn't understand why I didn't want to go to the GDR. I don't want to travel to the new federal states even now. Not because of lovely pictures and memories that I want to preserve, or ugly ones I want to avoid. I have hardly any pictures, and that's how I want it to stay. In the GDR we had city maps of Berlin, the capital of the GDR, on which West Berlin was just a big white blank, terra incognita. That was what the GDR became for me after my escape: a big white blank, terra incognita. It does need to be explored, but I have no interest in doing it.

I should. The GDR was my life for the first twenty years of it. How can I see myself, understand myself, prove myself, without accepting that time as part of me? How can I write about myself; how can I write about my daughter? It's not true, either, that I'm not interested in the GDR. I'm researching how orphans in the GDR grew up, the problems difficult teenagers faced, the homes where they were locked up. But I don't want to go there. Not to Paula, to find out whose doorstep she left the baby on; not to the pastor or the hospital or the orphanage, not to the adoptive or foster parents, not to the homes. Is Paula even still alive? I last wrote to her in 1979, and not long after that she stopped writing, too. I also stopped sending letters to my grandmother, mother and sisters, but I know from announcements Helga sent me that Grandmother and Mother died a long time ago, and Gisela died of breast cancer not long before the Wall came down. By now, it's possible that Helga is also dead and I just don't know about it.

I don't want to go there. It would feel as if I were right back where I was before my escape. As if I had only just had the baby, as if I had only just turned my face away when Paula tried to show it to me, as if I had only just waited for Paula to start the Trabi and drive off and take the baby elsewhere and dispose of it anonymously, somewhere where it is no longer mine. I must go there, I know. It is the start of the search for the child, my daughter, and it is part of the search for myself. I cannot find myself if I don't find her, or at least do everything in my power to find her.

I've reread what I've written, and I don't like it. Yes, I have good reason to look for my daughter. But if I'm experiencing such profound resistance, if my innermost being rebels against it, I also have good reason not to.

When I heard the Trabi drive off, I felt liberated. I had pushed out the thing that had grown inside me, and was rid of it. I was empty, I was light.

I am not a monster. I know that even pregnant women who want their babies sometimes feel as I felt. They sense in their belly, as I did, not a tiny creature that they love and stroke and talk to and whose boxing and kicking delights them, but a growth. Not malignant. But something that doesn't belong there. That needs to come out. They don't put themselves through the agony of birth in order to hold their baby in their arms, but to rid themselves of this growth. I felt no connection with the thing that was growing inside me. Sometimes Paula would try to persuade me to put my hands on my belly and listen to what my body was telling me. I refused to go along with it. But I did follow all her instructions for the birth. They say that, with a first labor, it can take a very long time for the final contractions to start. They came quickly for me, and the baby came quickly, too. It was an easy birth.

I had the baby at two or three in the morning. By the time the Trabi was out of earshot, I could hear the first birds. It grew light, and I saw that it was going to be a day of white sky and pale sun, when contours blur and colors fade. That suited me.

I, too, felt as if I were becoming less and less, empty and light. I fell asleep, woke when Paula came home, fell asleep again. I don't know for how many days I languished like that.

Paula helped me with the lochia, the sweats and the pain, and showed me what to do to make the milk stop after a week. When I felt like howling, she thought it served me right, and turned away. I thought it served me right, as well. Not that I thought I'd sinned and needed to atone for it. I'd got myself into a mess, perhaps I had even caused the mess, and when you're in a mess you feel like howling.

I didn't have much time, either. The winter semester started in mid-October, and I needed to be back in Berlin. I didn't know when I would see Kaspar again. And when would the escape happen, when would I be with him, when would he see me naked? I had done all I could to ensure I wouldn't come to him with stretch marks. Now I had to do all I could to ensure he wouldn't see me with a flabby stomach.

I had read about peasant women who, when their contractions started, walked from the fields to the farm, gave birth, and were back working in the fields the following day. I wanted to be able to do this as well. At any rate, Kaspar didn't notice anything when we met up again, and by the time I joined him three months later, after my escape, the last of the stretch marks had vanished and my belly was taut and flat again.

I was proud of this. It's only now that I wonder whether it wouldn't have been better if I had not been able to hide my condition from Kaspar when I arrived, or when we saw each other again in October, or even when we said goodbye in July. Alas for the hiding; alas for the silence.

But I've already written all I can about that.

Paula. I don't want her to see me, I don't want her to see through me, I don't want to speak to her, go to her, look for her. But whose doorstep did she leave my daughter on all those years ago?

Paula didn't stay long at the hospital; she soon became a district nurse. The last time she wrote to me, she was a district nurse in Briesen. I don't actually need to see her. Isn't writing to her enough? After writing to the local authority in Briesen to obtain her location and address?

Dear Paula,

You never reproached me, back then. You thought my decision was wrong, and you tried to change my mind. Not by lecturing me, but by asking me to listen to what my body was telling me. I didn't want to. I didn't want to meet the baby.

Now I do. I want to meet my daughter, the strong, vivacious, happy young woman she has become. I want to explain to her why I couldn't accept her, back then. I don't want to demand anything of her — how could I? I want to offer myself to her, all that I am and all that I have, and hope there's something there that she likes.

I'm trying to write a book. About myself, what else? Who was I, back then? Was I too immature to take on the responsibility for my child; was I right to leave that to others? Was I too egotistical? Must my life in the West outweigh what I could have been for my child in the East? I want to find all this out through my writing. I want to put myself on trial — and make the case for myself. What I write will be uncompromising and truthful.

Whose doorstep did you leave the baby on, back then? I ought to discuss all this with you in person, not in writing. I ought to come and visit you. I can't do it. I still can't go back to the GDR, what's left of it, not yet. When I can . . .

I hope you are well, and send my warmest regards

Then another letter:

Dear Pastor,

I am sure you remember that one night, just over forty years ago, a baby was left on your doorstep. She was – she is – my daughter. Please will you help me look for her?

I don't want to burst into her life. I just want to offer myself to her. She may even be looking for me.

Yours sincerely

And so on? Letter after letter? To the adoptive parents, the foster parents, the children's home? Would they even help me look for her? Would they have to ask my daughter first if she wants to be found? Or are they allowed to take the decision as to whether it is in my daughter's interest? Would she want to see me in order to decide? Would I have to tell her what happened, back then?

I can at least write to the local authority in Briesen and ask where Paula lives now.

My daughter, the strong, vivacious, happy young woman? Why do I keep repeating this? Even though I've researched orphans, problem teenagers and children's homes in the GDR? Even though I have seen the photo – have seen her?

I thought it was myself I was seeing. The young woman standing at the bus stop with the boys with jump boots and tattoos, looking straight into the camera, not insolent and defiant like the others, but superior and indifferent – there is a photo of me at the Humboldt University matriculation ceremony in which I, too, look like that, exactly like that. It wasn't how I felt, but it was how I wanted to come across, at the ceremony and in the photo: superior and indifferent. I can't put the photos side by side; all I have in front of me is the photo of the bus station, with the graffiti, and the beer and liquor bottles on the bench and on the ground, that they showed on TV and that I asked them to send me. But I clearly remember the photo of me at the matriculation ceremony, and I've got the photo from the *Sächsische Zeitung* of me in the Student Brigade. They seem to be photos of the same young woman. I recognize her in me again when I look in the mirror, even though I am decades older.

We don't have a TV; neither of us wants one. I happened to see the program at a friend's house. It was about the lost generation who were in their mid-twenties when the Wall came down, whose training was worthless in united Germany, who didn't have the heart or the energy to train all over again, who had no work, drank a lot, loitered about, mouthed off and sometimes beat up punks or foreigners or homeless people. The journalist had found quite a few among them who had been raised in homes in the GDR, and who had not only no training and no work, but no family, either.

I asked the television station where the photograph was taken. Frankfurt an der Oder. Should I have travelled there straight away and gone from bus stop to bus stop asking about her, looking for her? Hello, here I am! We look so alike – could we possibly be mother and daughter? Shall we sit and have a coffee or a beer together? I gave birth to you and abandoned you in 1964, sorry. I understand that you didn't and don't have it easy. Is there something I can do for you? You're welcome to come and stay with me, with us; my husband knows nothing about it, but that doesn't matter.

I couldn't bring myself to do it. And how do I know the photo shows what I think it does? You see the most astonishing, bewildering resemblances. They often hold conventions for people who all look like Elvis Presley or Bill Clinton, and if they're making a film about Queen Elizabeth or Abraham

Lincoln, they find an actress who looks like the queen or an actor who looks like the president. What would I be doing to a young woman if I started talking about mothers and daughters and making confessions and promises without being absolutely certain?

Besides, why shouldn't my daughter be a strong, vivacious, happy young woman? I've read that in Germany one million children were orphaned by World War I, half a million by World War II, a million in Vietnam by the Vietnam War, between fifteen and twenty million worldwide by AIDS. Some will have been traumatized, others will not; that's how it is. And there are so many famous orphans, in life and literature! No: whatever my daughter has been through, I refuse to stop picturing her as a strong, vivacious, happy young woman. She's not a young woman any more; she's in her forties, I know that. How could she understand me if she hadn't lived? All the same, I see her as young – as young as I was back then.

What would it have been like if I had fetched her and brought her home to us? A young woman who has grown up in children's homes and is traumatized and drinks beer and liquor with boys at bus stops and mouths off and gets into fights? How would Kaspar have reacted?

In all the years of our marriage, I have sometimes thought that deep down, deep inside, Kaspar knows, and has concealed it from his life just as I have concealed it from mine. I thought he must have sensed that I was concealing a secret, and that, out of love, he didn't probe, until his love let him guess, even know, what it was. And that then he shared it with me – you can share without words and without gestures – and that was why he was always so gentle with me. I know that he was also gentle with me because the things I did confused him. Leaving the bookshop, going to India, goldsmithing, cooking, writing – he didn't understand what drove me, and was afraid it would drive me away. He was also gentle because he didn't want to lose me. But I sometimes thought that wasn't the only reason.

People talked less in the nineteenth-century world, the literature in which Kaspar prefers to spend his time. People talked less in the GDR, as well. About emotional things, that is. Talk of fears and urges and childhood conditioning, psychological and psychoanalytical dilettantism, was something I only encountered after fleeing to the West. Women who don't know what's the matter with their men, who complain about how their men don't talk about themselves any more – how often have I heard this from my friends? As if everything needed to be described and explained! I usually know what's the matter with their men. You just have to watch and listen. It used to be something you learned; people don't learn it nowadays, or they've forgotten how to do it. Couples usually used to know what it was their partner couldn't talk about. That's why I sometimes think Kaspar knows what I can't talk about. That concealing it wasn't so wrong after all. That the day or night may still come when we sleep together and lose ourselves in one another.

How would Kaspar react if I told him today that my daughter was coming to stay with us, told him who she is? Would he lock away the valuables so my daughter wouldn't take them and pawn them to buy alcohol or drugs? Would he ask me how I thought that could work, me with my alcohol problem and my daughter with hers? Would he stock up on alcohol so we would drink at home and not go out crawling from one pub to the next? Would he think about which books my daughter might like to read, bring them home from the bookshop and put them on the bedside table in the guest room? Would he ask her if she could give him a hand in the bookshop? Would he want to take her to the theatre and concerts and the cinema?

Yes, he would do all of that. He wouldn't impose on her. As long as she wasn't dismissive and unpleasant, he would open his heart to her.

Why have I let all those years go by since I saw her on television? It's too late now to go to the bus stop in Frankfurt an der Oder and fetch her and bring her to live with us.

When Kaspar and I saw each other again, in October, we were relieved. Not that we were worried over the summer that we wouldn't love each other any more come the autumn. In some strange, wonderful way we knew right from the beginning that our love would last. But there were so many things that could happen in three months! An extension of the travel ban to cover not just West Berliners but all West Germans; an informer in our circle of friends, whose reports the Stasi took seriously enough to ban all contact between East German students and students from the West; an accident that might put me or Kaspar in a wheelchair. It is possible for people to love and lose each other.

We resumed our life as we had lived it in the summer. We met up at Ingrid's with our friends from East and West, went to the theatre and the cinema with them, and spent time alone together, for as long as we could, on the blanket in the park, then afterwards on long, cold walks, and in cafés and bars. We bought candyfloss at the Christmas market and went on the carousel and the Ferris wheel; Kaspar pretended he didn't see how pitiful it all was, and I bade farewell to my childhood and youth.

Kaspar didn't talk about his efforts to find a means of escape. When the time came, he explained to me what I had to do. I had to book one of the weekend trips to Prague that East Germans were being offered in the winter of 1964–65, for January 15 to 17. I would be given a ticket and papers; I would board the train to Prague with these on the fifteenth, and show the papers to the East German border guards. Shortly afterwards, I would show the Czechoslovak border guards different papers: with these, I would travel as a West German, in transit through Czechoslovakia en route to Vienna. Kaspar needed passport photos of me, my height, my eye color. When he brought me the papers on the fourteenth, he explained the rest of the escape: the arrival in Prague, the train to Vienna, the hotel in Vienna and then, the following day, the flight to Berlin. He would be waiting for me at Tempelhof. If, during my escape, someone spoke to me and said, 'I wonder what the good soldier Švejk would say?', there was a reason for that: the people who obtained the papers were sending one of their number to travel with me. Then Kaspar gave me a travel bag, a scarf he had bought in KaDeWe and a packet of Marlboros, and told me to put the new travel bag inside my old one for the GDR border control; for the Czechoslovak border control, I should hide my old travel bag inside the new one, put on the scarf, and smoke Marlboro, not Juwel.

I didn't ask who these people were, how they had got hold of the papers, whether they would be travelling with me because the border guards had to be bribed, why they might speak to me. Kaspar and I only discussed the essentials, and we did so calmly, as if there were no danger and nothing could go wrong. I was afraid when I learned he was crossing the border with my passport photos, afraid before he came with the papers, and afraid when I saw myself in the mirror – I could see in my face that I wanted to escape, and thought everyone else would see it in me as well. He must have been afraid, too, when he brought the passport photos and papers over the border: afraid of body searches like the ones to which he and other friends of ours had been subjected. Neither of us let our fear show on the fourteenth. But when we hugged each other goodbye, we held each other very close for a very long time.

I said goodbye to my grandmother, mother and sisters, saying I was going to Prague for the weekend. I didn't want to say goodbye for longer; not because they would have betrayed me, but because I feared that there would be a reckoning, Grandmother and Mother with me, and I with them. When I said goodbye to Ingrid, she hugged me for longer than usual; then she looked at me, took my head in her hands, and said, 'Good luck,' as if she knew. I was moved by all the places I was seeing for the last time, the journeys I was making for the last time: Unter den Linden, the steps of the Humboldt University, the S-Bahn with its wooden seats and smell of cleaning fluid, the old school opposite our house, the tram, the apricot tart in the bakery window. For a moment I even liked the enamel sign with the three blue arrows and the slogan 'Recognized Area of Exemplary Order, Security, Cleanliness and Discipline', which hung on our house and which I had always found absurd.

I slept badly. In my dreams I was sitting on a train, realized it was the wrong one, waited at a station where no further trains arrived or departed, dragged a suitcase over railway ballast and tracks to a train that pulled away just as I had almost reached it. Fear crouched in my body, a slight fever, cramp in my stomach, trembling and jumping at every sound and light. I was glad when dawn came, when day broke, when I made coffee in the kitchen and prepared breakfast and we all sat down together as if it were a day like any other.

The train to Prague was cold. I was sharing a compartment with an elderly couple and a student; I told myself they would notice I had different papers and identities at the different border controls, wondered how they would react, didn't know what to do. They got off at Dresden. I sat alone in the cold compartment, shivering because I was freezing and scared, stared out of the window at the river and forest and mountains, and smoked. The East German border guard shook his head and flapped his hand, waving the smoke out of the compartment. The Czechoslovak guard wrinkled his nose, turned away, took my papers out into the corridor, closed the compartment door and checked and stamped them outside.

With that, it was already over. I was relieved. And still afraid. What if the border guards talked to each other about the smoker in the compartment? Who couldn't be both East and West German? Would they come back and arrest me? Or would they call ahead to Prague? Would the police be waiting for me when I got off the train?

I was afraid to get off in Prague. I was afraid at the Czecho-slovak–Austrian border. After that, I shouldn't have been afraid any more, but the fear had lodged in my bones. In the bar of the hotel in Vienna, I drank for the first time in my life, to numb myself, and my fear disappeared overnight. I enjoyed the take-off and flying the next day – it was my first flight. Shortly before we landed, a man sat down beside me and smiled. 'I wonder what the good soldier Švejk would say?' He took my West German papers off me, praised me, said I had done well, got up and left.

I saw Kaspar as I was waiting behind the glass door that led from the customs area into the main hall. He was standing in the hall, had seen me, and was hopping about and fidgeting and waving. I waved back, and as soon as I was through the glass door we ran towards each other and fell into each other's arms.

It had only been two days since our last meeting, but we felt different. We were in another world, from another world. We took a taxi to Dahlem; Kaspar took me to his room, where he had put champagne on ice; he opened it, toasted me and wanted to hear all about my escape. More than anything, though, he wanted to touch, hold, stroke, kiss me. He wanted to sleep with me, sleep with me at last. I would rather have gone for a walk, in a park, in a wood, by a lake or river, felt the rain promised by the grey clouds overhead. But I thought I owed it to Kaspar, and I slept with him, his desire, his need, his impatience, his awkwardness. I fell asleep as the rain began to fall on the windowpanes and sill.

I woke in the middle of the night. Kaspar was asleep beside me with his fist in front of his face and his legs drawn up, like a child. I got up, opened the window and lit a cigarette. None of it was wrong; not Kaspar, not the bed, not the room. At the same time, none of it was right. I was no longer there, and I was not yet here. Gradually I would settle in. We would push the bed over to the other side of the room and gaze up from it at the tree and the sky; we would find a desk for me and put it in front of the window; we would walk the streets, first around the block, then in ever-widening circles. The heating gurgled, and I thought of how, at home, I had to get the tiled stove going in the morning; sometimes, if we had wrapped it tightly in newspaper, the briquette would still be glowing, and I only had to blow on it hard to light the fire. I thought of the nocturnal noises of home: my grandmother's shuffling footsteps and my mother's hurried ones when they went to the toilet, Helga's smoker's cough, the chiming of the clock on the quarter-, half-, three-quarter and full hour, which sounded beautiful to me as a child and, later, rather jangly; the screech of the tram as it rounded the corner, the last shortly after eleven, the first just before five. I thought of my bed: Mother and Grandmother had one bedroom; Helga had one she used to share with Gisela and didn't want to share with me; I slept on the sagging, uncomfortable, creaky sofa in the living room. Nothing that came to mind was particularly nice or particularly important. But I was swamped by a wave of homesickness, and no longer knew why I was here and not there.

Then Kaspar woke, saw me standing at the window, sat up and asked, 'What is it?'

I said, 'Nothing.'

I said it on many nights that followed, even after the initial, powerful wave of homesickness had passed. As with my homesickness, I didn't want to talk to Kaspar about what I was thinking: about the baby, or my worries about studying and work, or about him and me. Those first weeks were not easy, in various ways: I was interrogated for three days in the Marienfelde reception camp; the financial support Kaspar received from his parents was modest; the five thousand marks he had borrowed from various people to pay for my escape had to be paid back. There were no women in the apartment, and they didn't want any women, and pressured us to move out; when I went to the authorities to get a new identity card and passport, and the orphan's pension to which I was entitled because my father had been killed in the war, I was treated like a troublesome petitioner. And the shopping! As a refugee, I was given vouchers for an initial outfit, clothes and shoes; they were only enough to buy shoddy things, and when I didn't want to make do with the shoddy things the shops laid out for me, and wanted to pay extra for better ones, it was made clear to me that I should take what I was given and not ask questions, and not express a preference.

Kaspar put up with me standing and smoking and saying nothing in the middle of the night, accompanied me to the authorities and to the shops and the student advisory service and the matriculation office so I could start studying the following semester, moved the bed and found a desk for me, made the bed in the morning, cleaned the room, and cooked in the evening. He was loving, helpful, patient – until he reached the end of his tether. I brought home a little portable radio; I'd always wanted one, and had finally bought one for myself. I had done so without speaking to Kaspar first, and he was furious. How could I spend so much money! I knew how hard up we were; he understood it wasn't easy for me to rearrange my entire life, but he'd had to rearrange his as well; he would have to stop studying to work and earn money; I was acting like a princess; this couldn't go on. He wouldn't stop, and he started to talk about us: no, being together was not a mistake, but we had to be together properly, if we weren't together properly we wouldn't survive. He didn't mind if I studied and he gave up his studies, but if we were living in two different worlds, me at university and him at work, it was even more important that we should be together properly. If he woke up again and saw me standing at the window smoking, he would grab me and shake me until I told him what was wrong; yes, he knew that this was unacceptable, but he didn't care.

I was shocked. My homesickness, the pain of my humiliation by the authorities and in the shops, my dithering over which subject to study, my disappointment at sex with Kaspar, which still wasn't good, my worries about money – it was self-indulgent behavior with which I was trying to get out of living, living for myself, living with him.

'You're right.'

He stared at me in astonishment. It took a moment for him to see from my expression that I meant it, that I had understood him. Then he smiled. 'You're my princess. When I said you were acting like one, I didn't . . .'

'How about queen?'

'Queen's good, too.'

'Let's start again.'

★

And so we started again. I overcame my shyness, told him what I liked and didn't like, where and how I wanted to be touched, what roles I wanted to play and which he should play. He was a quick learner, and became an imaginative lover. When he saw me standing by the window at night, smoking, and asked me what was wrong, I told him everything, except my thoughts about my daughter. But I didn't get up as often any more. We talked at length about studying and work. He said studying wasn't important to him and he would be just as happy apprenticed to a bookseller. At first I didn't believe him and urged him to continue with his studies, but then I realized he was serious and went with him to look around Berlin bookshops. I enrolled on the German and Theatre Studies course at the Free University. We found a small apartment: a living room with a stove, a bedroom without one, a kitchen where the sink doubled as a washbasin, a toilet outside on the landing. We bought a shower cabin and installed it in the kitchen.

There were two months until the start of his apprenticeship and the start of my semester. We wanted to pay off our debts and earn money, and we found work at Siemens. It was Kaspar's first experience of a factory, my first of a West German factory. It was more hierarchical than the East German ones I had worked in; the bosses were more important, the tone was harsher, the processes faster. Two of my female colleagues were students; the other women treated us with friendly condescension. It would have been better if I hadn't told them that I had just escaped from the East; I was often treated not only with condescension but with faint contempt, as if I were spoiled and were being pampered and coddled at the expense of others. I realized that the indignities I had been subjected to by the authorities and in shops had deeper roots. At university, no one, professor or student, treated me with condescension, but if I introduced an East German perspective or used an East

German term, I irritated them. They expected all things East, because Soviet and communist, to have been cast off when I escaped, and that I would now be just like them.

What happened to me was a small-scale version of what I saw happen to East Germans after the fall of the Wall. At first, they were welcomed with delight. People asked, with interest, what it had been like in the East, how they had lived there. But they were asked the way people are asked about their travels. When it became apparent that they had not simply been travelling and had now returned, but that they came from another world, a world where some things had not been to their liking, but a world that was theirs, one they had built and preserved, a world to which they had been and were still connected, the interest quickly waned. Had the East actually created something of its own? In the East there had been oppression, injustice and unhappiness; since oppression and injustice had ended, formerly oppressed East Germans could be like unoppressed West Germans again, and no longer had any reason to be different. If they were, it was inappropriate, and ungrateful, too, because so much had been given to them to make them as happy as happy West Germans.

It is best for us East Germans, when we are among West Germans, to leave all things East behind. It was true then, and it is still true now. My daughter was not the only reason I erased the GDR, made it a blank, terra incognita.

It also spoiled my studies for me. I didn't belong. Lectures were fine; all of us sat there silently and listened and took notes. But the seminars and colloquiums were attended by the students who had read everything and more, who asked the right questions and gave the right answers and came out with incisive criticism. They weren't just clever – or, if they weren't, they didn't just act clever – they were suave, skilful and eloquent, with precisely the right degree of arrogance for the rest of us to accept it as an expression of genuine superiority. The rest of us – I wasn't the only one who kept quiet, I wasn't the only one who lowered her head when the professor asked a question of the group, I wasn't the only one who stammered when I had to speak. With the others, though, it was shyness. I was afraid I would say something that would betray my Eastern origins, to which the professor would respond with, 'Ah, our student from the East,' or, 'So, what does Karl Marx have to say about this? I'm sure you'll know,' or, 'We learn this in high school here, but you don't have it over there.' Or else that one of the suave students would find my origins exotic and chat me up after class, and I would just feel inferior and horrible.

Also, nothing was ever taken seriously. I wanted to know who the author was and when and why, his purpose in writing the text, the effect the text had had in its day, and to feel the effect it had today, to find myself in the text and allow it to touch and change me, to see its power, its beauty, its greatness, to understand and love it. In class, no one wanted to see and understand the power, beauty and greatness of the texts or allow the texts to touch and change them. It was all about quibbling, about metaphors, symbols and allegories, about immanence and reception, structuralism, synchrony and di-achrony, sociology and politics, about narratological concepts that concealed banalities such as the fact that one could tell a story in flashback or as a glimpse into the future, and could tell it once or several times, in direct or indirect speech. I didn't understand what anyone might get out of this approach to lit-erature: the professor, the student, the German teacher, or the children he would teach.

The best thing about my studies was the reading. Kaspar would be in the bookshop or the vocational school; I would lie on the bed and read. I read everything we were assigned and everything recommended to us – the literature, not the books about the literature. In the second semester, I attended a seminar on Thomas Mann's *Doctor Faustus*, and although I had to work in the holidays, because we still had to pay off our debts, I managed to set aside two weeks to read it. I lay on the bed with my back against a pillow and my head against the wall and read. On the bedside table was a glass of vodka and orange; Stephan had made me one once, and I had liked it ever since. Two ice cubes, one-fifth vodka, four-fifths orange juice. It was cheap, I could keep a clear head, it made me sleepy but only for a while. I read twenty or thirty pages, drifted off into sleep, woke up, read another twenty or thirty pages, drifted off again, woke up again. What I read accompanied me into and out of sleep; I was conscious and unconscious, waking and sleeping and dreaming in the story. Never before and never again was I so immersed in, so lost in, so at one with a book.

And I learned that you can drink alcohol without your breath betraying you. Kaspar didn't notice anything, and didn't get to see the vodka bottles, full or empty. He enjoyed me recounting *Doctor Faustus* to him as an evening serial.

I dropped out of university after two semesters, and did not regret it. I was happy to become a bookseller as well. The bookshop where Kaspar was training would also have taken me on as an apprentice, but we were determined to have our own bookshop as soon as possible, and thought it would be a good idea if we could contribute experience from two different places. We lived in Kreuzberg; his bookshop was in Zehlendorf, mine in Schöneberg, and we cycled part of the way together in the morning.

Because I had a high-school leaving certificate, my apprenticeship, like Kaspar's, lasted two years rather than three. My bookshop was small; I soon familiarized myself with it, and after six months the owner often left me in sole charge. At vocational school I learned about the book trade, bookkeeping, business administration and social studies; I was let off German classes because the teacher said I already knew enough. I liked being at school again, two half-days a week. Being entertained by information, participating a bit, switching off a bit, sometimes listening, sometimes not, joining in if it's interesting, daydreaming if it's dull – you only have this at school. At eighteen, it's effectively over, and I had it again at twenty-one. I felt light and free; Kaspar and I got to know Berlin, made new friends, and were able to celebrate repaying the last of the debt along with my passing the exam.

Then Kaspar came into a small inheritance, and we looked for a bookshop and an apartment. We wanted children, which I was both looking forward to and afraid of, and after two years we found an apartment and a bookshop and renovated both. The apartment was grand, but in a terrible state; the bookshop was smaller than we would have liked, but there was a big storeroom on the courtyard side that could be incorporated into the shop. We did most of the work ourselves: in the apartment we uncovered and restored the stucco on the ceilings, laid cables under plaster, sanded the floors and painted and tiled the walls, installed new fixtures in the bathroom, insulated the floors and walls, put in new windows, floorboards and shelving. We worked well together, didn't fall out over setbacks, and celebrated our progress. Finally, there was a big inauguration at the bookshop and, the following year, a big housewarming. I remember we were very worried in the beginning: had we overstretched ourselves by buying both the apartment and the bookshop; would a bookstore chain open a branch in our neighborhood; would we have enough customers; would we turn enough of a profit? But it all started smoothly, and our life acquired its fixed pattern, its routines, its rituals.

I remember those early years very clearly. The train compartment I travelled in from Berlin to Prague; the view from the plane on my flight from Vienna to Berlin; the interrogation room in the Marienfelde reception camp; the classroom in the vocational school; the bare walls and rubble in the apartment and bookshop during the renovations – I see it all in my mind's eye. My memories of the years that followed are fainter and paler. Is that how it is when life proceeds at a leisurely pace, without shocks or surprises? When alcohol becomes your companion? Life was not uneventful: we leased an allotment, bought a grand piano for the big apartment and took lessons, learned Italian, organized readings and started a book club for adults and another for children, travelled a lot – not long trips, because we didn't want to leave our staff to run the bookshop for too long, but short, quick ones to the capitals of Europe. I remember exactly all the things we did. But I don't see them in my mind's eye. I carry images of the renovated apartment and the extended bookshop with me; I live in the apartment, and I'm often in the bookshop, even though I don't work there any more. But I don't see Kaspar and myself at our piano or Italian lessons, or on our trips; the Eiffel Tower and St Peter's Basilica are no different in my mind than if I had seen them on television or postcards. It's as if a fog of memory has settled over all those years; occasionally it parts, but in it I take uncertain, fumbling steps.

This is true even of the months in India, my great departure and awakening. I read an article about Bhagwan Shree Rajneesh and his ashram in Poona, and not long afterwards I recognized a woman in the bookshop, in orange robes and with a small picture of a bearded man in a round wooden frame on a long wooden chain around her neck, as a sannyasin, a follower of the Bhagwan. I spoke to her; she had just got back from Poona and was transported by her experience. She talked about the Bhagwan's lectures, the groups, the meditation, the dancing and the loving. She talked about her fears, her ambition, her successes and her ego, and how Poona had liberated her from all that. When I asked her what she planned to do in the future, she smiled. She was in the here and now. Here was the goal, now was the fulfilment; all we had to do was let it be. Let it be, and let go.

She said it cheerfully, with conviction, gazed at me as if she could see into my soul, stroked my head with her hand, and I began to weep. I didn't know why; why the idea of letting it be and letting go touched me so deeply. But a longing arose in me and grew stronger and more purposeful, a longing to cast off and sail away, to leave behind my harbor and my shore and lose myself in the vast expanse of the seas, to be myself, devoid of ego. I couldn't stop crying, and she took me in her arms. When I had calmed down and released myself from her embrace, she held me by my shoulders and laughed at me: 'You have to go.' I gulped, looked into her laughing face, and I, too, started laughing, hesitantly at first, then loudly. 'I have to go.'

I was glad, and also somewhat aggrieved, that Kaspar let me go without protesting. I want him to respect my independence, to let me make my own decisions and do as I please, but I want it to be obvious that he finds it hard. He said that he didn't like being without me, that he would miss me. But he said it as if he had already come to terms with it, and that hurt me. In the encounter group in Poona, I accused him of being unable to let go, of being an emotional cripple, a wimp who repressed his own sexuality and mine, and I rained down blows on the man whose face and body reminded me of him. Whom I slept with the very same day.

With him, and with others. I thought I had understood what love was: that it takes and gives joy without needing, without demanding, without clinging. That sex, if it is spontaneous, natural and conscious, opens a door to the universe. That first in sex, in orgasm, then in dance, in ecstasy, in kundalini, and finally in meditation, I would experience the summit and the stillness and leave my ego in the valley. When I took sannyas and received the mala, the Bhagwan's picture in a wooden frame, I also received a new name: Prem Raga, the song of love. I felt a new love for all things and a new enthusiasm for all things; increasingly, it was enough for me to listen to the Bhagwan's lecture in the morning, sit and meditate by the river during the day, and listen to music and dance in the evening. When I was offered the chance to live in the ashram and work in the kitchen, I was going to write to Kaspar and say that I wasn't coming back to Berlin.

I kept putting it off. I sat by the river and tried to meditate; the days I spent in meditation are among my clearest and most beautiful memories of Poona. The fog of memory parts, I see the fast-flowing river, I hear it rushing along, and the brightly colored birds fly low over the water, which reflects the blue sky and white clouds. Again and again I succeeded in consigning my thoughts, memories, feelings to the river, which took them and carried them away. But the decision to stay in Poona and not return to Berlin blocked my meditation. And yet I had already made it – all I had to do was tell him!

No, I hadn't made it, not yet. I had told the sannyasins with whom I shared an apartment in Poona about the offer, and they had congratulated me. I was so lucky! The Bhagwan's presence, his energy, his clarity, the dynamics and music of the ashram, the work with the sannyasins. They yearned for an offer like the one I had received, and took it for granted that I would accept and stay. I had not decided; I had allowed myself to be carried along by their congratulations and by what they desired for themselves.

And this wasn't the first time. During the months in the ashram, I had allowed myself to become infected by the others' yearning for a life without rationalism and materialism, without greed and fear, without ego. The yearning was not mine. I did not believe in rationality, and was not attached to material things; I had no ambition, no fear of loss; I didn't need to be liberated from them. The Bhagwan, I realized, was for people from the West who cared about career, success, prestige and riches, who had had enough of them, who were seeking enlightenment – and then pursued a career in the ashram and were successful and acquired prestige by being closer or not so close to the Bhagwan, more or less enlightened, important or not so important in the ashram's organization and in the leadership of the groups. I was a child of the East: none of it made any sense to me.

Although I did not return to Berlin as a sannyasin, I was not the same. I had cast off and sailed away, had left behind my harbor and my shore and lost myself in the vast expanse of the seas. Lost and found – I was fully present, I needed no enlightenment and no new name and no orange robe, nor did I want children any more; I liked my world and my life, and I saw enough that appealed to me, that I wanted to do and try. I was happy to see Kaspar again, to be with him morning and evening, to share the bed with him and sleep with him. The rest of the time, I lived my own life. First training to be a goldsmith, but not working as a goldsmith for long; then training to be a cook, but again staying only a short while in the kitchen; finally, retreating to write in a little room overlooking the courtyard – perhaps that doesn't sound like a real life of my own, more like a chaotic, aimless muddle. For me, though, each step was the right one, even if I don't know why. Sometimes I think that, first of all, I wanted to give my daughter something pretty. The little silver cup, my first piece of metalwork, might have been a gift in honor of her birth.

Then perhaps I felt that what my daughter really needed, more than a pretty cup, was a good meal. What she needs even more urgently is a face, a form; she needs to become a person. For that, I have to look for and find her, offer myself, expose myself to her, and I hope I can do this by writing it all down.

This is how I envisage my novel:

Part 1: Me

Childhood and youth, Leo, Kaspar, the birth, escape, apprenticeship and bookshop, India, goldsmithing, cooking, starting to write, writing as search

Part 2: The Search

The search for Paula; the conversation with her; the lead, following the lead, stages along the way

Part 3: Her

One day I will stand in front of a door, will knock or ring, and she will open it. Or her husband will, or a child. I ask if I can speak to her. 'What's it about?' 'May I come in for a moment and explain inside?' And the child calls: 'Mummy, there's a woman who wants to come in and explain something.' She comes out now, and looks at me suspiciously. 'Yes?' I say it's a complicated matter that I would rather not have to discuss on the doorstep or in the hall. Perhaps she asks if it's to do with this or that, an accident involving her husband, or her daughter having a problem in school, or a complaint by a neighbor, things she wants nothing to do with that could cause her anxiety and trouble. I say no; she lets me in, and we stand in the kitchen. I would like to speak to her in private, but what do I do if she insists her husband stays with us? Do I start by saying that she presumably knows she was found on the doorstep of a parsonage or hospital on the Baltic coast? That I left her there. That I am her mother. I can't make up for failing her back then. But if I can be something to her now, if there's something I can give her, I would like to do so. If there's a place for me in her life, I would like to be part of it.

Do I prepare a slip of paper with my name, address and telephone number, to leave there if she throws me out? What do I say if she doesn't throw me out, but is brimful of rejection and hostility? Forgive me? I'm sorry? I don't know whether I am sorry, or how sorry I am. It's so long ago; it has become a part of me that I accept as I accept myself. I can tell her that I understand her rejection and hostility, take the slip of paper out of my bag and put it on the table and leave. If at that point she sits down – she's been standing until now – and invites me to sit as well, if she looks at me across the kitchen table and asks, 'Why?', I have to talk. If then she says, 'You chose to look after yourself in the West rather than look after me here,' I shrug my shoulders. I say again that I detested Leo; that I wouldn't have wanted to keep her even if I had stayed in the East, that I would have aborted her if I could, and besides, all I did was leave her to a fate thousands of children experienced during and after the war. What do I say if then she asks why I wanted to find her? Yes, I'm allowed to cry, to say to her through my tears that I longed for her, for the daughter who is flesh of my flesh and bone of my bones, for the woman who can understand me, and whom I can understand, like no other, for that kindred spirit in the true sense of the word. And what then?

These are idle questions. Rather than fantasizing about the encounter, I should make it happen. What am I afraid of? That the very building at or in which I knock or ring at her door will be so wretched it will break my heart? That when faced with my daughter's fate and her accusations and reproaches, I will feel guilty after all? So guilty that I cannot bear it?

The letter from Briesen town hall has lain on my desk unopened for several days now.

Paula is alive. She worked for years as a district nurse; then, after the Wall came down, she met a doctor from Berlin who was curious about the Germany behind the Wall, wanted to get to know it, spent the weekends driving around between the Baltic and the Ore Mountains, the Elbe and the Oder, and got stranded with a flat tire in Briesen. They married, and opened a practice in Rietzow, the only practice for miles around. Dr Martin Luckenbach became a proper country doctor, and Paula Luckenbach, as his receptionist, remained a district nurse; now past retirement age, between them they are still providing medical care for their rural area. Their address is An der Kirche 1, in Rietzow.

A good thing I marked my letter for the mayor's personal attention. He is happy to be able to give me good news of my old friend. She is a much-loved district nurse, is invited to all the festive occasions in the Briesen area, and sometimes comes. She had a child, incidentally, at quite an advanced age; her son studied medicine, is doing his specialist training, and his parents hope that one day he will take over the practice. Young people don't want to move out to the countryside these days. But Martin Luckenbach Jr has spent so long out in the world that perhaps he would like to settle in his old home.

I've looked it up. Just under two hours by car; three hours and twelve minutes by train, then eleven kilometres on foot or by taxi. I will go there. But I'll finish Part One first, rework what I've written about my time with Leo up to my return from India, add what happened before and afterwards.

★

That was weeks ago. I've done neither one nor the other. I have at least been cycling every day, even though I don't like getting numb hands and a runny nose in winter. Apart from that, I seem to be paralyzed; I sit at my desk looking out at the courtyard and the bare chestnut tree, at the buildings opposite, the church tower. You're depressed, you can and must do something about it, Kaspar would say, if he realized what was wrong with me; but I don't let on, and he just thinks I drink too much. He's right: I drink too much. So?

I read through it all again. All that research, the cuttings, the commentaries I prepared in the beginning! And all I found was what I already knew. The children's homes and juvenile detention centers and camps in the GDR were as GDR as everything else in the GDR, like the restaurants and the bookshops and the universities and the trains. Ugly, pedantic, narrow-minded, infantilizing, degrading, paralyzing. I could have spared myself the research. What a stupid idea, anyway – wanting to know the worst that might theoretically have happened to her so the reality could not be worse. If it were winter, I would have burned the whole lot in the tiled stove.

The poems were just a thin notebook. I tied a stone to the notebook with the leather ribbon. Then I went to the Tiergarten and threw it in the Landwehr Canal. For a moment the notebook floated on the water, as if the poems wanted to take a few last breaths. Then they succumbed and sank. Despite Klaus's friendly interest in publishing them, none of the poems were as good as I wanted them to be.

And the novel? These few pages, in almost ten years? I was so disappointed with it, and with myself, that I threw the computer at the wall. Since then, I can't find the novel any more. I can still write, and when I save what I've written, the text whisks off the screen and a chime sounds. It's as if everything I write is falling away down a deep well. Maybe I could get the computer repaired. But it seems fitting to me that the novel falls away and sinks. Maybe now I can go on writing it. Maybe now I can even go to Rietzow and begin the search. The writing and the search are one and the same, and if what I write falls away, maybe the burden of the search will fall away as well.

So. I've written something again, for the first time in weeks. Because I've gone back to vodka and orange juice? I bought every variety they had in KaDeWe: freshly squeezed juice and juice from concentrate, blond orange and blood orange juice, blood orange with grapefruit, blood orange with pomegranate. Blood orange with a bit of pulp and vodka is the best. I should leave off the wine, which I can't hide from Kaspar. I should leave off the vodka, too, I know, but I think I need it until I've really got stuck into the search.

Oh, Kaspar. Every day, in the weeks when I didn't write anything, I looked at the book you gave me for our first wedding anniversary. A yearbook of poems: you chose a poem for each day and wrote them all out by hand. Many are short, but there are some long ones and some ballads as well. So much work! And, unlike the poetry calendars in the shops, there's not a single poem in your yearbook that I don't like. Every May 17, spring sends its blue ribbon fluttering through the air once more.

Sometimes I look at you when you carry me to bed and lay me down, and I wake but I don't let you see. You sit on the stool, and you're looking at me with your eyes, but you're dreaming. Are you dreaming of the children we didn't have, the companion I never was to you, the woman I would be if I didn't drink? Or are you dreaming of the young woman you fell in love with? You still love me, I know. It is the great comfort of my life: that whatever in my life I am not, whatever I am not to you, I am enough that you love me to this day.

Part Two

I

It was early afternoon when he finished reading. There were times when he had been unable to go on, and had sat there trying to take in what he had read, to comprehend it, make sense of it. She really did that? That was how she had seen him? That was how she had seen herself? And he hadn't realized? She had thought that, deep down, deep inside, he knew everything? Was that a sign of her love? Or was she just evading responsibility, making it easy for herself — she didn't need to talk to him, because he already knew?

The final sentences — were they a message of farewell? Had Birgit taken her own life after all? No: if they were a message of farewell, Birgit would have written in the past tense, not the present. They were a message. He would rather have read a message about her love for him instead of his for her. But at least she had recognized, and had needed, his love. There was a truth to her final sentences that made Kaspar both happy and sad, and he wept.

He wept silently. Sitting there, eyes blinded by tears, he reached across the desk and opened the window, let the warm wind blow in and dry his tears, heard the sound of children playing in the courtyard, the slap of rope on ground, the counting of jumps, the glee of the jump miscalculated. In one apartment, someone was practicing 'The Entertainer' on the piano, untalented but undaunted, while a loud argument was coming from another.

Was it because of the life going on outside? All of a sudden, what had passed between him and Birgit and what they had missed out on appeared to him in all its mundanity. For all their closeness, there had been a gulf between them; he had loved her more than she him; she had wanted to find herself, and had gone looking without him; she had kept secrets from him, slept with other men, started many things and seen few of them through to the end – so? He hadn't known everything deep down, deep inside, but he had known that she could never give herself completely, and that she was never completely his. They had both known it; they had shared it, and in that respect, they had been close.

Had she been writing for him, as well? Was her text a mandate for him? If he found it, was he meant to finish the novel and send it to Klaus Ettling? What he could do was seek out this daughter and offer himself to her. Was that what she had wanted? Was that what he wanted?

He turned back to the folders and found the letter from the mayor of Briesen. Paula Luckenbach, An der Kirche 1, Rietzow; two hours by car, or three hours and twelve minutes by train plus another eleven kilometres.

He spent a long time considering the question. Even with Birgit he had once felt that he was intruding, although she had wanted him. The daughter didn't want him; this time he certainly would be intruding. Was what he had to offer good enough to justify the intrusion? Was that also why Birgit had hesitated – because she had asked herself the same question and had not been able to answer?

In the end, he made the decision because he couldn't bear his monotonous, joyless, functional life between apartment and bookshop any longer. He wanted out. He didn't feel good about it; the urge to get out didn't justify anything, but it was irresistible.

2

He found no website or email address for Dr Martin Luckenbach's practice in Rietzow, only a phone number. Should he
call, introduce himself, and ask if he could come? What if
Paula didn't want that, and wouldn't talk to him on the phone,
either? If he were standing in front of her, it would be harder
for her to turn him away. He rented a car and drove there.

He came off the autobahn at the exit for Briesen. He wanted
to see where Paula had worked for so many years. The village was spread out. Most of the houses were modest, and still
coated in the plain, sand-colored render of the GDR; some had
upgraded to yellow or white; there were sheds where things
were presumably being manufactured or stored, and a small
church with a new red-tiled roof on the tree-lined village green
that gave the village a focus and a center. Kaspar drove slowly,
hoping for a bakery or shop where he could get coffee and a
bread roll, but there was nothing. Nor did he see anyone on the
street. The parents were at work, the children still in school,
or, if they were home already, eating lunches their grandmoth-
ers had cooked; the sick were in bed; the unemployed in their
gardens, or out mushrooming, or fishing at the lake on the
map – Kaspar didn't want to see the emptiness of the village as
bleak, he wanted it to have a reason.

He left Briesen behind and drove through the rolling countryside. Fields of corn, sunflowers, stubble; sometimes a wood, still green, but with the first leaves turning yellow; sometimes a village with a few houses and an old church of brick and stone; above it all a big sky, with sun intermittently breaking through the clouds. Then the road cut through a range of hills down to the Oderbruch plain. The terrain was flat; the elevation in the distance had to be an embankment, with the Oder flowing along behind it. Kaspar drove to the embankment and got out of the car.

It was very quiet. For a moment Kaspar held his breath, and looked around to reassure himself that nothing was making a sound, that he had not gone deaf. Then he climbed up the embankment. The blue-green Oder flowed along beneath him; grass and bushes grew on the banks, and there were geese resting and sheep grazing on the opposite side. Kaspar sat down and began to hear: the murmuring of the river, the soughing of the wind, the cackling of a goose, the quiet hum of an engine that died down and started up and died down again, Kaspar didn't know on which side of the river. He thought of Birgit. He was angry with her. Why hadn't she said anything? Why weren't they on this quest together? Why weren't they sitting together beside the Oder, with the sun on their skin and the silence in their ears? He would have liked to put his arm around her, would have liked to feel her head on his shoulder.

Rietzow lay at the foot of the range of hills, under one that rose up high and fell steeply down to the Oderbruch. Glancing to left and right, Kaspar counted about thirty houses. The church was a ruin; the tower had no cupola, the nave no roof. The plain, two-storey early-eighteenth-century house beside it had once been the parsonage. Now it was the house and practice of Dr Martin Luckenbach.

Kaspar had arrived during opening hours. The front door

was open; waiting patients were sitting and standing in the corridor. As Kaspar looked around, a woman pointed to a book lying on a chest of drawers at the end of the corridor beside a water cooler and cup dispenser: he should sign in, she said, and he would be called when it was his turn. 'People are seen in order.' When he had signed in, and was leaning against the wall at the end of the queue, the woman nodded and repeated, 'People are seen in order.'

Most of those waiting were elderly, sitting quietly; two young women were chatting about a Turkish hairdresser's new salon; three children were playing on smartphones; a young man tried to strike up a conversation with the young women, but they ignored him. Kaspar thanked the woman who had directed him towards the book; she informed him that the doctor treated everyone the same, new patients and old, and that you could tell from his accent that he was from the West, but not otherwise. The door at the end of the corridor opened; a mother came out, carrying a child in her arms, and behind her a woman in a white coat, with red hair and a red birthmark on her right cheek. Paula. She glanced at the book, called the next patient, and turned to everyone waiting. 'Sorry, I'm afraid we're running late. There was an emergency.' Her voice, her demeanor, her gestures – all indicated that she was secure in her authority. She was taller and thinner than Kaspar had imagined, not beautiful, but attractive by virtue of her confidence and liveliness.

Kaspar counted the people waiting, and calculated that it would be at least two hours before his turn. He walked out of the house and over to the church, saw the scaffolding in the nave that stopped the walls from falling down, and the steel girders that must have been stored there for the renovation. The tower had been covered over with a flat roof, and inside the tower hung a bell. Walking through the village, he found an old pub that bore the name 'Zur deutschen Einheit', celebrating German unity; its menu offered German and Asian dishes and pizza. He went in. There were men sitting alone, drinking beer in silence; one stood by an old fruit machine. Kaspar said hello; they did not respond. He sat at the counter and ordered coffee and a bread roll from the landlord; they were brought to him by the landlady, who looked Asian. A church with a bell, a doctor, a pub – Rietzow was a proper village. When Kaspar resumed his walk around it, he also found a shop selling eggs, milk, fruit, vegetables and potatoes from the farm. He climbed the hill and found an old cemetery with a wrought-iron fence and a pretty view across the plain, the village and the Oder.

Then he was back outside the doctor's surgery. The front door was still open, but the corridor was empty. Kaspar went in and sat down. Paula showed the woman who had informed him that life happened in the correct order out of the consulting room, said goodbye, and glanced at the book. 'Herr Wettner?' She smiled. 'You're the last. Please would you close the front door?'

Kaspar had already started to speak as he was walking back towards her. 'I'm not a patient. I'm Birgit's husband – Birgit's widower. Please excuse me for intruding like this. I would welcome the chance to talk to you. If now is no good, I can . . .'

'Birgit's husband? The man Birgit went to in the West?' She spoke with friendly curiosity.

Kaspar was relieved. 'The same. I found some things Birgit wrote. She writes about you. And about her daughter.'

She nodded. 'I thought Birgit would come one day. And you've come instead.'

'Birgit wrote to Briesen and found out your address, but then she died.'

'What of?'

He frowned. 'Of impatience, alcohol, sleeping pills, a deep bathtub. It's complicated.'

Paula nodded. 'Do you want to stay for dinner?'

'I'd like that. Thank you very much.'

'I just have to tidy up. Then we'll go into the kitchen.'

She picked up a water cup that was lying on the floor. Kaspar said, 'I'll do that.' She nodded, went into the consulting room and busied herself in there. Kaspar picked up everything that was lying around, put it in the wastepaper basket, lined up the chairs neatly side by side, and replaced the empty water bottle in the dispenser with a full one from beside the chest of drawers.

'I see you know how to tidy up.'

'I have to do it every evening. I own a bookshop.'

'I remember Birgit used to read a lot. Right until the end?'

'Less so over the years. Perhaps because she started to write herself. She wanted to look for her daughter, and find her, and write about it.'

Paula stepped out of the doorway and gave him a hug. 'I'm sorry you've lost her. You wouldn't be here if you hadn't loved her.'

3

In the kitchen, Kaspar washed lettuce, tomatoes and herbs that Paula brought in from the garden, mixed the herbs into quark, sliced bread, and opened a bottle of Riesling. She put plates, bread, ham, sausage and quark, lettuce, oil and vinegar on a tray, and he followed her to a table in the garden, carrying the wine and a carafe of water. The vegetable bed was well tended, the lawn had not been mowed for a long time, the hydrangeas looked lovely even with their faded blooms, and the apple trees where the table stood were full of small apples. It was a homely garden.

'Isn't your husband going to join us?'

'My husband's away. He became a country doctor, but he's still interested in tumor viruses. That was what he was researching early on in his career; he wanted to carry on with it and become a professor. These days he sometimes goes to conferences, and comes back sad and relieved: sad because he could have done all that, too; relieved that he's away from all the posturing.' She saw Kaspar's astonished expression and laughed. 'You're wondering who was holding the consultations this afternoon. Me, who else? We can only manage by running the practice together. Don't tell the health authorities. Though they probably already know.'

She ate quickly; she drank the wine as if it were water, and the water, too, glass after glass. Then she leaned back. 'Do keep eating. I need to tell you things, not you me. Although – when I've finished my story I'd like to hear more about Birgit. Would you fetch another bottle from the fridge?'

Kaspar went into the kitchen. This time, on the wall above the fridge, he saw the photograph of a young man with freckles like Paula's and a serious expression. He brought the bottle and corkscrew to the table and asked, 'The photo above the fridge – is that your son?'

'We're hoping, against all odds, that he'll take over the practice. Detlef's got what it takes to be a researcher and professor – any hospital would take him – and there are better practices than ours. But then there's Nina, the daughter of the head of the last agricultural co-operative, who snaffled the whole thing after the Wall came down. She's studying agriculture, and may want to take over that business, make it organic, regenerative, holistic – "beyond farming", it's called. Detlef and Nina loved each other once; he doesn't talk about her, but he doesn't talk about anyone else, either. That's what we're banking on.' She smiled. 'You don't like to ask why we want our son to be our successor – why we don't want him to do better than us. We have a responsibility to the country, and to the people – not just us, everyone – but we have the wit to see that responsibility, and the opportunity to take it on, and we earn enough to live on without making major sacrifices.' She laughed. 'Martin's set up a cinema in the cellar. We sit in the best seats, and a projector beams the films onto the wall.'

'You'd stay here?'

'Yes. We'd travel a bit more, maybe even for a couple of months, but we'd always come back here. When we don't have to run the practice any more, we want to try to get a school and a kindergarten here again. And police and a bigger shop and a pastor. Then maybe someone will come and set up a small business. They used to process textiles here; there are lots of nimble-fingered women, and there are no shops that do invisible mending any more in the whole of Berlin. You could . . .' She laughed again, and Kaspar liked her affirmative laugh. She waved her hand dismissively: 'I like to dream.'

'Whose . . . whose doorstep did you leave Birgit's daughter on, back then?'

'Could you have done that? I couldn't. A few days before the birth, I called Leo Weise and arranged for him and his wife to take her. I drove to the nearest telephone box with the daughter, told him that it had happened and they had to come, and handed over the baby six hours later.'

'I don't know what I could or would have done. Birgit and I didn't have children; we never tried to find out why, we just accepted it. I would have liked to. I would have been happy to take on her daughter, as well. Maybe they could have escaped together. Maybe, as a mother, Birgit wouldn't have become an alcoholic. Maybe . . .' He couldn't go on, raised his arms and let them fall. Tears were running down his cheeks.

Paula stood, came over and clasped his head against her stomach. 'Yes,' she said. 'Yes.' When she sensed that he had stopped weeping, she stroked his head, and sat down again.

'In her writing, Birgit wondered whether perhaps deep down, deep inside, I actually knew everything. I didn't. Should I have? Should I have noticed she was pregnant in the summer of 1964?'

Paula shook her head, frowning, as if she thought this absurd. 'Birgit made it easy for herself.' After a while she asked, 'Do you want to find her daughter?'

'I want to find her and do what Birgit wanted to do: offer myself to her. Maybe she can relate to Birgit's story somehow, and to me, and to what I can offer her. Maybe . . .' He smiled.

'How many times have I just said "maybe"? Birgit's death, her daughter, her keeping it secret – I feel as if the bottom has dropped out of my life. As if it were all just a "maybe".'

It grew dark. Paula put everything on the tray, carried it into the kitchen and came back with a lantern. 'I can tell you that Leo Weise and his wife called the baby Svenja. At our brief meeting they were over the moon: excited, solicitous, affectionate. I don't know how they managed the adoption, but he was the first district secretary; he had the power to do it. He invited me to her Jugendweihe, the socialist coming-of-age ceremony. It was a big party; I didn't stick out, I didn't speak to Svenja. But I did see her, and she looked like Birgit. And she looked happy.'

'You wrote Birgit a card.'

'Yes. The chocolate girl reminded me of her. I had to go to Niesky a few times after that, and I walked around with my eyes peeled, but I didn't see her again. I thought about her sometimes, during the reunification period. About her and all the other children whose training meant they could have been someone in the GDR, but suddenly it wasn't worth anything any more. Older people, too: often, what they'd studied and worked at in the GDR wasn't worth anything any more, either. But if you're young and you end up with nothing, even though you've just worked hard and completed your training, it can easily knock you sideways.'

'Do you miss the GDR?'

'Oh no. Maybe I would if I hadn't found Martin. Maybe I would miss the independence district nurses had in the GDR that nurses don't have today. Things worked out well for me.' She laughed her affirmative laugh again. 'If I didn't keep telling them not to over and over again, the patients would call me Doctor.' She looked at the clock. 'It's late. Why don't you stay the night?'

4

The practice opened at seven. She woke him at six. They drank coffee in the kitchen and ate bread and jam, and he told her about Birgit's life. She made him a ham and cheese sandwich.

'For the road. You'll want to speak to Leo Weise next. I think at some point he was promoted to first district secretary in Görlitz. Niesky is on the way; you can ask after him there first.'

At the door, he thanked her. 'I was afraid of starting the search. Birgit was afraid of it, so I was afraid, too. But my search has begun well with you.'

'Call me when you find her. Better still, bring her to visit us. I'd like to see her.'

He drove to Niesky. The plain, the range of hills and the road that cut through it, the flat hilltops, the little villages, the expanses of fields and occasional woods – the countryside was starting to feel familiar to him, and he began to love its simple beauty. He particularly loved it when a village lay in a hollow and the church spire rose up to greet him above the roofs. The big sky arched over it all again, and beneath it Kaspar felt not lost, but protected. This was how he had imagined the countryside as a child: fields, woods, villages with church spires.

He arrived in the late afternoon. On the main square he

found an old man sitting on a bench opposite the church. He sat down beside him and asked after Leo Weise.

'What about Leo?'

'I'd like to speak to him.'

'You're from the West.'

'I'm from Berlin. To West Germans, we Berliners are in the East.'

The old man took a packet of cigarettes from the pocket of his coat, lit one, coughed, and shook his head as if he didn't know why he was coughing or why he was smoking or why he was sitting there. 'You're just a speck of dirt, the lot of you, a speck of dirt on the map. And you want to tell us what's what.'

'I don't want to tell you what's what. I don't know myself.' He watched the old man suck in smoke, exhale and cough again. 'Do you know whether Leo Weise is back living in Niesky, and if so, where?'

'Are you a reporter?'

'I'm looking for his daughter. She's inherited some money.'

'He was good as first secretary. He was good in Görlitz, too.' The man laughed bitterly. 'I was good, too.'

'What did you do?'

'I . . .' He stopped. The reflexive response, to retell the story he had told so often, was no longer there. He had told it too many times. 'He lives out by Mücka, where Ernst Thalmann Strasse turns into Niesky Strasse.' He shook his head, coughing. 'Inherited? From the West? Can you inherit anything good from the West?'

5

The house was on the main street, an old single-storey house surrounded by old single-storey houses, with a small garden at the front and a big garden with a shed at the back. The attic had been converted; the sand-colored render of the other houses had here been painted white, the grimy red roof tiles replaced by bright, shiny red ones. Leo Weise wasn't rich, but he wasn't poor, either.

Kaspar rang the bell and listened but didn't hear anyone coming to the door. When he rang again, a woman appeared around the corner of the house. 'What do you want?'

Kaspar introduced himself, and was told that she was Frau Weise. He explained that he would like to speak to her and her husband.

'Well, come into the garden and tell us what it's about.'

Based on the photos in Birgit's papers, Kaspar had pictured Leo Weise as tall, slim, relaxed and friendly. He would not have recognized him in this hulking old man, small eyes sunk in a puffy face. This man loved Birgit, he thought. If he and his wife had separated, Birgit would have become his wife. I wouldn't be here, would not have married her, would not have met her. Perhaps he's on cortisone? Does he have bad rheumatism?

Leo Weise had risen heavily to his feet on seeing Kaspar. He stood upright, one hand resting on the back of the chair, motioned to Kaspar to take the other seat at the table, sent his wife to fetch another chair, and waited for her to join them before sitting again.

'And you are?'

'Kaspar Wettner. I'm the widower of Birgit, Svenja's mother. Birgit wanted to find Svenja, but she died before she could start looking. This search was a legacy for me; it led me first to Birgit's friend who handed Svenja over to you back then, and now to you.'

Leo Weise looked at his wife, and she looked at him, and in their looks Kaspar saw pain and reproach and the memory of disappointments and hurt. Then Leo Weise looked away, stared into space, and his face grew hard. His wife stroked her hand across her forehead.

'Birgit was a slut, no offence, and Svenja had it in her blood. Maybe Birgit was different later on. I wasn't the only one she seduced back then; she . . .' He waved a hand dismissively. 'Water under the bridge. Svenja was a sweet girl and a dedicated Young Pioneer. She was a Young First-Aider, she wore the red cross on her left arm and wanted to be a doctor, and we were happy; do you remember, Irma, how happy we were?' He looked at his wife, who nodded, her eyes closed. 'When she was in the FDJ, she fell in love with a boy who was two years older, a little shit. He wasn't in the FDJ, because he was in the Evangelical Church youth group, but he didn't want to stay with them, and they didn't want him, either: he was an unstable type who blathered on about anarchy and shaved the side of his head and dyed his hair and went on to deal drugs. All the talks we had with Svenja – didn't we, Irma? We understood that she needed freedom, and we let her take her driving test and gave her a moped, a Schwalbe, second-hand, but in good condition. She didn't ride it around our beautiful countryside, to the Ore Mountains and the Baltic, but to the city, where she amused herself by scaring people, riding straight at them. Then she had an accident; she'd been drinking, and we thought that would bring her to her senses. But things didn't get any better; they got worse. Until, in the end . . .'

'You shouldn't have done it, Leo.'

'You couldn't think what else to do, either. She was always out, we never saw her any more, we couldn't talk to her any more, she wasn't studying and she wasn't working, she was living with that guy, they were breaking into one empty apartment after another – don't you remember when you spent a whole day looking for her and finally found her in that derelict house on Winterstrasse, and she screamed at you? That it was suffocating to be around you, she would have died being around you, and now she could live at last?' He shook his head. 'Oh, Irma. You know how hard it was for me. I thought the reformatory was the only thing I could still do for her; that she wouldn't understand it at the time, but she would later on.'

'You shouldn't have done it. We should have been patient. When the police called me and I picked her up from the station, she was insolent and loud, yes, but she was my girl, and in the car, after ranting and raving and then refusing to speak, she eventually said a very quiet "Thank you".'

'And when she got home, your girl said that here, with us, was not her home any more, and she trashed her room.' He took a deep breath. 'It was the only thing I could still do for her, and what she would have been like without Torgau – better, worse – I don't know.'

'Why did you have to have her recommitted after six months? She—'

'She still hadn't understood.'

'Don't you remember what Raul told us? That she tried really hard and stuck it out because she thought: six months, and it would be over. Another three . . . It broke her.'

Leo Weise was grinding his teeth, hands clenched around the arms of the chair. He must have been about eighty, but he was still a powerful man. What was he capable of when he lost his temper? Kaspar wasn't afraid of him; Leo had forgotten that he was there. Had his wife said more than usual, because she knew he wouldn't do anything to her in front of Kaspar? Was he capable of being violent – had he been violent towards her and Svenja?

Leo Weise became aware of Kaspar again. 'When she came of age, she was discharged. She went to Berlin; all her kind went to Berlin.' He laughed. 'She didn't stay, though; none of her kind stayed, they just came back here again. She worked for the railway carriage construction company until the Wall came down. She would have ended up in prison otherwise. I know, you think everything in the GDR was wrong. Paragraph 249 of our criminal code was right: anyone who won't work when they're capable of doing so should be punished. After reunification, she got back together with the guy it all started with. He was a skinhead by then, in a bomber jacket and combat boots, and now they beat up the kids with the dyed and partially shaven hair, and the Vietnamese. "Swatting ticks", they called it. And he was a drug dealer on such a grand scale that he didn't think anything could happen to him. The police didn't get him, but in 1991 he was shot dead outside the brothel he'd opened with a bunch of Czech girls. After that, Svenja disappeared.'

Irma was about to speak, but Leo Weise shot her a look. 'Now then, Irma, aren't we going to offer our guest something? Coffee? A slice of your apple pie?'

6

'Did Birgit speak of me from time to time?' asked Leo Weise, when his wife had gone into the house.

'While Birgit was alive, I knew nothing about her daughter and nothing about you. After her death, I found some notes of hers; she wrote about you in them.'

'She's too young to be dead already. How did it happen?'

'It was an accident. She fell unconscious and drowned. Did you ever tell Svenja that your wife was not her biological mother?'

'Why would we have done that?'

'Just asking. May I use your toilet?'

Kaspar followed his directions, through the kitchen to the door beside the entrance. On the way back, he stopped in the kitchen and observed Frau Weise.

'I can carry the tray.'

'Thank you.' She sliced the pie. 'I last heard from Svenja nineteen years ago. She was in Frankfurt. She called me and asked for money.'

'Did you see her?'

'We met at the train station. She looked terrible; it broke my heart, and I wanted to help her and talk to her. She just wanted the money. She gave me a kiss – my girl gave me a kiss – and then she was gone.'

'Who's Raul?'

'He came to see us years ago. He'd gone to West Germany after the Wall came down, done well for himself, and he wanted to see Svenja again. They kept the boys and girls separate in Torgau, but they did sometimes manage to become friends. He left his address here so Svenja could reach him. I'll give it to you later. We mustn't keep Leo waiting.'

They drank the coffee and ate the pie, and the conversation petered out. Kaspar asked what Svenja had been interested in when she was a girl, what she had liked doing, and received the terse response that she had been good at sport – volleyball and basketball – had read a lot – history and adventure stories – and had, of course, been a good Pioneer. Then Kaspar ventured to ask how Leo had fared during reunification.

'They stood outside my office shouting, "Stop killing our town," as if I'd let the old part of town go to rack and ruin! Ninety per cent of building capacity was allocated to prefabricated buildings; that was the plan. I couldn't change it, no one could change it. I couldn't preserve the old town with the ten per cent that was left.'

'You were in your mid-fifties – what did you do after reunification?'

'I was voted onto the local council as a representative of the new Party of Democratic Socialism. The municipal government wanted me, as well, but the high-ups in the capital wouldn't accept a former GDR functionary in the new Görlitz administration. Because I'd had dealings with the Stasi. Of course I'd had dealings with the Stasi; how could I have run the town without having dealings with the Stasi?'

Irma put a hand on his arm. 'If you'd joined the municipal administration, we wouldn't have been able to afford the house. It was a blessing in disguise.'

'I worked for Volkswohl Insurance. I knew my clientele; I was good.' He laughed. 'If I'd been in the Stasi, instead of just having dealings with the Stasi, I'd have been even better. They could get anyone to buy anything.'

Again Kaspar wanted to know: 'Do you miss the GDR?'

'Miss it? What would be the point of that? We lost, that's all there is to it. Whether we only lost one round or the whole fight, whether the fight is still going on, I don't know. We made plenty of mistakes we can learn from. I was against Ulbricht and for Honecker back then, as well. I didn't know enough, and I didn't think enough. Think!' he exhorted Kaspar, staring at him and tapping his head with his finger. 'Think!'

As they said goodbye, Frau Weise slipped Kaspar a note. 'Raul Buch, Taubenstrasse 12, 53125 Bonn, 0228 411788.'

7

When he got back to Berlin, Kaspar called Raul Buch. He was willing to talk to him, and said he was working from home over the next few days; Kaspar could come by one afternoon. They arranged to meet on Wednesday. Buch sounded friendly and businesslike; a practiced telephone voice, the kind that Kaspar, who had always found it difficult to talk on the phone and still did, would have liked to have had.

Kaspar took the train. It was raining when he left and it was raining when he arrived. It had already been raining when he woke up, and after glancing at the clock he had been glad to be able to stay in bed a little longer and listen to the pattering of the rain. Looking out of the train window at the wet towns, squares, streets and fields, he thought of Svenja being homeless. Had she always found apartments to squat? Had she lived on the street, as well? Under bridges when it rained? In shopping arcades and the entrances to buildings in winter? Can you set yourself up there and get used to it? Is it not so bad then? Does there come a point when you can't, don't want to, do it any differently, the way he couldn't sleep with the window closed?

But we are creatures that need a home, and if we are nomads, repeatedly putting up our tent and taking it down again, that tent is our home. Kaspar remembered the dog and cat he and Birgit had had for a while. They had found the dog in the road, hit by a car and injured, while they were driving in the countryside, and the cat had come from a friend who couldn't keep it. How happy the two animals had been to have a home! Kaspar remembered how they had slept snuggled up together beside the hall cupboard. What had driven Svenja out of her parents' house? Leo Weise had probably been a strict father, but he seemed to have been satisfied with her apparent good conduct as an excellent Young Pioneer and Young First-Aider, and not to have harassed her by demanding that she believe unquestioningly in socialism. Irma Weise was a loving woman, and Svenja must have felt that love. The Weises would surely have lived a well-ordered life – oppressively so? Had Svenja wanted to break free? Or had something happened to destroy her trust in the way the world was ordered? Losing her mother immediately after her birth? Kaspar couldn't believe that the handing over of the child from Birgit to Paula and from Paula to Irma and Leo Weise could have caused any damage, or that Svenja would remember it. His own childhood memories began at the age of five.

The journey through the rain, the drops streaming across the window, fast or slow, leaving shorter or longer trails – it made Kaspar sad. Some drops remained small; others merged together and grew large, and sooner or later they were all blown away by the wind. He knew, of course, that the drops were not a manifestation of the transience and futility of life. Nor were they a manifestation of how people follow their paths in life and do not find each other unless the wind of fate merges them together. Yet all these thoughts tormented him. He was on the trail not just of Svenja but of Birgit, too; he didn't know whether he was really getting closer to Svenja, he only knew that Birgit was slipping away. Birgit had made it easy for herself. Birgit was a slut. He didn't believe either of these things.

But the Birgit of her writing, the Birgit she had concealed, hidden from him, had been authenticated by his meetings with Paula and with Leo Weise. She wasn't just a written character, a person on paper. She had actually existed, far removed from him, a stranger.

On arrival in Bonn, he took a taxi. It drove him to a new estate of white detached houses and duplexes with small gardens and young trees. Back when he and Birgit had still hoped for children, he had imagined a world like this for their family: one where there were no secrets, as there had been in the old parsonage beside the old church where he had grown up; no past full of bomb sites and bullet holes, as there had been in Berlin for many years; not flooded with impressions, as around a house or apartment in the city, but a white blank they would have entirely to themselves. Others found new estates dull, characterless, amorphous; that was what he wanted. But not even Birgit could see why he liked them.

Raul Buch's house had two doors and two doorbells, one for his home and one for his company. Kaspar pressed the second. A young man opened the door, asked, 'Herr Wettner?', and led him down to the basement, to a large room with desks and computers and a glass wall overlooking the garden. A man in his mid-forties was sitting at one of the desks. 'One moment,' he said, raising his hand. The young man pulled up a chair for Kaspar and sat down at another desk. Kaspar remained standing, looking out at the garden, a patch of lawn with shrubs at the bottom, and at the drops on the windowpanes. Eventually Raul Buch stood, greeted him, apologized and led him into a small, adjacent office with the same view of the garden.

'I met Svenja a few times in Berlin, after she got out of Torgau. It was a long time ago. You said on the phone that you were looking for her – I don't think I can help you, I'm afraid. I tried to contact her a few years after reunification; I visited her parents and left my address, but she never got in touch. I don't even know if she's alive. She was taking drugs, beating up gays and foreigners, surfing trains and the S-Bahn; she was doing stuff that people don't always survive.'

'Her mother said you had the impression she was doing well after the first six months in Torgau. That the extra three months had broken her.'

'You weren't supposed to stay in Torgau longer than six months. We knew that, and it helped. We knew there were sometimes readmissions. But those were the exception, and you always think others will be the exception, not you.'

'Svenja's second admission . . .'

'Was arranged by her father, like the first. Normally, people came to Torgau from another institution, and it helped to have that institutional experience, as did having the support of your family. Coming there with no experience of an institution, yanked out of ordinary life by your own father . . .' He shook his head. 'The admissions procedure was intended to be a shock, and it certainly was for Svenja. Standing to attention, stripping naked and handing everything over, being physically examined as if you were cattle, institutional clothing, then a solitary cell with a plank bed and bucket. You were told how to answer and how to make the bed, and you had to learn the rules off by heart. Three, four, five days of solitary confinement. After that you understood that, in there, you were just a piece of shit.'

'How did you get to know each other?'

'During roll call. Up at five thirty, exercises, wash, make the bed, listen to the news, breakfast, roll call.' Raul Buch had barked out the schedule; he paused, sighed and smiled. 'Do I sound military? It was like the military. We were supposed to learn to obey. Obey, work, subordinate ourselves to the youth workers and integrate with the collective. Anyone who didn't toe the line was punished – duck-walk circuits of the yard, press-ups, knee bends; scrubbing the corridor on your hands and knees, and then they'd lead a group down the corridor and you had to start all over again. Detention of up to two weeks, and if the youth worker didn't like you, you had to stay standing from morning till night. And if you answered back, they would throw the bunch of keys at your head. And the beatings . . . my God, the beatings I took. And the fox earth . . . the wire cage . . .' He stared into space, lost in his memories.

'Wire cage?'

'You asked how we got to know each other. Boys and girls reported together for roll call, and we worked alongside each other, us boys in our area and the girls in theirs. That was where I saw her. I wrote to her, and she answered; not straight away, the third time. Contact between boys and girls was forbidden, and smuggling letters was risky, but you could do it in the kitchen, and there was one youth worker who wasn't as strict at the weekend. Svenja wanted nothing to do with me at first, because she only had a few weeks left and didn't want to ruin anything. Then, when she came back, she didn't care what they thought. My time was almost up by then, so now I was the one who wanted to be careful. But Svenja . . .' He got up, went over to his desk and came back with a photograph, which he handed to Kaspar. The young woman reminded Kaspar of Birgit: the same curve of the mouth, the same dark eyes and dark hair, but her expression was unapproachable, challenging, alluring, a woman to whom you would want to prove yourself, a woman you would want to conquer. 'You can see for yourself. You couldn't be careful with Svenja. I spent my last two weeks in Torgau in detention.'

'What was it like when you saw her in Berlin?'

'We just reminisced – that was it, for a while. I trained as a skilled worker for data processing, because I wanted to get out, and I hoped to put it to good use, which I did. She got involved with the far-right scene; not for the politics, for the violence. She wanted to destroy what had destroyed her. I was the square and she was the rebel.'

'But after reunification you wanted to see her again.'

Raul Buch stared out of the window. 'If I'd found her, and if she'd wanted to, I'd have married her like a shot. I've done well, I'm successful, I don't have a Saxon or Berlin accent, I don't use East German expressions, so no one can tell I'm from the GDR. Certainly not when I show up with my wife; she's from Bonn, she's got that reassuring Rhineland sing-song, good taste, lots of shoes, and she's a good mother. But . . .' He stared out of the window again.

Kaspar nodded. 'I understand.'

'I don't think you do. You're thinking, he's homesick, and when a person's homesick they like to be with someone from home. It's not that. Svenja's real. We were real over there – you see how I even say "over there"? Svenja didn't rebel because she was fed up, or because she was bored, or because it's cool and a way to show off. She was serious about it, and she paid the price. We were all serious about it and paid the price, even the informers you're all so quick to criticize. I was never approached by the Stasi, thank God; I would have had to say yes or no, and it would have mattered, and it would have marked me, one way or the other. Here in the West, nothing matters. Which is nice for you.' He laughed. 'Nice for me, too. Nice and easy and dull.' He stood up. 'You came by taxi. I'll call one to take you back to town.' He swiped and tapped his phone.

'Where would you look for her?'

'No idea. I didn't only visit her parents back then. I looked in Berlin and Görlitz, and I went to Frankfurt because someone said they'd seen her in Frankfurt. Like I say, I don't know whether she's alive or dead.'

Kaspar pointed to the photograph in his hand. 'Can I get a copy?'

Raul Buch took it from him, went out to the main office, made a copy and gave it to him. He led him back up the stairs to the main entrance and waited with him for the taxi. 'If you find her – will you let me know?'

8

Frankfurt – Raul Buch hadn't said so, and Kaspar hadn't asked – had to be Frankfurt an der Oder. When had they filmed the bus stop there, the one where Birgit had recognized Svenja? Fifteen years ago? A hopeless lead.

Birgit, who had researched her daughter's life in the children's homes of the GDR and, at the same time, fantasized that she had grown up to be a strong, vivacious, happy woman; Birgit, who had been unable to cope with her great fears and timid hopes, and had preferred not to know the truth – Kaspar understood now why she had not embarked on the search. If she had, the difficulties involved would have crushed her every step of the way. But how wonderful it would have been if she had been able to write, and could have given her life the shape that she was seeking.

He got home late. Unable to stop thinking about it, he sat down and wrote the letter he had been composing in his head on his journey through night and rain. Perhaps he could finish the novel for Birgit.

Dear Herr Ettling,
  Please forgive me for responding to your kind letter only now. The reason for this is not just grief, which continues to sap my

energy. I still have not found the novel Birgit mentioned to you.
I am confronted with mountains of paper and an encrypted
computer.

I have, however, come across some texts that might be the
beginning of the novel. They touch on the theme of escape,
which Birgit had spoken of to you. I will keep you informed
about the progress and outcome of my search. I do not hold out
any hope of finding the leather-bound notebook with the leather
ribbon in which Birgit wrote her poems. However, if I find the
novel that mattered so much to Birgit and on which she worked
for so long, I would be happy if you were to publish it.
Yours sincerely

The following day he left his colleagues in charge of the bookshop again and travelled to Frankfurt an der Oder. The police
were a fifteen-minute walk from the station. At the counter,
a woman was deep in conversation with a policeman. Kaspar
waited.

The woman was outraged that her neighbors were putting
the rubbish next to rather than into the bins, and extracted
a promise that a police patrol would come around to check.
The policeman couldn't say when that would be, only that the
officers would ring her doorbell so she could show them and
explain the situation. He was patient and friendly, even when
the woman complained that this was all too vague and was
going to take too long. She took her time packing the map and
photos she had brought with her back into her bag, and left
without saying goodbye.

'How can I help you?'

'I'm looking for this woman.' Kaspar placed the photo of the
bus stop on the table and pointed to the woman who might be
Birgit's daughter. 'That's a bus stop here in Frankfurt.'

'Yes. Why are you looking for this woman?'

'She may be my late wife's long-lost daughter. If she needs help, I'd like to help her. It doesn't look as if things are going too well for her.'

The policeman picked up the photo, studied it again and shook his head. 'That was years ago. The skinheads used to meet up at the bus stop. There's a petrol station over the road that sells alcohol all night.'

'Yes, it's an old photo. It's the only lead I've got.'

The policeman turned and called to one of his colleagues. 'Alex, could you come here a moment?'

A policeman got up from his desk, a heavy, slow-moving man with a tattoo that peeked out from under his collar. He came over and let his colleague give him the photo. 'Yeah?'

'Do you remember her?'

The policeman stared at the photo for a long time. Finally, he nodded. 'We've got her in the system, too. Why?' The first policeman pointed at Kaspar and explained. The other shook his head. 'You're not her father. I remember her. The first time we picked her up she was still seventeen, so we called her father; he was first secretary in Görlitz, and he came and took her home. But she ran away, and the next time we picked her up she was of age.'

'Why did you pick her up?'

'Rioting, drinking, fighting, smashing bottles at the bus stop, harassing customers at the petrol station – the usual. Who are you?'

'You're right: I'm not her father. But my late wife was her mother. The Weises adopted the girl, and I've been tasked with looking for her and helping her, if she needs it.'

The policeman waited to see whether Kaspar had anything else to say, then continued. 'I don't know where she is. In the late nineties, the skinheads went their separate ways, got jobs, got married, had children. A few of them live out in the countryside. This guy from Lower Saxony showed up with a bunch of nationalist slogans; he wanted to set up a farm with the skinheads, and get others to take over other farms, so that in the end they'd have a liberated nationalist village. There are a few villages like that.' He gestured vaguely into the distance.

'Might I find Svenja there?'

'You could look for her there. Where you might find her – no idea. At some point she stopped calling attention to herself, and since she called attention to herself as long as she was here, I assume she isn't here any more.'

'Do you know what the man from Lower Saxony was called?'

'The police don't give out names. You should know that.' He turned and went back to his desk.

'Was that everything?' the first policeman asked.

9

Kaspar found reports online about the far-right völkisch settlements in Schleswig-Holstein, Lower Saxony, Mecklenburg–Western Pomerania and Brandenburg, far too many to drive from one to another asking about the man from Lower Saxony and Svenja Weise. Most of them seemed to be near the town of Güstrow, so he hired a car again and started there.

The pastor sent him to the school principal; the school principal sent him to the school counsellor. He knew which of his pupils were from völkisch settler families; they were disciplined and hard-working, never expressed social or political opinions, and only occasionally gave themselves away; the parents also kept their opinions to themselves, but they always pitched in when the school needed parents to help out. The teacher didn't know where the families came from. The Kegelmanns might know more, he said: a married couple, artists; he was a sculptor, she was a painter; they'd settled in Perlewalk before the Völkische came with their national-socialist ideas. 'No one knows the far-right scene better than those two. They keep an eye on what the Völkische are up to, and every year they organize a music festival as a kind of resistance. Their farmstead is easy to find: there's a sculpture of a hand by the entrance. Do you remember the yellow logo of a hand, with the slogan

"Leave my mate alone!"'? The sculpture's based on that yellow hand with the slogan.'

Kaspar drove to Perlewalk and found the farmstead. Beside it were the ruins of a barn; Kegelmann was picking through the charred planks, looking for whatever could be salvaged. He told Kaspar about the fire, which had been started by the nationalists, who wanted him out of the village. 'There's no way they're getting rid of me now. We'll have music again next summer, and maybe we'll find someone sensible to buy the farmstead next to mine before a Völkischer does. You're not looking for a farm, are you?'

Kaspar explained what he was looking for.

'The man from Lower Saxony.' Kegelmann nodded. 'Sure, I remember him. He showed up in every village, and in every village they laughed at him. Taking skinheads off the street and setting up a farm with them – what an idea! I think he was from one of those völkisch clans. You have to picture it: the great-grandfather has a farm in Lower Saxony and is in the SS; the grandfather takes over the farm and is a representative of the Deutsche Reichspartei, which was formed after the war by old Nazis and then banned; the father buys the farm next door for his brother, so the village will be more völkisch, and sets up a branch of the Patriotic German Youth; the eldest son inherits the farm, and the second son, our man from Lower Saxony, goes out into the world, as second sons have done since time immemorial. He goes to the East, because he wants to make something of himself and at the same time to serve the cause and make a village völkisch, so he looks for a farm. He didn't find one, our man from Lower Saxony – I'd have heard about it – but I don't know whether he's still hoping to buy one, or has gone back home because one came on the market there. Taking skinheads off the street . . .' Kegelmann shook his head.

Kaspar thanked him and was about to leave when something occurred to Kegelmann. 'Lohmen. Try Lohmen. I have a feeling someone told me the guy from Lower Saxony was living in Lohmen and running a snack bar. There is, or was, a snack bar there, that's for sure; I had a plate of smoked sausage and kale there years ago. And that's a Lower Saxon dish.'

There was no snack bar any more, just a wooden shack with a canopy and counter, and a table with two benches alongside. Kaspar got out and walked around the shack; the grass was tall, and the lock was rusty. No one had cooked or eaten anything here in a long while. On the other side of the fence, a woman was gardening; she kept glancing at him. He went over and spoke to her.

'They served good food, but who passes through here? They were supposed to upgrade the road so people could get from Güstrow to Bredzow faster, but they never did.'

'Lower Saxon cooking, I heard . . .'

'They did black pudding, boiled, fried, roasted, with cabbage. What d'you mean, Lower Saxon cooking? Just because he's from the West?'

'What about the young people who came with him? Did it work out?'

'Well, he's married to the woman. The men have all gone. Did you want to buy the snack bar?'

'I'd have to take a look at it. And I'd have to dismantle it and take it with me.'

'Have a word with him. His house is the one by the water tower.'

IO

Kaspar left the car where it was. The main street of the village had no pavements, nor did it need any; there were no cars, no bicycles, no tractors. Two houses further on, another woman was working in her garden; she looked up, and Kaspar said hello, but she didn't return the greeting. None of the houses were farms; they were houses for commuters or pensioners, and one had a signboard for an insurance company. The house to which Kaspar had been directed, like the others, would not have looked out of place in a suburb.

Kaspar knocked and listened. No one came down the stairs, or along the corridor inside. He turned and looked at the village street, the neighboring houses, the church without a spire, the big building behind it – a barn or warehouse – the gardens and fields, one of which had a pair of horses in it. He couldn't see any people. He couldn't hear anything: no children playing, no barking dog, no birds, no agricultural machinery. All was silent and empty.

He was about to walk back to the car when the front door opened. 'Yes?'

A woman in a short-sleeved, calf-length blue dress, buxom, with strong arms, a full-figured matron. Was this Svenja from the bus stop in Frankfurt? Kaspar saw none of the superiority and indifference Birgit had detected in the young woman's gaze. Nor did he see any of the challenge and allure Svenja's expression had conveyed in Raul Buch's photograph. The woman looked tired, not as you do after a couple of nights' bad sleep, but as if everything had been too exhausting for a very long time. And yet she reminded Kaspar of Birgit: the mouth, the dark eyes, the dark hair; her voice, too, sounded familiar.

'Frau Svenja Weise?'

A girl of about fifteen, red-haired, gangly, in a colorful skirt and blouse, came and leaned against the doorpost and observed Kaspar attentively. Then a man in a white T-shirt appeared beside the woman, half a head taller, with a buzz cut and tattooed arms, and answered for her. 'Renger. And who are you?'

'Kaspar Wettner. Frau Renger, may I speak to you for a moment? In private? What I have to say only concerns you.'

'I decide what does or doesn't concern my wife. Go into the kitchen with Sigrun, Svenja; I'll hear what he has to say.'

Kaspar hesitated, then shook his head. 'I'd like to speak to you, Frau Renger. Then it's up to you what you tell your husband.'

'It doesn't work that way,' said the man, raising his voice.

She put a hand on his arm and replied softly, 'Say what you have to say; my husband will hear it, too. But, Sigrun – go into the kitchen, will you, child?' The girl did as she was told. The man was preparing to complain and get indignant; she put an arm around him and looked up at him. 'Like you said: we'll hear what he has to say.'

Kaspar didn't like the situation. He was standing two steps down, with the loud man and the tired woman above him, like a supplicant about to be rebuffed and chased away. But he wasn't going to get a better opportunity to speak to her. He pulled himself together. 'You grew up as the Weises' daughter.

You're actually the daughter of Leo Weise and Birgit Hager. Birgit gave you away right after you were born. Later, she and I got married. After reunification, she started looking for you. But she died while she was still looking, so I took up the search, and found you. For a long time, I didn't know you existed; I only found out after Birgit died. She wrote about you, and I read what she'd written.'

'Has Svenja inherited something?'

'Never mind that, Björn. Let's sit down first and have coffee. Will you come in?' She nodded to Kaspar, and gestured unenthusiastically to invite him in. She did look superior and indifferent now, as if steeling herself against any unpleasantness Kaspar's surprise visit might bring.

Kaspar followed her into the kitchen and remained standing by the door. Svenja made coffee. Sigrun was sitting at the table reading, and Björn sat down with her. No one spoke. Kaspar looked around the kitchen: sideboard and dresser on the left, old, wooden, with decorative carving; fridge, shelves, oven and sink on the right; a long wooden table with six chairs in the middle. On the other side of the room, double doors opened onto a cottage garden with flowers and shrubs and flower beds. The kitchen was light, welcoming, comfortable.

Then Kaspar recognized the man in the photograph above the sideboard as Rudolf Hess, and deciphered the saying that hung alongside: 'The highest good a man possesses is his nation. / The highest good a nation possesses is its law. / A nation's soul resides in its language. / True to nation, law and language / this day finds us, as will each day more.'

Björn sat in a chair with a carved back and arms at the top of the table, the place of the head of the family, and observed Kaspar. Sigrun, too, kept raising her head, looking at Kaspar, looking at her father; she seemed to be waiting for something to happen.

'You know who that is? Martyr for Germany, martyr for peace?'

'Rudolf Hess. Born Alexandria, 1894, died Berlin, 1987.' Kaspar hoped that by indicating his knowledge of Hess he would be spared a lecture about him. It didn't work.

'Died? Do you say "died" when someone is murdered?'

'I thought he . . .'

'You thought a ninety-three-year-old man who could barely walk and couldn't lift his arms had hanged himself? You thought the British accidentally let his organs disappear during the autopsy? You thought if it's in the history books, it must be true?' Björn spoke derisively, cunningly; he was waiting for Kaspar's answer to reveal his gullibility or delusion.

'He couldn't tie his shoelaces any more,' said Sigrun, firmly and proudly, looking first to Kaspar, then to her father.

'That's right, Sigrun. He couldn't tie his shoelaces any more.'

Right now, thought Kaspar in a flash, I mustn't put a foot wrong. If I want to have contact with Svenja, I can't make an enemy of her husband. But if I pretend to be something I'm not, it'll come out sooner or later. 'I've never concerned myself with Hess's death.'

'What did you concern yourself with?'

'I'm a bookseller.'

'There are lots of books about Hess. Have you never seen them?'

'I don't remember all the books I've seen. And most of the books I've seen I haven't read. A bookseller can't read everything that passes through his shop.'

'Have you got shelves full of books everywhere?' Sigrun looked at him curiously.

'We have shelves on the walls, and between the walls, and they're all full of books. But there are bookshops that are even bigger and have even more books. What are you reading?'

'You can sit,' said Björn, and Kaspar took a seat opposite him.

'*The Great Elector's Shipboy.*' Sigrun held the book up; it was old, and on the cover a boy with an axe in his hand was leaping from the deck of one ship to the deck of another beneath the flag of Brandenburg. 'The Dutch, the mean old moneybags, didn't want us to have the colonies. They lied to us and betrayed us. Everyone was against us. But the negroes were on our side.'

11

Svenja put cups and plates, coffee spoons and cake forks on the table, and Sigrun jumped up and handed them round. Then Svenja brought coffee and plum cake, poured the coffee, served the cake and sat down with them.

'Why didn't your wife want me?' Svenja stirred her coffee with her spoon, not looking at Kaspar.

'Forget it, Svenja. She had a guilty conscience, and she wanted to find you and give you something. She's left you something, that's why her husband's come. Right?' Björn stared defiantly at Kaspar.

'I haven't found a will. But I haven't looked for one yet, either.'

'The daughter inherits. You don't need a will for that.'

Svenja frowned. 'What are you talking about, Björn? I'm still the daughter of Irma and Leo Weise, and whether I'll ever be anything else . . .'

'He' – Björn pointed to Kaspar – 'said you're his wife's daughter, and his wife has died. He's got her fortune, and he knows you're her heir. I advise him' – Björn leaned forward and glared at Kaspar menacingly – 'I advise you not to try anything on.'

Try anything on? I will take advantage of your greed, Kaspar thought to himself, and I will get to know Svenja and I will get to know Sigrun and I will find out everything Birgit would have wanted to find out. 'I'll start looking for the will. I didn't have any reason to before now. There won't be much; you don't get rich running a bookshop. But don't worry – Svenja will get whatever she's due.'

'A quarter.'

'What?'

'Half of what you own comes from your wife. Half of that goes to you, and half to Svenja. So a quarter of what you own belongs to Svenja.' Björn considered. 'An eighth, at least.'

'Oh, Björn. Let's find out what this is all about first. Did you go and see my parents?'

'Yes. Frau Weise said she last saw you in Frankfurt, many years ago. Have you had any contact with your father?'

Svenja shook her head. 'I don't want it. Not with him, and not with her. And I certainly don't if they lied to me all my life. Björn's parents are dead, and it's a shame that Sigrun's growing up with no grandparents. But better no grandparents than them.'

'If we need them to get what's rightfully ours, you will speak to them. I don't want any sentimental nonsense.' Björn was getting louder.

Again Svenja was able to soothe him with a soft voice and a hand on his arm. 'Let's take our time and think it over. As far as inheritance is concerned, as long as the Weises are still my parents, I'll inherit from them, which may be more than I would from him.' She jerked her head at Kaspar. 'We don't want to make things any worse with my parents than they already are. And Herr Wettner is going to look for the will, and when he finds it, or doesn't, we'll see what we do next.' She turned to Kaspar. 'Do you live in Berlin?'

'Yes.'

'What's your bookshop called?'

'Kompass.'

'I'm the best with the compass.' Sigrun sat up. She had been bent over her book, but she was listening, not reading. 'Is this man my grandfather?'

No one answered straight away. Svenja and Björn looked at each other, surprised by what Sigrun had picked up and pieced together.

'I'm your step-grandfather.' Kaspar smiled at Sigrun, then at Svenja. 'And I'm your stepfather.'

Sigrun regarded him seriously, as if considering whether she wanted him as a grandfather. Finally she smiled back. 'Do you want to come to the fete at the weekend?'

12

So it was that Kaspar found himself back in Lohmen at the weekend. Björn, clearly displeased by Sigrun's invitation, but too proud not to want to show himself and his family and his people off to Kaspar now that they had come to his attention, had told him to be there at three; they would make their way to the fete together. When Kaspar arrived, the streets were already full of parked cars, minibuses and delivery vans, and families were milling around. Some of the men wore a traditional carpenter's waistcoat and trousers, while some of the women were in dirndls.

Björn greeted him with, 'Have you found the will?' Kaspar nodded. 'Then we'll sit down first.'

They sat around the kitchen table again, without Sigrun this time. Svenja tried to ask whether Kaspar had had a good journey. Björn interrupted. 'What's with the will?'

'It's a bit complicated. Presumably Birgit wanted to spare me the trouble of having to lay hands on so much money all at once. But she also wanted to help you, Frau Renger, if you had children. She wanted you to have a quarter of her assets, so one-eighth of our joint property, to be paid out in annual instalments until the last child came of age. Then another quarter was to go to the children, for their education, and to help set them up in life. Birgit also wanted the children to spend five weeks a year with me: three weeks in summer and two stays of one week each, in the autumn, winter or spring. If you had no children, you would receive one quarter now and the other in ten years' time.'

'The other in ten years – what's that about? Why should Svenja have to wait ten years?' Björn was angry.

'Birgit wasn't good with money. I assume she thought the same might be true of her daughter, so it would be better if she didn't get the inheritance all in one go.'

'How much is it?'

'Our joint property – the apartment and the bookshop – is worth eight hundred thousand euros. How old is Sigrun?'

'Fourteen.'

'That means' – Kaspar calculated – 'you get twenty-five thousand for four years in a row, and Sigrun gets one hundred thousand on her eighteenth birthday.'

Svenja smiled, first at Björn and then at Kaspar. 'That's . . .'

But Björn brought his hand down heavily on top of hers. 'We won't be fobbed off with charity. We want the whole lot, and we want it now. If you don't cough up, we'll contest the will and see you in court.'

'Oh, Björn, let's . . .'

Björn raised the hand that held Svenja's, and slammed both their hands back down onto the table. Svenja cried out softly and tried to free herself, but Björn gripped her hand firmly.

'If you think that just because we're country folk . . . We have lawyers in our ranks who know their stuff, and who know how to deal with people like you.'

'Yes, Herr Renger, please do speak to your lawyer. I've spoken to one as well. In order to claim an inheritance from Birgit, Svenja has to prove that she is Birgit's daughter. She has to persuade the Weises to disclose what happened back then, which wasn't done by the book, and in doing so she risks offending the Weises and being disowned and disinherited by them. If she succeeds in proving that she is Birgit's daughter, perhaps through exhumation and genetic testing, and then rejects Birgit's last will and testament, she will receive only the statutory portion – one hundred thousand. And it will take years.'

Björn listened, frowning and clenching his jaw. 'I'll be looking into all this, don't you worry. You can transfer the first instalment in the meanwhile.'

Kaspar took his time. He looked at Svenja and Björn: she yielding to her pain with a faint, tired smile, but pleased about the money; he full of rage, and full of fear that he would look like a loser in front of his wife. Kaspar was sure that Svenja was acquainted with Björn's fear and knew how to handle him so that, in front of her, he could be the big man, the strong man, the victor. That was how it should be.

'You win. I'll transfer twenty-five thousand when I get back to Berlin. If you accept the will and send Sigrun to me for five weeks a year, that'll be the first instalment. If you contest the will, we'll offset it against what you receive at the end.'

'Twenty-five thousand.'

'Twenty-five thousand.'

Svenja had freed her hand, and put it on Björn's arm. 'Kurt's coming to the fete. You can ask him there.' She turned to Kaspar. 'Doctor Kurt Maier is a lawyer in Schwerin.'

Björn didn't reply. He looked at the clock. 'We have to go.'

13

But they didn't go. Sigrun burst into the kitchen in a long-sleeved white blouse and a calf-length grey skirt, her red hair in a single plait wound around her head, flushed and breathless. She looked lovely, but it was a shock for Kaspar to see the girl in uniform.

'I want to take Grandfather to the fete!'

He stood. 'I'd like that.'

'And I'll show you my room first.' Before her parents could say anything, Sigrun took Kaspar by the hand and pulled him up the stairs into her room. A desk stood beneath a window in the sloping roof, to the left a bed, a bedside table and a wardrobe, a bookcase on the right. Everything was tidy; there were notebooks piled up on the desk and pens arranged in a glass, the bed was neatly made, and the books were organized in groups and bookended. Kaspar looked in vain for things familiar to him from his friends' daughters' rooms: cuddly toys, dolls, dinosaurs, a box of make-up, necklaces and bracelets hanging from a nail. Then, on the ceiling above Sigrun's bed, he saw small, dark blue stars, outlined in gold, some thickly and some thinly, a whole sky.

'How lovely!' Kaspar turned to Sigrun. '"Can you count the stars that brightly twinkle in the midnight sky?"'

It was the opening of an old German lullaby, but it meant nothing to Sigrun. Perhaps she was embarrassed that Kaspar had spotted the girlish element in her room, which wasn't meant to be girlish. She pointed to three portraits, neatly framed prints hanging on the wall above the bookcase. 'That's Rudolf Hess, that's Irma Grese, that's Friederike Krüger. They're my heroes.'

Kaspar recognized Hess's oafish, credulous face; not a print of a painting, like the one in the kitchen, but a photograph. It hung between a woman with long blonde hair, a determined mouth and fierce expression, and another with the sweet, chubby face of a child. 'Who are the two women?'

'Irma Grese served in the SS, was executed by the British and died like a man, unlike her commandant, who wept and wailed. Friederike Krüger cut off her hair, wore trousers, joined up as a soldier and fought against Napoleon. She was wounded, made an officer, and awarded the Iron Cross and the Order of St George.'

'That's impressive. And you have so many books!' Kaspar studied the bookshelf. Some of the titles he recognized: *Rulaman*, *The Cave Children*, *Kaiser, King and Pope*, *The Last Horsemen*, *Hitler Youth Quex*, *A People Without Space*, *The Decline of the West*. 'Have you read that, as well?'

'No.' She shook her head. 'There's a bookstall in Güstrow where you can take and leave books; I found it there. I like books in two volumes.'

'So do I. If you're immersed in the story, you don't have to worry that it'll finish when you finish the book.' He tried to make a mental note of the titles: would he have to read them all in order to get through to Sigrun? 'Do you have a favorite book?'

'I don't know. I liked *A Girl and Her Führer* and *Dora Does National Labor Service* for a long time, but now I prefer to read about history rather than girls. Do you know *Baska and Her Men*? What books do you read?'

'I'm a bookseller, so I try to read books that have recently been published. Customers want advice; I need to be able to tell them which of the new books they might like.'

'But what do you read for pleasure? What's your favorite book?'

'*War and Peace* by Leo Tolstoy.' And because Sigrun gave him a querying look, he started to tell her the story of Natasha and Sonya, Pierre and Nikolai.

At first Sigrun listened; then her gaze began to wander, then she turned her head away, then she couldn't keep her hands and legs still. 'Why isn't your favorite book a German one? Why Russian — it is Russian, isn't it?' She took his hand. He hoped it was just his imagination, but the gesture didn't seem as blithely natural as before. He wanted to squeeze her hand, but was afraid of getting something wrong.

14

At first glance, it was a village fete like any other. A band was playing; they were just following up a folk song with a rousing rock number. One stall was serving drinks, another had grilled sausages and a hog roast; there were tables with bowls of salad – potato, pasta or green – as well as baskets of bread and cakes on platters. The older people sat at beer tables while the younger ones stood around in groups, and the little children ran between the two. Sigrun let go of Kaspar's hand and found some other girls in grey skirts and white blouses, so Kaspar strolled about on his own.

People kept looking at him in astonishment, and he could understand why: in his jeans, T-shirt and jacket, he looked out of place among the men in journeymen's clothes and women in dirndls or dirndl-like dresses. He returned their gaze with a friendly smile, and sometimes the astonished look grew friendly, too, but most people looked away. When he went to get himself a beer, he noticed that they were serving juice and water, too, but no cola. The beer came in a glass, the food was served on plates with steel cutlery, and the girls, including Sigrun, went around collecting the dirty plates and cutlery, took them into the big building nearby, and brought them back out again, washed and clean. He took his glass and plate and sat down at the end of a beer table beside an elderly couple.

Here, too, he was met with the same astonished look. 'How do you come to be here?'

'Sigrun Renger invited me.'

The man looked at his watch. 'They'll be starting in a minute. She won last year. I wonder if she will again? Our girls are getting better and better; our boys need to watch out.'

'What are you celebrating today?'

'Harvest festival. Haven't you been up to the big field yet? The competitions will be held there at half past four, then the festivities.'

At half past four Kaspar was standing with the other visitors at the edge of the field. A sort of straw altar had been erected at the end of it; sunflowers were sticking out of the straw, and a harvest crown was enthroned on the altar, made of ears of corn decorated with flowers and colorful ribbons. A tightrope was strung across the field between two trees, three or four metres above the ground, and a line was marked on the field itself where nine girls and ten boys were waiting, the girls in grey skirts and the boys in short lederhosen, each with a white blouse or white shirt.

'We want to feel our feet on the soil, we want to feel the force of the earth. Prepare for the barefoot race!' An umpire raised his arm, lowered it, and the nineteen children started running. Sigrun didn't really stand a chance in her long skirt, but she came third, to loud applause. 'We fear no enemy, we fear no danger, we fear no abyss: we overcome them all. Prepare for the rope! The best time last year was one minute fifteen seconds.'

The winner of the barefoot race was the first to climb the ladder. At a given signal, he swung himself hand over hand along the rope across the field, looking grimly determined, timed by the umpire and spurred on by shouts of encouragement from the crowd. Just before the end he began to slow down, and the shouts of encouragement turned to jeers, but when he reached the finish he jumped elegantly from the rope to the ground.

Sigrun was the third to step up. She performed the exercise effortlessly; there was no strain on her face, only concentration. She swung herself forward quickly and easily, hand over hand, and by the time she reached the finish line she had set a new record. Kaspar shouted and cheered and clapped along with everyone else.

The third discipline was hand-to-hand combat for the boys, gymnastics for the girls. The umpire spoke of life as a fight and the fight as life, got the boys up first to fight on his right, then called up the girls on his left. The boys were doing what looked to Kaspar like judo, though their clothing didn't really fit Kaspar's image of judo. In their long skirts there wasn't much the girls could do with hoops, balls and ribbons, but what they could do they did with dignity. The umpire was about to declare Sigrun and Horst the winners when Horst said something to Sigrun; she looked at him, pounced on him, turned her back, pulled him over her shoulder and threw him to the ground. There was more cheering. Horst got to his feet; he was about to launch himself at Sigrun, and Sigrun was readying for the fight, but the umpire held Horst back, declared the games over, and said that because they had both broken the rules neither she nor he would be declared the winners, but another girl and boy instead.

Then Björn stepped up to the altar. It was getting dark; two of the boys who had just taken part in the games and the combat stood either side of him, with black kerchiefs above their white shirts and torches in their right hands. The crowd moved forward – Kaspar guessed there were between seventy and eighty people – and silence fell. Björn spoke.

To his surprise, Kaspar found that Björn was no bad speaker.

He spoke in a calm, firm voice, building up to points that invited applause, resuming as the applause died away. First he gave thanks for that year's harvest: a völkisch family from Berlin, the husband an architect, the wife a mother of five, had just bought a farmstead in the village and would soon be moving in. They were sorry not to be able to be with them today, but were looking forward to life in the community and sent their greetings. Then he talked about the period that followed the harvest. They would need to prune the trees soon, or they wouldn't have a good harvest the following year. It was like that everywhere: whatever hindered growth and the bearing of fruit had to be cut off and removed. To approving laughter, he continued: 'We had to lend a bit of a helping hand to make the farm available for the family, and there are other farms where we need to do a bit of cutting and removing. That's how our community will grow. People on the outside don't know what community is any more; they live for themselves, degenerate by themselves, die by themselves. The only ones who still know the meaning of it, apart from us, are the clans: the Mussulmen and headscarf women and their families. They want to take over Germany – they want to make our country their country. But we won't let them. We are ready to fight. We grow on German soil; we derive our strength from German soil. The German future belongs to our völkisch community.'

During his speech, the boys and girls had stacked up a pile of wood in the middle of the field. The torchbearers processed down a passage through the crowd and ignited the wood, while the crowd spread out to form a circle around the bonfire. As the flames flared up, the band played a tune and everyone joined in. 'Rise, flames, arise, / Blazing towards the skies.' Kaspar didn't know the song and didn't catch it all, but he understood that we were standing in a sacred circle watching the flames burn to the glory of the Fatherland, that the flames summoned the youth and gave them courage, that the enemy paled at the sight of them, and that we swore at the altar of the flames to be Germans. The singing continued with 'A Young Volk Arises' and 'Brothers in East and West', and again all Kaspar understood was that, whether townspeople, farmers or workers, we were young soldiers, we were marching, Europe shone before us and the Reich within us. The next songs were more subdued, sadder, more wistful: in 'The Wind Blows Over Fields' the emperor's cavalry rode across Flanders to their deaths, and in 'Make Way, O People' the last of the Goths set off across the grey sea for faraway Thule. Kaspar knew 'Wild Geese Are Flying Through the Night' from his time in the Evangelical Church youth group; he sang along to this, and to 'By the Well in Front of the Gate' and 'No Land More Beautiful', songs that had imprinted themselves on his memory when his grandmother sang them with him as a child.

He looked around. During the last few songs, the faces had softened in the firelight. How could it be otherwise? he thought. Why shouldn't people of the far right be just as capable of dreaming, of being as pensive, as wistful as us? He thought of General Governor Hans Frank, the Butcher of Poland, who had played Chopin with feeling at the castle in Kraków, and Hitler, who loved his dog. Kaspar didn't want his enjoyment of the songs to create a sense of solidarity with the people standing around the fire and singing with him. He liked Chopin, and he liked dogs, but he didn't want to hear Frank play Chopin, or to play with Hitler's dog. He slipped away from the circle, walked over to the church and sat down on the doorstep. The singing continued, concluding with 'Deutschland, Deutschland über alles'; then the crowd dispersed, heading back to the stalls and tables, and the band livened up again and played some more rock.

Kaspar got up and returned to the fete. Björn approached, holding two glasses of beer. 'Here! Let's drink to the women.

What was yours called? Birgit? Let's drink to Birgit and Svenja and Sigrun.' He raised his glass to Kaspar and gave him a piece of paper. 'And to the money you're going to transfer to me. Here are my bank details and account number. And to the holidays Sigrun will spend with you.' He took a sip. 'And to Germany.' He took another. 'I'll introduce you to our lawyer, too, so you know what's what.'

Björn took Kaspar's arm, steered him over to a table, introduced him to Dr Maier and left the two of them alone. A young man with an intelligent face – why shouldn't the far right have intelligent faces? As he understood it, if the Weises didn't play ball, Svenja would have to take them on, and would need Kaspar to get involved. Would Kaspar testify that Svenja was Birgit's daughter? Would he agree to Birgit's exhumation? Would he let him take a look at Birgit's will? No? And what if he were to sue him?

In the end, he laughed. Kaspar's offer was a decent one; they should leave it at that. And Svenja should show her face with the Weises and put the screws on about her inheritance. How often did someone get a chance to inherit from two sets of parents?

15

Kaspar walked across the site to say goodbye. Björn was sitting with a group of men; they were drinking, talking and laughing loudly, slapping each other on the back and banging the table. Sigrun was by the fire, her head on a friend's shoulder, staring into the flames. Kaspar thought he would find Svenja with the women on the stalls. But she was standing off to one side, leaning against a big pile of wood, without a beer or wine glass and without a cigarette, and Kaspar wondered whether turning her back on Frankfurt had also meant turning her back on alcohol and drugs. She smiled at him as he approached, a cautious smile, ready to disappear again at any moment. He came and stood beside her, and they watched the crowd.

'Are you going? Before you do, tell me why your wife didn't want me.'

'She never talked about you to me. I didn't know you existed until I found her notes after her death.' He should have anticipated this conversation and prepared for it. He was glad when Svenja waited patiently. 'I think she just wanted to escape. She hated Leo Weise; she'd had a relationship with him and he had lied to her and tried to use her; she was afraid that it would be possible to arrange for her to escape, but not both of you; maybe she was also afraid I wouldn't want her any more if I found out

166

about her and Leo and you. She would have terminated the pregnancy if she could, but Leo strung her along, and by the time he walked out on her it was too late. She may also have projected her hatred of Leo onto you. I don't know. There's so much I don't know.' Svenja didn't speak, and he carried on. 'I know it tormented her, later on. She wanted to find you. But she was afraid of that, too. And because she was afraid of finding you, she was afraid of even looking. Instead of looking for you, she read, about orphanages and reformatories and re-education camps and labor camps. She had asked her friend to leave you on the doorstep of a hospital or parsonage, and she was afraid that from there you would have ended up being sent from one home to another. At the same time, she hoped that, when she met you, you would be a strong, vivacious, happy woman.'

'What would she have wanted with me, if she had found me?' Until now, Kaspar had always heard Svenja speak in a subdued voice, and, when she wanted to calm Björn, a gentle one. Now she sounded as if she was controlling herself only with great effort, as if suppressing grief or anger, or possibly hatred towards the woman who had abandoned her and whom she despised and rejected. She pressed her lips together, and just as her mouth reminded him of Birgit's mouth, her tightly pressed lips reminded him of Birgit's closed expression when she was upset or annoyed, but controlling herself.

'She wanted to tell you who she was and how it happened, and she wanted to offer herself to you. She was prepared to give whatever you might want of her. That was what she hoped for: that you would want something of her. She didn't dare to want anything of you.'

'Offer?' She laughed. 'Offer, or force on me? You made that up about the will. You want to keep an eye on me and Sigrun. All right, fine; I'm happy for Sigrun that she can have a grandfather, and I'm happy for her to see the city, too. The autumn break starts in three weeks; Björn will bring her to you. But don't think you can buy us. If I see that Sigrun isn't my Sigrun any more, that's it. You can take your money and – you know what you can do with it. Björn's after the money, as you know, but that won't help you then, either.'

Kaspar heard her resistance, and was moved by it. He thought of Birgit's resistance, her defiance whenever he confronted her and she defended herself, her readiness to break off, to stop working in the bookshop, to set out for India, to retreat to her room, to drink. Svenja wouldn't hesitate to break with him. 'What makes Sigrun your Sigrun?'

'That she's proud of herself and of us and of Germany. That she's strong and doesn't let anyone push her around or put her down. That she knows who she is and what she wants.'

And in this Kaspar heard the Svenja who had not been allowed to find out who she was and what she wanted, who had been pushed around and put down, who had had nothing of which she could be proud. She had left it all behind: the parental home, being committed by her father, Torgau, the years with the skinheads. In Björn, and believing in völkisch values and pride in Germany, she had found something that sustained her, and she wanted to pass it on to Sigrun. Still, Kaspar wanted to try to establish a bridge between them.

'I'm not proud of Germany. Why should I be proud of something that isn't my doing? But I can't imagine being anything other than German. Is that enough?'

'We'll see.' She produced a piece of paper from the pocket of her dress, and another, and a pen. 'I've written down our phone number for you. Will you write yours down for me?' When he had done so, she smiled at him again, as she had earlier, when he saw her standing there and came to stand beside her. 'I know it was your wife who didn't want me, not you.

You didn't have to come. You can call me Svenja, by the way.'

'And you can call me Kaspar.'

'Kaspar – like the clown?' She laughed out loud, a bright, cheerful laugh he would not have expected from her; then she covered her mouth with her hand, still laughing quietly, and apologized. 'Don't be cross; I wasn't making fun of you, I've just never met anyone called Kaspar before.' Still laughing, she gave him a kiss on the cheek. 'Safe journey home, Kaspar!'

16

He drove out of the village the way he came in. He remembered passing a timber yard, located it in the darkness on the opposite side of the road, and parked up between two woodpiles.

What should he do? He was too tired to drive to Berlin, and had probably drunk too much, as well. Rietzow couldn't be far; he thought of asking Paula to put him up for the night, but he was reluctant to drive even such a short distance; besides which, by the time he got there, it would be too late. He couldn't recall passing a guesthouse anywhere along the way. He would sleep in the car.

With the seat back lowered, he had a flat bed, and could use his coat as a blanket. He lay down but couldn't sleep. Sigrun would be coming in three weeks. She couldn't sleep on the living room sofa. She needed a room of her own with a bed, wardrobe, table and chair – he would have to set up Birgit's study for her. She needed books – he would have to speak to his colleague at the bookshop who curated the books for children and young adults. He needed games he could play with her. What could he show her in the city? Which museums would interest her? How did she feel about theatre, cinema, opera, concerts? He had to prepare himself, have a program for each day; he didn't have to follow it, but he had to have one.

Did she need girls her own age to play with? Where would he find them?

He grew increasingly uneasy. How was he to manage all of this? Even the strongest people fall prey to helplessness and defencelessness when they lie awake at night, and for Kaspar the tasks ahead began to take on alarming dimensions. His colleague would recommend books for him, but if the recommendations were no good, he would have to read his way through the entire section of books aimed at young girls. What sort of picture should he hang in her room? Not Frederick the Great or Bismarck, obviously, even if Sigrun might like that; but nothing that would feel like a provocation, either, nothing her father – who knew? – might have shown her along with pictures from the 1937 exhibition of degenerate art, and ruined for her. A Feuerbach painting of a woman, full of dreamy longing? Koller's *The Gotthard Post*? A mountain landscape by Hodler? Was there a musician or film star who transcended politics, popular with both right and left, someone Sigrun was keen on and whose picture on the wall of her room would immediately reconcile her to him, and to her stay in his world? Whom could he ask? Then there was the money. He didn't have it in the bank; he couldn't take it out of the bookshop. Could he get a loan from the savings bank? Would he have to mortgage the apartment?

He pushed off his coat and sat up. He had to get out. He groped for the door handle, couldn't find it, and started panicking that he was trapped in this darkened carapace, unable to sit up, barely able to stretch out, bumping up against it on all sides, his head, his arms, his feet. Then he managed to open the door, pushed himself out head first, propping himself up on his hands, pulled his legs out after him, slipped, fell, crawled, and finally sat down on the ground beside the car, panting.

When his breathing quietened, everything was silent. As silent as it had been a few days earlier beside the Oder, Kaspar thought; and that the silence in the East was both familiar and eerie. He listened, but no twig snapped, no owl screeched or hooted, no wind rustled in the trees. He could smell the piles of cut wood. Why, Kaspar wondered, do we like the smell of wood? Because people lived in wood before we built houses of brick? Because our first tools were made of wood? Because wood is alive; because it grows and ages as we grow and age? Kaspar heard a distant roar and got to his feet. The sound was fast approaching, growing louder; the bright lights dazzled him, and before he knew it the speeding car with its growling exhaust and headlights on full beam had passed. Was it going to the fete?

Even if he did manage to get everything ready – the room and the picture and the books – and Sigrun felt comfortable, what was he actually doing? What right did he have to intrude upon her life? Had Birgit had a right to do so, and had he inherited it? A right because Sigrun was Birgit's granddaughter? What on earth had he been thinking when he invented the will and commandeered Sigrun for the holidays? Had it seemed to him such an obvious thing to do because she was in danger in her far-right environment? Because he wanted to save her from moral and intellectual corruption?

Kaspar had always avoided getting involved. He was a member of a church, and occasionally went to services without believing in God, but had never taken on any responsibilities there. He was a member of the Chamber of Industry and Commerce and the German Publishers' and Booksellers' Association, but had never held any office. Occasionally, politics would get him riled up and he would consider joining a political party. Occasionally, he would be invited to get involved in the 'Citizens for the Park' initiative. But he had never got beyond reliably voting in elections, and occasionally picking up paper, plastic cups and bottles on his walk through the park. And now suddenly he wanted to save – no, not the world, but Sigrun, which seemed to him no less exotic and presumptuous.

He was freezing. He put on the coat, walked up and down, sat in the car again, raised the back of the seat and switched on the engine and the heating. The noise and the dry, dusty air it blew into the car's interior soon bothered him, though, and he switched them both off again. The colder he got, the more he sobered up, and he decided to drive to Berlin, but fell asleep as he was making the decision and awoke as dawn was breaking.

He drove off. It was too late to avoid getting involved. He already was. He had to get on with Björn and Svenja and be a grandfather to Sigrun, as best he could. He would have liked to have had children; he'd had none – and now he had a grand-daughter. And now that he had her, he had to tend her soul. He laughed. Sigrun's soul, the German soul . . . What am I letting myself in for?

17

Back in Berlin, Kaspar took out a loan from the savings bank and transferred twenty-five thousand euros to Björn and Svenja. He went into Birgit's room, stood in the doorway, sat down at the desk and looked around. If he took Birgit's big desk and big bookcases down to the cellar, he could fit a bed along the left-hand wall, a little desk under the window, a little bookcase to the right of it and a wardrobe against the wall on the right. Kaspar set to work. He put Birgit's things in the cellar, found a bed, a desk and a wardrobe in an antiques shop, got a carpenter to put drawers in one side of the wardrobe and a rail across the other, and make a bookcase narrow enough not to look empty with the ten books he wanted to put in it, and the few Sigrun might want to bring with her. He brought Birgit's chair back up from the cellar; it was more modern than the rest of the decor, but it would be good for Sigrun's back, and a reminder of her grandmother.

He read his way through the books recommended by his colleague, books that were read and enjoyed by fourteen-year-old girls. He understood that, at that age, they liked to read about girls a little bit older. But did the very first book have to be about sixteen-year-olds who were cool because they drank alcohol, took drugs and had sex?

He hadn't read about fourteen-year-olds, either, when he was fourteen. Back then, he and his classmates had started to read their way through the literature of the world, from Tolstoy and Dostoyevsky to Stendhal and Hugo. There was a lot he had not understood, and had not appreciated as it deserved. But it had been exciting, and despite his not understanding it, or because he didn't understand it, it had provided plenty of food for thought and discussion. The recommended girls' books did the same. Only – what sort of role models did they provide?

But then, what sort of role model was Julien Sorel, who seduced two women, or Rodion Raskolnikov, who had killed two women? They existed at a remove of more than a century, but when he had read about them they had been as close and challenging to him as if he and they lived in the same time and the same world. The girls' book ended well – should he count on the alcohol, drugs and sex being sublimated into the happy ending for Sigrun, just as, for him, the murders committed by Raskolnikov were overridden by his reclamation through Sonya's love? Was his assessment of the reading comprehension skills of fourteen-year-old girls simply too low? But while the murders did not make Raskolnikov attractive, alcohol, drugs and sex made the sixteen-year-olds cool. Was that what he wanted Sigrun to learn?

He kept reading. The next book was about seven fourteen-year-old girls who survived a few weeks in the forest one summer, during which they encountered strange people, friendly dogs and three boys. No alcohol and no drugs, and tentative affection rather than sex. But what was there about surviving in the forest that would impress Sigrun, who had gone on long hikes with far-right groups and camped in fields and forests?

He liked the story of a sixteen-year-old Black girl who lives in a ghetto but who, thanks to her parents' ambition and their careful economizing, is sent to a white private school; her Black boyfriend, the same age, is shot by a policeman for no reason, and she learns to stand up for herself, against the police and against the gang in the ghetto. But you could smell grass before the end of the first page, and there was reference to a condom on the second. What if Sigrun asked him about them? Grass he could cope with; the protagonist doesn't like it and doesn't smoke it, and doesn't like the smell of it, either. Nor does she use the condom. But should he, her grandfather, be the one to explain to fourteen-year-old Sigrun what condoms were for? Or had she already known for years?

He plumped for the adventures of a young girl who, after meeting the wrong boy, eventually meets the right one: a Native American, who takes her with him into his world and introduces her to nature and a new way of experiencing and thinking and feeling; she falls in love with him, and he with her, and she decides to stay with him despite the differences in their worlds.

Then he remembered his own children's books: *The Jungle Book*, *The Black Brothers*, *Treasure Island*, *Robinson Crusoe* and *Oliver Twist*. He had loved these books; he had lived with them. He didn't have them any more. So he got hold of them, along with *Little Women* and *The Lord of the Rings*, which he hadn't read but had heard about. Those that were out of print he found second-hand. Eight books – that ought to be enough. Kaspar put them in the bookcase. Then, unable to resist, he picked up *The Jungle Book*, read it, and was as delighted by Mowgli's friendship with the panther and the bear as he had been as a child. Whichever book Sigrun made friends with, he would share that friendship.

He bought tickets for *The Magic Flute* at the Komische Oper, and for a concert of Bach, Glass and Brahms at the Philharmonie. He checked the opening times of the museums. On one of the days, he would take Sigrun to the bookshop with him and let her help with the packing and unpacking and sending of books; on another, he would take her to the cemetery to visit her grandmother's grave. On the evenings when they had nothing else planned, he would play games with her: at home he found a chess set with wooden figures and board, inherited from his grandfather, and he bought Nine Men's Morris, draughts, Reversi and Scrabble.

The evening before Sigrun was due to arrive, he went up to the study and sat on the chair. This was where he had sat after Birgit's death, after the police had gone. It had been Birgit's room then; now it was Sigrun's. Then, he had still known nothing about Sigrun; now, what he knew about Birgit had become confused. She had written that her great comfort was that he had loved her. Why hadn't she let him love her more deeply? Why had she remained by herself, alone with herself? What did it mean that she had bequeathed him Sigrun? This was what she had done; this was how it felt to him. With Sigrun, he would go to the opera and to concerts again, something he could not have imagined doing any more after Birgit died.

He stared at the blank wall. He hadn't been able to decide on a picture for Sigrun, and had remembered that, as a child, he had liked to look at the blank wall by his bed.

18

Björn called in the morning to say that he and Sigrun would come at five, and at five they were there. Björn was wearing carpenter's trousers and a white shirt, Sigrun the colorful skirt Kaspar had seen her in before, and a white blouse. She was carrying a small, old, leather suitcase.

'Can I take a look around?' asked Björn, after they had greeted each other, and without waiting for a reply he went into the living room and dining room, cast an eye over bedroom and kitchen, and glanced around, looking for something. 'Where's Sigrun going to sleep?' Kaspar showed him the room. 'Where's she going to wash?' Kaspar showed him the guest toilet with shower and washbasin. 'Where've you put the television?' Kaspar assured him that he didn't have a television. Sigrun, who had not said a word until then, said, 'Nor do we,' and Björn nodded and put his hand on her shoulder.

He didn't want to stay for dinner. But he did want a beer before driving home, a quick one, at the table in the kitchen; and over first one beer, then another, he made clear: no television and no cinema, no Internet, no cigarettes, no jeans, no lipstick, no piercings. Sigrun listened, expressionless. Kaspar nodded. 'That's clear, then.' Björn got to his feet. 'I'll pick her up in a week's time.' But he didn't go to the door as resolutely as he had spoken and got to his feet. He turned to Sigrun. 'Take care, my girl.' He bent down, kissed her forehead and left.

Kaspar and Sigrun sat at the table and looked at each other. Her red hair, her freckles, her eyes – green or brown, or both – her mouth, the curve of which was the only thing about her that reminded him of Birgit. Where might her red hair have come from? Not Björn, not Svenja; not Leo, either. Had Paula brought it into the family, by bringing Sigrun into the world and accompanying her on her first journey? Kaspar shook his head; he couldn't believe he was thinking something so silly.

'How old are you, Grandfather?'

'Seventy-one.'

'I'm fourteen. I'll be fifteen in December.'

Kaspar nodded. 'That's a good age. Do you want to unpack and make yourself at home? Can I help you?'

'I can manage.'

'What made your father think I would get you a piercing?'

'Me, not you. Irmtraud got a piercing, a tiny silver swastika at the top of her ear; it looks great, I like it. Irmtraud lives in Berlin; she's with the autonomists, and when I'm older I want to go to Berlin and join the autonomists, too. My parents think that's the wrong path to go down.' She laughed. 'Now they're afraid I'll run away from you and end up with Irmtraud. I thought Father was going to warn you of what he'll do to you if I run away.'

'Do you want to end up with Irmtraud?'

'No, I just want to see her. You can come along, if you like.'

Kaspar carried her suitcase up to the room, showed her the wardrobe with the rail and the drawers, the bookcase and books, the switch for the overhead light and the one for the lamps on the desk and bedside table, then stood in the doorway, unsure what to do next. 'Do you like pizza?' Sigrun nodded. 'Then come down when you're ready and we'll go and eat.'

She came down as he was reading a Wikipedia article about the autonomous nationalists. Was this really what she wanted to be?

They went to an Italian restaurant, and everything they saw along the way impressed her: the tall buildings, first with front gardens, then without; the wide road with lots of shops and restaurants; all the cars, all the people. She had never been to Berlin before; she wouldn't tire of the city in the one week they had ahead of them. She was impressed by the restaurant, too, where the owner greeted Kaspar as an old friend and her as a young lady; by the dining room with its red walls and subdued lighting, by the waiters in their long white aprons, by the white tablecloths and white linen napkins. 'Proper table napkins,' she said as they sat down, unfolding hers and spreading it over her knees. She talked about the pizzeria in Güstrow, where most people just went for takeaways, and the few who ate in sat at awful plastic tables under neon lights. She also talked about the boys and girls from her school who hung around outside the pizzeria in the evenings, drinking, or at the petrol station – the independent one; they didn't go to the Shell – and used to hang around the kebab stall, drinking, before it was torched.

'Torched?'

'The two who ran it were Africans and Mussulmen. We don't need people like that.'

'The people who buy from them need them. If no one needed them, they wouldn't be there.'

'Oh, Grandfather, why are you being so difficult! I only know what happened, I wasn't there. I don't do stuff like that. I don't hang around the petrol station, either, and I don't drink beer. I think they should sell their kebabs in Africa, but maybe you're right and it would be better if no one bought from them any more. Is it true there are buses here that are like one bus on top of another?'

Kaspar promised to take her on a ride around Berlin on top of a double-decker. He told her about the tickets for the opera and the concert, about the museums, the bookshop, and the games they would play together. Her eyes shone as she listened. She was looking forward to all of it.

'How far is it to Ravensbrück?'

'Ravensbrück?'

'Irma Grese – I want to see where she worked. Once or twice a year my parents take me to a gathering somewhere, but they never take me where I want to go. Will you go to Ravensbrück with me?'

'When you come back and stay for longer. We already have a full program this week.'

Sigrun could see that this made sense. She ate her pizza, ordered a cola, hesitantly, with a mixture of curiosity and guilt, then went on to drink another. She asked about the size and population of Berlin, whether the U-Bahn really ran underground, how she could help in the bookshop. Suddenly she asked what Grandmother had been like. Kaspar promised he would take her to Birgit's grave and tell her about Birgit there. Sigrun was satisfied with this, and by the end of the meal she was satisfied with everything, tired after her journey, tired after all the questions, and ready for bed. When he came up to say good night, she beat about the bush until he realized that she was a bit frightened to go to sleep in the unfamiliar room, and didn't want to admit it to him, or to herself. He sat down on the edge of the bed and told her the story of *The Magic Flute*. He told her about Tamino, the monster pursuing him, his fear and helplessness, and about Papageno, who introduces himself to Tamino with a song after the latter comes round from a faint. He told the story slowly and calmly, and watched Sigrun's eyes grow heavy. 'I'm going to go downstairs. I'll leave the doors open and play the song, and you're going to fall asleep.' He placed his hand briefly on hers, got up, went downstairs, found the CD and Papageno's song and played it. Then he went to the bottom of the stairs that led to Sigrun's room, called up quietly, 'Sigrun?', received no reply, and quietly said, 'Good night!'

19

He finished reading the Wikipedia article about the autonomous nationalists. He couldn't believe that Sigrun wanted to eradicate the political system by way of revolution, and replace it with a national and socialist community – that she could even conceive of what the political system and revolution and a national and socialist community were. Did the revolutionary rhetoric sound exciting to her? Did the black trousers and hoodies, baseball caps and gloves look cool to her, after the prim skirts and blouses? Did she want to be one of the few girls who asserted themselves in the autonomist movement?

Then he read about Irma Grese and was even more baffled. At seventeen she had wanted to be a nurse; at nineteen she became a guard at Ravensbrück; then, at Auschwitz, she at times had the supervision of more than thirty thousand women, and finally led a death march to Bergen-Belsen. She was exceptionally cruel, beat and whipped people, set dogs on them, was described as the worst female guard in the camp and nicknamed 'the Hyena of Auschwitz'. She proudly confessed in court that she had done her duty to the Fatherland, and maintained her composure on the gallows. Was that enough for Sigrun? Did it not matter to her what Irma Grese had done? Did she not know? Did she not want to know?

ERNHARD SCHLINK

When Kaspar came into the kitchen to make breakfast at seven o'clock the next morning, Sigrun had already laid the table. She had pulled a chair over to the window and was sitting reading *Treasure Island*. She jumped up, explained that she always got up that early as the school bus picked her up at seven, switched on the oven, in which she had already placed the bread rolls, and put water on to boil. When he tried to do something, she said, 'Let me,' and made black tea for him and a hot chocolate for herself, revealing that she had inspected the cupboards and drawers and familiarized herself with the kitchen. Kaspar found the ease with which she moved around the kitchen and availed herself of objects and supplies a little discomfiting, but he enjoyed being waited on.

It was a grey autumn day. Sigrun wasn't bothered by this; she didn't want to postpone their exploration of the city. They were out and about all day, rode below and above ground on the U- and S-Bahn, sat on top and at the front of double-decker buses, where you are king of the world, while on other buses and in the tram they sat at the back, where you ride away from it. They walked and walked. Kaspar remembered the Sunday after his arrival in Berlin all those years ago, his first walk around the city, his first visit to the East. He also remembered how, back then, he had wanted to be at home in all Berlin and in all of Germany, and it wasn't possible. Now he was, and he was glad of it.

With Sigrun, he walked down Karl-Marx-Allee again from east to west; he showed her Alexanderplatz, the Museum Island, Berlin Cathedral, the Neue Wache memorial, the university and the Gendarmenmarkt. She had questions and things to say about all of it. She would have liked everything to be bigger, more imposing, more magnificent; only the cathedral passed muster, both outside and in. At the Neue Wache, she spent a long time contemplating the pietà by Käthe Kollwitz.

184

'Is that a German mother with her dead son?'

'Yes, and when it was installed many people interpreted it as a commemoration of the German victims of the war, but not the victims of German tyranny. Hence the inscription on the ground.'

'"For the victims of war and tyranny",' Sigrun read aloud. She shook her head. 'Why not "for the German victims"? Why can't we remember our victims, and the others theirs?'

'All are equal in death. And it's good to remember not only what one has suffered oneself, but what one has inflicted on others, as well.'

'Always the others.'

'No, Sigrun: the others as well.' Kaspar didn't want to get into an argument about Germans and others and the question of whether Germans portrayed themselves too negatively and others too positively. 'I came here once in winter. I was alone; it was quiet, it was cold, it was snowing. Snow was falling through the skylight, the snowflakes were dancing and whirling down and settling on the mother's head and shoulders, and the sight was so sad, so painful – it was a grief and pain for everything that is not right. It's not right that people kill and die in war, that they are violent towards each other and oppress each other. The Earth is so big and so abundant that we can all live on it and have good lives.'

Sigrun didn't answer, and Kaspar didn't know whether what he had said had got through to her, or whether she was silent as he would be silent, as a child, when his mother voiced a moral standpoint and he just wanted to get the moralizing over and done with. He also didn't know what it signified that she took his hand when she said, 'Shall we go?' Outside, she let go again, and chatted away cheerfully as before.

On the way home, she insisted that they should cook together that evening and should go shopping for ingredients.

He couldn't cook but didn't like to say so. He saw some fresh chanterelles, remembered the pasta with fresh chanterelles that he had eaten in the restaurant, and bought them, along with some onions, bacon and cream, spaghetti and lettuce. When they got home he set to work, chopping the onions unevenly until Sigrun told him to start cutting the bacon. In the blink of an eye she had chopped the onions, taken over the bacon as well, and set him to washing the lettuce. She did the cooking, but made out that she was helping him. Was that something girls learned in völkisch communities? How to give the man who's no good at managing things the illusion that he is nonetheless in charge? Kaspar had read about the traditional male and female roles cultivated by the far right, and he didn't want to reap the benefits of this. Once the chanterelles were in the frying pan with the onions and bacon and the spaghetti was in the boiling water, he sat down. 'You're good, Sigrun. Thank you very much for cooking. You'd have found it even easier and quicker without me. But I've learned from watching you, and tomorrow I'll be better.'

'Tomorrow we'll cook something else.'

'Did you learn from your mother?'

'She doesn't cook. That's why I learned.'

After the meal she wanted to play chess, and she was so good that he lost the first game, and the second. A few times she pointed out a mistake and told him to make a different move. She was sweet, as she had been when cooking, but he sensed a determination in her, as if they were engaged in a battle that she had to fight and win wherever they encountered each other. The battle of youth against old age? Woman against man? A political battle?

But she let him recount the next instalment of *The Magic Flute* at bedtime, and before he left her, to put on a recording of 'This Image Is Enchantingly Beautiful', she gave him a kiss.

20

The next morning, Sigrun had spread out the map of Berlin on the kitchen table. 'It's a lovely day. Can we go for a walk?'

It was a lovely day. Kaspar and Sigrun went out onto the balcony; the sky was blue, the leaves were glowing, and there was a promise in the air that, when autumn and winter were over, spring would come again.

'I don't know. We did enough walking yesterday. I need to stop by the bookshop, as well, and the concert starts at seven.'

Sigrun shook her head. She had thought it all through: S-Bahn to Wannsee, ferry to Kladow, then back to Wannsee on foot through Sacrow, the outskirts of Berlin and the Berlin forest. 'This is a bad map. It can't be more than twenty kilometres, though. We'll be back in time for the bookshop and the concert.'

'I don't want to walk twenty kilometres, not today, and not tomorrow, either. I saw at the fete how strong you are; I'm sure you can do it. I can't.' Kaspar was annoyed. The map of Berlin belonged in a pile of papers and brochures with notes about senate and district institutions, customs posts, hospitals, doctors, wholesalers, workmen, emergency services, postal tariffs; nothing secret or private, but not something you would come across by chance, either. As with the kitchen the previous day, today Sigrun had familiarized herself with everything in the living room. Not that he would have refused her permission, if she had asked. But without asking?

Sigrun was oblivious to his irritation. She smiled – had she scored another victory in her battle against him? 'I did the Wolfsangel hike last year. A hundred and fifty kilometres in four days, with a fifteen-kilo pack. It's meant for boys, but they often don't manage it. It's not really meant for girls.'

'Wolfsangel hike?'

'If you finish it, you get the Wolfsangel. Because then you're able to defend yourself, and the rune stands for the ability to defend yourself.'

'Will you show me?'

Sigrun ran up the stairs, ran back down again, and stood in the kitchen holding a silver badge with pride. She placed the little shield in his hand; on it was a picture of a rod with hooks at either end that pointed in opposite directions. She saw him looking at the badge in puzzlement, and asked, 'Don't you know the runes? I'll explain them to you. Our Germanic ancestors speak to us in them.'

Over breakfast, Sigrun drew runes on a piece of paper: the 'sig', or victory, rune – her rune, but it had been used by the SS and was now banned; the fourteen rune, the rune for her age; the othala rune, which symbolized freedom; and the black sun, the symbol of completion. Sigrun had given up on learning the whole runic alphabet. There wasn't a lot you could actually do with runes. But she did explain them to the völkisch youth. 'I also teach them to respect the German language and say *Handtelefon* instead of *Handy*, *T-Hemd*, not *T-Shirt*, *Übersicht*, not *Résumé*, *Weltnetz*, not *Internet*.'

Kaspar remembered the saying on the wall in Sigrun's kitchen. 'A nation's soul resides in its language?'

Sigrun beamed. 'Yes, Grandfather! You read that at our house.'

Did the nation's soul reside in the *Handtelefon* and the *Weltnetz*? Kaspar stopped himself from asking the question. The saying had an element of truth, even if it wasn't the one Sigrun was teaching the völkisch children, and Kaspar didn't want to make fun of either Sigrun or that truth. He wanted to take Sigrun seriously – how else would he get through to her?

'You've already taken on responsibility for younger children?'

'My favorite thing is leading a youth group – a group of girls' – she laughed – 'when we go camping in a scouting tent. We have a campfire in the middle, I read out loud to them every evening, we sleep with warm feet and cool heads, wake up in the morning feeling fresh, and after five days we're a proper fellowship. I also like that everyone has to take turns keeping watch during the night, and is responsible for keeping the fire burning for an hour. I make sure that my group really does the morning run and the press-ups and knee bends properly; I want them to be strong, and for us to win the field exercises.'

'Do you win?'

She laughed. 'What do you think?'

'I think you win.'

'Not the singing. Winning that's a question of luck. You can make the lazy and the fat ones run, but if all someone can do is croak, thrashing them won't make them sing.'

'You like singing?'

'So do you. You sang along at our fete; I could see that you enjoyed it. Next time I'll bring my songbook and show it to you. Do you know "Our Lives Belong to Freedom"? It's my favorite song. With "Brothers in East and West"; I like that our honor is loyalty – loyalty to people and country. What's wrong with that?' She pushed back her chair, sat up straight and sang in a high, clear voice: '"Our honor is loyalty, / Loyalty to people and Reich. / Let us build on this faithfully, / For future and people alike.'"

Once again, Kaspar was tempted to challenge her. To explain to her that the melody of the song she was singing was stolen from the workers' movement song 'Brothers, to the Sun, to Freedom'. That the workers' movement was deeply hostile to the völkisch movement, and the theft was a way of mocking the workers. That 'My honor is loyalty' was the motto of the SS. That loyalty is only honorable if it is loyalty to the right thing; that people and country don't always do the right thing, and that it is therefore sometimes necessary to rescind one's loyalty. But Sigrun had spoken and sung so innocently that, once again, he didn't feel he would be able to get through to her.

'When I was a boy, I was in the Evangelical Church youth group. I wore its uniform jacket, slept in a tent and sang the "Song of the Wild Geese". I think we all have to take responsibility for our own honor. If someone does something dishonorable, it doesn't become honorable just because they did it out of loyalty to someone else. Come on, though,' he said, looking at his watch. 'We have to go to the bookshop, and before that I want to show you what's in store this evening.' Kaspar played Sigrun the first movement of Bach's G minor piano concerto and the beginning of the second, Glass's first Etude, and the beginning of Brahms's Symphony No. 4. 'When I hear Bach, it feels to me as if the music contains everything, the heavy and the light, the sad and the beautiful, and reconciles them with each other. With Glass, I think of the flow of life rushing past, with rapids and waterfalls here and there but rushing on and on. Brahms, to me, is passion and the controlling of it. I don't mean that when you're at the concert you should feel the same as me. Everyone hears it in their own way. But when you're listening to music, it's good to listen to yourself, as well, to see what the music is doing to you.' Kaspar suddenly felt embarrassed. Had he lectured her? He didn't want to do that. Had what he'd said gone over her head? 'Do you know what I mean?'

'Yes,' she said, gazing at him seriously, as if she really did understand.

'Good. Then let's go.'

21

In the bookshop he asked her first to unpack the boxes that had been delivered, then to take the order forms that had been put in a tray while a member of staff was off sick, and put them in alphabetical order. After dealing with all the calls and conversations and decisions that were waiting for him, he went to see how she was getting on, and found neatly stacked books, folded boxes and sorted order forms, but no Sigrun. He thought of Irmtraud, panicked, went out into the street, couldn't see Sigrun, told himself that if she really wanted to leave she wouldn't let him find her in the street, and turned back. He scoured the bookshop. She wasn't in the children's and young adults' section, or in fiction. She was sitting on the floor in front of the shelf of contemporary history books, reading.

'You do have a book about Rudolf Hess. It's full of lies. All the books here are full of lies. Hitler didn't want the war, he wanted peace. And the Germans didn't murder the Jews.'

Kaspar sat opposite her on the floor. 'These are books by historians who spent years researching them. How do you know they're lying?'

'They've been bought. They're being paid. The occupying powers want to keep Germany down. We're supposed to bow our heads and be ashamed. Then they can suppress and exploit us.'

'If you look at the books, they're based on the records of the German government and of the National Socialist Party and of the concentration camps, and on eyewitness statements, and on things Hitler and his men wrote themselves. Do you think all of that is lies?'

'They're lying about Auschwitz. People can't be gassed with Zyklon B, or at least not as many and not as fast as they claim they were in Auschwitz. Papa says that's not politics, that's chemistry. And if they're lying about chemistry, which you can't actually lie about, then they're lying about everything else as well.'

'Do you want to read one of the books? So take it with you. I have a book on chemistry at home, as well.'

Sigrun took the Hess biography, to show Kaspar the lies that it contained; and because she had room for more books in the tote bag he gave her, she picked up a YA book as well. Kaspar was slightly reassured that she had checked out the children's section before she went looking for Rudolf Hess.

Neither of them brought up the bookshop conversation again. They went to the Alte Nationalgalerie, and Sigrun enjoyed the paintings of Caspar David Friedrich and Adolph Menzel, and asked questions about their life and work – Kaspar was glad he had read up on them the previous evening. She also enjoyed the concert. It was her first, apart from a far-right rock festival her parents had taken her to in Saxony; now that they were a bit older, they didn't really like the music any more, but at the festival they met up with old friends they wanted to stay in touch with. Sigrun put on the best dress she had brought with her – a dirndl – pinned up her red hair and threaded a blue ribbon through it, and instead of walking half a step ahead and telling him to hurry up, as she usually did, she walked calmly at his side through the foyer and up the stairs. He couldn't tell from her expression and demeanor to what extent it was the hall of the Philharmonie that impressed her, or the sight of the orchestra, conductor and pianist, or the actual music; perhaps she didn't know herself. But she didn't fidget in her seat, didn't look at her watch, and when the audience went out in the interval and at the end, she didn't leap to her feet. On the way home, she was quiet.

When they got back, she made camomile tea with honey and stirred her glass without speaking.

'I'd like to know more about the composers. Bach and Brahms were Germans. What was the other one?'

'Did you like him?'

She nodded.

'He's still alive. That's all I know.' Kaspar got up, fetched his computer and searched. 'Philip Glass, American, born 1937, Jewish parents, musical upbringing, learned violin, flute and piano, played in an orchestra at the age of ten, first composition at eighteen. He said that the musical material you find in daily life is the most interesting. That's good, isn't it?'

'I don't know.' She spoke as if she wanted to revise the pleasure she had taken in Glass. Because he was American? Because he had Jewish parents? Should Kaspar say something? She pointed to the living room. 'There's a piano in there. Can you play?'

'I haven't played for a long time. Birgit used to play a lot.'

'May I try tomorrow?'

'Of course. We can find you a teacher, too.'

'But then I'll go home and I won't be able to carry on.'

'There are electric pianos that sound like normal ones. If you enjoy playing the piano, we can buy you an electric one. It's just a keyboard; it'll easily fit in your room.' She looked sceptical. 'I'm sure there are piano teachers near you as well.'

Still she looked sceptical; he laughed, and said, 'Völkisch piano teachers that your parents won't object to.'

'There's no need to make fun of us.'

'I'm not making fun of you.'

She gave him a doubtful look and finished her tea. 'I'm going to bed. Will you put on the music that didn't have piano in it for me to fall asleep to? You don't need to come up; I'm fine by myself.'

He heard her wash, go upstairs and get into bed. He called up, 'Sleep well,' she called back, 'You, too,' and he put on the second movement of Brahms's Symphony No. 4. Yet despite the serene call of the horns, despite the measured pizzicato, the beguiling entry of the strings, the gentle start of the melody, even before the horns grew more urgent, the strings more determined and the melody more sombre, Kaspar felt anxious. Was this music to fall asleep to? It agitated him – did it agitate Sigrun, too? Why did she want to be on her own this evening? Had he offended her; had he lost her? At least she hadn't closed the doors and rejected the evening music.

When the movement ended, he switched the music off. He took the book about the technique and chemistry of murder in Auschwitz from the shelf and considered where to put it. She should be able to find it easily, but shouldn't feel that he was pushing her to read it. He got up, looked around, couldn't find a good spot. Then he felt ashamed. He didn't know whether he would eventually be able to get through to her, but if he did, it wouldn't be with tricks. He put the book back. If she wanted to find it, she would.

22

He was woken by tentative notes on the piano. Sigrun was trying to play a tune. By the time he emerged from the shower, she had found it. It wasn't a tune he knew.

She had laid the table in the kitchen again. Before breakfast, he showed her how to play the eight keys with her five fingers, how to switch from the middle finger to the thumb when playing a scale with her right hand, and from thumb to middle finger with the left, and she kept going until she could play the tune with her right hand instead of note by note with her index finger.

'You're really talented.'

She shrugged, but he could see that she was pleased with the praise.

'Have a lesson and see if you like it.'

'Why did you stop playing?'

'Your grandmother played so well that I didn't want to hear myself play any more. She didn't take it up until after we were married, but she practiced so hard that she was soon way ahead of me. Shall we go and visit her grave today?'

On the way there, they walked back down the wide road with all the shops, restaurants, cars and people that had impressed Sigrun two days earlier. Now she was critical. Why were people seduced into consuming so much; why didn't they cook for themselves; why did they drive when they could walk or take the train or bus? Kaspar didn't know how to respond. He left the wide road and turned down smaller streets, past tatty shops, pubs, offices, repair shops that mended everything from shoes to computers. He told Sigrun about the old graves in the cemetery that you could take on and have restored, and that Birgit had selected one of these and was buried there. One day he would lie beside her, and he was glad of that, although he wasn't bothered about the old grave.

They walked through the big, open gate, past the chapel and up the central axis of the cemetery. It was an avenue of tall, old trees, wide enough for a carriage – black, with a black-clad coachman on the box and a coffin under a black cloth, pulled by four black horses – that was slowly making its way up the slope before disappearing over the summit, where the gaze passed through the trees and on up into the sky.

Birgit's grave was beside the wall; the S-Bahn line ran along behind it. A stone slab between two pillars, an angel on each pillar, a stone slab in front of them on the ground. The upright slab bore the weathered names of those buried here a hundred years ago and more; the slab on the ground bore the name of Birgit Wettner.

'Do you know who the people were?'

'Merchants, officers. The last members of the family were four sons; they were all killed in World War I, one in each year.' Kaspar pointed to the stone bench on the neighboring grave. 'Let's sit down. I want to tell you about your grand-mother.'

Kaspar wanted to give Sigrun a picture of what Birgit was like. He told her about her family, about Leo Weise and her escape, then about her studies, her work, her piano-playing, her time in India, her activism on behalf of nature and the climate, and how she had got involved with one thing after another and walked away from them, one after another.

'She didn't find her place in this world.'

'Because she lived first with us in the East, then with you in the West?'

Kaspar was astonished by Sigrun's question. Then it occurred to him that Birgit had started drinking when she was a student, when she first experienced alienation in the West. Was this alienation the root of Birgit's placelessness? And had Birgit drowned both the placelessness and the alienation in alcohol?

'I don't know, Sigrun. Does living both there and here mean you don't find your place in the world?' By the time he realized his question was open to misinterpretation, she had already misinterpreted it.

'I'm only with you for a visit. That's all right. If I lived here longer – without my parents, I mean, and without my people and without my own ground under my feet – how could that work?' She frowned. 'What else can you tell me about Grandmother?'

He told her about Birgit's hopes: that she would write the story of her life, and that she would find her daughter, and that the two were connected, and that she hadn't done either of them. Yet she had been a good writer. It was sad, he said, that Birgit was talented in so many ways, and at the same time so at odds with herself, so blocked. 'Do you know that feeling when you want something but you don't dare try to get it?'

Sigrun considered. 'No,' she said, 'I don't. I think either you do or you don't.'

'Yes, that's how it should be: you do or you don't. But some people have almost no fear, and others have a lot. Perhaps your grandmother was especially fearful. She wanted to find your mother. But she didn't know whether your mother was doing all right or not, and if she hadn't been, your grandmother would have thought it was her fault. She feared the guilt. And she feared being accused and condemned by her own daughter. She accused herself, and condemned herself, and she couldn't bear any more accusation and condemnation.'

'Would we have liked each other?'

'She'd certainly have liked you. No one could help liking you. Would you have liked her? She would have made a great effort with you. But she had good days and bad days, and on the bad ones she could be unapproachable and unwelcoming. I don't know how you would have gotten on with her.'

'What else are we doing today?'

'What else would you like to do today? We can go to the museum of modern art, we can go on a boat trip across Berlin, I can call your grandmother's piano teacher and ask if he can give you a lesson today, you can beat me at chess, or I can beat you at Scrabble; we can cook together again tonight.'

Sigrun nodded. 'Call!'

The piano teacher didn't actually teach amateurs, and certainly not beginners. He had taught Birgit because she and his wife had been in the same yoga class and had become friends. He and Kaspar had also become quite friendly. When Kaspar told him about Sigrun, he declared himself willing to sacrifice his midday siesta. Kaspar showed Sigrun the graves of the Brothers Grimm and other famous people, and ate curried sausage and chips with her, then took her to the piano teacher's apartment on the banks of the Spree. He sat in a café for an hour and picked her up. When he asked what the teacher had taught her and what she had learned and whether the lesson had been fun, she gave only the briefest of answers, and didn't speak on the way home or while they were out shopping; her thoughts were elsewhere. The teacher had given her a notebook to take home, and when they got back to the apartment she took it out of her bag and put it on the piano without showing it to Kaspar. 'Will it disturb you if I play? Could you leave me alone?'

Kaspar went into the dining room, closed the door and listened to her practicing. It sounded as if she was trying to learn to read music, and to play little tunes from the notation. Two hours later she was still playing. She improved. When it got dark outside she stopped, paced up and down in the living room, occasionally standing still, went up to her room, came down again, and knocked.

'Yes?'

'He said that if I want, I can come tomorrow at nine. Every morning at nine, for as long as I'm here.'

Kaspar was so moved that he rose to his feet. 'Do you know what that means? He believes in you. He takes on very few people, and only the best.'

She shrugged again. But she blushed, and pressed her lips together and clenched her fists in triumph. 'Shall we cook?'

When they had eaten and were sitting together at the table, she said, without looking at him, 'You don't think much of us. You think we're stupid, we see things all wrong, there's no talking to us. You think you're better than us.'

Kaspar immediately wanted to contradict her. But wasn't she right? He looked at her. She had bowed her head, and her red curls were falling over her face; she may have been staring at her hands in her lap. She had hunched her shoulders and was all loneliness, all defensiveness.

'I've never for one second thought you were stupid. You understand everything I say, you beat me at chess, you're getting piano lessons from a teacher who takes very few people on. You're strong, and you persevere, whether it's at learning or hiking.' He paused. Should he also tell her that he was proud of her? But he foresaw a conversation in which she would say she was proud to be a German, and he would reply that you couldn't be proud of what you were, only of what you had done, and he certainly couldn't take any credit for Sigrun. He decided not to say that he was happy she was his granddaughter, either: he ought to show his happiness so that she was aware of it, on many occasions, in which case there was no need to put it into words; and putting it into words was no use if he didn't show it and she wasn't aware of it. He didn't wish for any other granddaughter; he had found this one, and he wanted to keep her. Should he . . .

Sigrun roused him from his thoughts. 'Is that all?'

'See things all wrong – do you need to see things right or wrong already? Don't you just need to *see* most of them first? You're fourteen: no one has seen everything at fourteen, or knows in each case what is right or wrong.' Sigrun's expression was still unconvinced. 'Why don't you just take a look at all this?' He spread out his arms as he spoke, to encompass himself, his apartment, his bookshop, Berlin, everything he was going to show and do with her.

'And will you take a look at my world?'

He smiled. 'Go camping with you? Play scouting games and accept challenges? Walk a hundred and fifty kilometres in four days with a fifteen-kilo pack? The grandfather with the Wolfs-angel? Oh, Sigrun.'

She considered. When he stood and started washing the dishes, she stood as well, picked up a tea towel and dried them. Eventually she said, 'You've got *The Diary of Anne Frank* on your bookshelf. You should read *The Truth About the Diary of Anne Frank* some time.' She finished drying up and hung the tea towel back on the hook. 'I'm going upstairs to read. Will you come and say good night in an hour? And put on some music? Piano?'

In the living room, he saw that the book about the techniques and chemistry of murder in Auschwitz was missing. It was the first of many books that she took and put back without a word of comment. Nor did he mention them to her. Sometimes he spotted the gap. But even if he didn't see it, she was still reading a book from his library. When he asked her about the books he had put in her room, she didn't have anything to say about them.

When he went up to say good night, she was looking forward to her piano lesson the next morning. He put on the *Notebook for Anna Magdalena Bach*.

23

The piano teacher gave Sigrun lessons on Saturday and Sunday, as well, and even on the morning of her last day with Kaspar, although Björn was collecting her at five, she still went to her lesson. By then she was making her own way there. Every day, after the lesson, she would sit down at the grand piano and practice for two or three hours. Kaspar couldn't tell whether it was more out of pleasure or determination, whether she had fallen in love with music or just wanted to prove herself to him, and to herself. In any case, she paid close attention in *The Magic Flute*, getting caught up in the action, shaking her head, laughing and gasping.

In the music shop she was suddenly shy; she nodded at everything Kaspar said and suggested, but wouldn't let him buy her an electric piano. She didn't know what her father would say if she loaded it into the car and said she wanted to take it home. She was afraid – no, she knew – that he would say no.

Kaspar could see that Sigrun was worried at the thought of a confrontation. He suggested ordering the piano online and having it sent to her. Wasn't her birthday in December? The third? That was six weeks away; she had time before then to explain it all to her parents. Still she was worried, and said she would call him if her parents forbade her to get the piano.

She lasted longer than he had expected in the Museum Berggruen. First, they went through all the rooms quickly, from bottom to top; she wanted to start by getting an overview. Then she spent a long time with Giacometti: Sigrun saw in his sculptures the long shadows of people in morning or evening light, and liked them. She approached the paintings of Matisse and Klee hesitantly, cautiously, as if she didn't know whether she really ought to, or wanted to, look at them. She spent longer in front of Matisse's paintings than Klee's; Kaspar had the impression she liked them more and more, but he didn't want to embarrass her by asking, because Klee was a German painter, while Matisse was French. Picasso was the only name she already knew. She disapproved of him. She didn't like it; it wasn't art. He explained Picasso's development to her as they walked past the many pictures, and she was intelligent enough to show an interest. But she would not be swayed in her disapproval of him, and when she described the painting of a woman as 'degenerate' he brought their visit to an end, without haste or argument.

Had she been trying to provoke him? Something was up with her; she was stroppy on the way home and over dinner, snapped at a woman who accidentally brushed past her in the U-Bahn, snapped at Kaspar because he was slow getting off the train, and complained about everything he put on the table. It was her last evening. Kaspar served a starter of prawns in a yoghurt and dill sauce, then there were grilled steaks, because Sigrun liked meat cooked over a campfire; these were accompanied by salad and baguette, and there was chocolate mousse for dessert. He had made quite an effort, preparing the sauces himself and thinking carefully about his choices. She talked about home, how good Father was at cooking and barbecuing, their contempt for buying things ready-made that you could make yourself, and how she couldn't see how Kaspar intended to survive the catastrophe, with no garden or provisions.

'What catastrophe?'

Sigrun's tone was condescending. 'You've all closed your eyes to what's going on, but anyone can see that the Mussulmen want to take over Germany, from inside and out. We can surrender, or we can fight back. If we want to be victorious, we have to be stronger. We have to be prepared. If we're not stronger, the others are.'

'Is that what your father says?'

'It's an eternal law. You've forgotten it. Father hasn't forgotten it, and he's always reminding us of it.'

'Always?'

'Always when we're tired and would rather just relax or have fun instead of working.'

'What work do you do?'

Sigrun stared at him as if he were slow-witted. 'We're settlers. We don't have enough land yet, but one day we will. We do what farmers do – what did you think we did?'

'Your place doesn't look like a farm. I thought your father, or your parents, worked in town.'

'I told you: we don't have enough land yet. And we don't have cattle yet, either, only chickens. But there's plenty of work for Mother to do, and for me to help with. Father has big pieces of equipment and he takes them wherever they're needed. His brother who inherited the farm in Lower Saxony bought new equipment; Father got the old pieces, and he keeps them in good condition and works with them.'

Again Kaspar had underestimated Björn. Björn had built up a business, and had perhaps also offered Svenja and the others the prospect of something more than the bus stop and petrol station and beer and fighting. Was what he had interpreted as subordination in Svenja actually gratitude?

When Kaspar went up and sat on the end of Sigrun's bed, he looked at her seriously. 'This hasn't been an easy week for you. I wouldn't have coped with this many new things as well as you have when I was fourteen. It'll be easier when you come back in the spring. We could go on a trip somewhere in spring, as well – what do you think?'

'I didn't visit Irmtraud.'

'Should I have thought of it?'

'No. We'll do it next time.' She frowned. 'I don't know whether I can invite you for my birthday. I don't know what my parents will say.'

'Don't worry about it. I'm glad I found you. I'm going to miss you.' He placed his hand on hers for a moment, as he had the first evening. 'Sleep well.' She didn't say anything; he left her, and put on one of Schubert's *Scenes from Childhood*. As the last notes died away, he heard Sigrun's feet on the stairs: she scampered down, ran over to him, gave him a kiss, ran back upstairs and shut her door.

24

The next day, after the piano lesson and practice and lunch, there were only three hours left before Björn was due to arrive. Sigrun wanted to go back to the bookshop. Could she choose three books?

When they got there, she told him she needed some time but could manage on her own, and went over to the history and contemporary history sections. Half an hour later he went to check on her, and found her lying on the floor on her stomach, playing with a little cat. Before he even had a chance to wonder what a cat was doing in his bookshop, he was captivated by their play. Sigrun had taken off her socks, tied them together with an elastic band, and hung the ball from another elastic, and it seemed she would never tire of enticing the cat to hunt and pounce and bat at the ball. It was a black creature with white paws, part clumsy child, part canny hunter, part menacing tiger. It, too, seemed not to tire of their play, which was accompanied by Sigrun's coaxing, teasing, laughing cries, until suddenly it had had enough, arched its back, stalked off and lay down. Sigrun crawled after it, laid her head beside the cat's, pulled it gently towards her and delicately stroked and tickled it.

Kaspar had seen Sigrun assertive, independent, decisive, combative. He had forgotten that, at fourteen, she was still a child who wanted to play, who craved affection and needed tenderness. She was so happy playing with the cat, so content snuggling up to it, that she didn't notice he was there. More tenderness . . . His hand placed briefly on hers, a hug in greeting and another in farewell, a kiss on the forehead on special occasions – more than that was not possible. Would a little cat help? Would Sigrun be happy to have one? Would he have to get used to having a cat in the apartment so she would have one in the holidays?

One of his colleagues had brought the little cat in. She knew she should have called and asked. But she'd had no choice; Lola had to take a pill every two hours, and there was no one at home to help. Kaspar enquired of the colleague what keeping a cat would entail, and didn't know whether the prospect of being greeted by a cat whenever he came home should please or alarm him. Finally, he asked whether people ever lent out their cats, whether he might borrow Lola when Sigrun came to visit, and was firmly told no: cats were not dogs, they were more attached to territory than people, and it was cruel to tear them away from their people and their territory. Sigrun and Lola could meet at the bookshop, though.

When Sigrun came to the front desk, she was bleary-eyed, holding Lola in her arms. 'We fell asleep together,' she said, surprised. 'We actually fell asleep together. Is it time to go? I left my books at the back.' She returned with three books: *Murder on the Orient Express* by Agatha Christie, a novel by Joyce Carol Oates about a girl who loses her mother in an accident, and a book about the expulsions of Germans and Poles during and after World War II. Kaspar was very surprised by her choices, but didn't comment.

Back at home, Sigrun wanted Kaspar to keep an eye on her while she packed, to make sure she didn't forget anything. She placed the books from the bookshop at the bottom of the suitcase; he didn't ask if her parents were not supposed to see them. They sat at the kitchen table, drank their last camomile tea together, and said little; yes, school started again next week, and she had to be on the school bus at seven; no, she didn't know when the spring holidays were next year; if his computer said two weeks before Easter, that must be right; she hoped her parents would let her have the piano keyboard; as well as the book for beginners, the piano teacher had also given her the *Notebook for Anna Magdalena Bach*; Kaspar should send a photo of Lola with his letter when he wrote.

Björn arrived, inspected Sigrun, drank a beer, very quickly again, demanded the next instalment on Sigrun's birthday – the instalments were owed for each year of her life, he said, not each calendar year – wanted to know whether his prohibition on films had been observed, and announced that Sigrun's next visit would take place the week before the week before Easter.

Then Sigrun was gone.

25

She had left her bedroom tidy, bed stripped and linen folded, towel folded and placed on top, books replaced on the shelves, the wardrobe emptied, the chair pushed in under the middle of the desk. It made Kaspar feel sad. A T-shirt – or *T-Hemd* – in the wardrobe, a photo of her parents on the wall by the bed, one of the conkers she had collected under the trees by the Neue Wache and put in her pockets on the table – if only she had left something behind to show she had felt a little at home and wanted to return!

As she had left the room in such a well-brought-up manner, he assumed he would also get a well-brought-up thank-you note. But nothing came: no letter, no card, no phone call. She didn't call to say he shouldn't send the electric piano, either, so he ordered one and, tracking it online, saw that it had been sent and delivered. Again she didn't call; nor did her parents thank him for the transfer of the second instalment. Should he write to Sigrun? Would her parents intercept the letter? What should he do at Christmas? Send her a present? Bring her a present? Did the family celebrate the Yuletide festival instead of Christmas? Did people give each other presents at Yule? He read that, at Yuletide, people's houses were open to guests who came and went and were lavishly entertained. Could he assume that he would be able to hand over his present and would not be turned away at the door?

He noticed how good it had been for him to have Sigrun around; in the apartment, in the city, in the bookshop. That he had been lonely in the months after Birgit's death, and was getting lonely again since Sigrun had left. He functioned; he was careful not to neglect his clothes and cleanliness, was as efficient and friendly as ever in the bookshop. But this took all his energy, and in the evenings it was all he could do to put a ready meal in the microwave and, after dinner, to sit on the sofa with a book. Pretty soon he found himself staring at the pages without reading them, dwelling on thoughts and memories that wouldn't fully take shape; they were just scraps that made him feel as if his life had fallen apart, the inner life and the outer. He was drinking too much, as well – to forget Birgit, and to forget himself. Every evening, and soon every morning as well, he promised himself that, this evening, he would stop after half a bottle, but then he would drink the whole thing after all.

The few friendships Birgit and Kaspar had shared had cooled even before she died: Birgit's drinking, then Birgit drunk, was embarrassing both for their friends and for her. He had sent notices after her death; he had received condolences, was invited over, but when he didn't invite them back, the friendships dried up. Before Sigrun's visit, he hadn't missed them. Now he wondered whether and how he might revive them. Or should he try to make new friends? How do you do that at seventy-one?

He looked for a café where he could play chess, partly because he thought it would help him connect with Sigrun. He found one, but the owner explained to him that chess players didn't meet in cafés any more, they met online, so these days he only held chess evenings on Mondays. Kaspar went a few times, won and lost. He enjoyed browsing the chess books in the cupboard with the chess boards and chess pieces and chess clocks, and he ordered one that promised to turn amateurs into masters. He studied it at home, and felt he learned more doing that than playing in the café, where in any case he never managed to strike up a conversation with his opponent.

Joining a gym and going to Pilates classes didn't help him to connect with people, either. But he didn't stop going; if Sigrun suggested another long walk, he wanted to be fit enough for the challenge. Because he didn't want to look foolish beside her in the kitchen again, he went on a beginners' cookery course; and because he was thinking of possibly taking her for a week to Venice or Florence or Rome, he started attending Italian conversation classes at the adult education center to refresh the Italian he had learned with Birgit years before. On the cookery course he met young men who wanted to, or had been instructed to, hold their own with their wives or girlfriends, whereas on the Italian course it was young couples dreaming of a house in Tuscany. He didn't make any new friends there, either. But at least he wasn't spending all his evenings at home.

Time and again, though – at work, while exercising, during his evening classes – the situation he was in felt unreal; as if it were all a performance, as if he were playing a part and playing it badly, and the others only had to look at him to see through him and reject him. He didn't belong in the world. He belonged to Birgit, who was dead. Birgit, who was dead, who turned towards him with love and liveliness, who lay on the sofa or the floor, whom he carried to bed, who moved him as he sat on the stool and watched her; Birgit, whom he loved. But she was also the dead Birgit of her notes, of the writing and not-writing that she had kept from him; of the searching and not-searching for Svenja that she had kept from him. So much that she had hidden from him, withheld from him, with which she had betrayed him! He understood that she was all these things at once, that he just needed to see them as a whole, to piece them all together. But when he pieced her together she became a construct; she became, for him, unreal, and just as he didn't belong in the world, he didn't belong to the dead Birgit, either. He didn't belong anywhere.

What had been real was the week with Sigrun. Sigrun had really surprised, shocked, challenged him. None of it had been a performance; none of it was playing a part. Had the things he had done and talked about with Sigrun had an effect? At least they had been real. Whether or not he was able to make an impression in this reality, he wanted to stay in it. He wanted to find a way of getting through to Svenja, too. At any rate, he had to ask her whether he could tell Raul about her, and whether she wanted to go with him to visit Paula. He had to find the right Christmas or Yule present for her. He had to find one for Sigrun. Yes – he would ring their doorbell in Lohmen on December 25, and when they opened the door he would immediately start talking about the lovely custom of open house at Yuletide, thank them for the welcome, and not give Björn the opportunity to turn him away.

26

He rang the doorbell on December 18. He had read that the Yuletide festival was usually celebrated on the twenty-first, not the twenty-fifth, and had started to worry that, lovely custom notwithstanding, they might feel he was intruding if he turned up during the festival itself. Visiting a few days beforehand seemed like a better idea.

Svenja opened the door in a kitchen apron, hands white with flour, said, 'Oh, it's you,' and went back into the kitchen. Kaspar followed her. She had started to roll out dough on the table, and carried on until the dough looked like France, more or less square with a winding coastline and border. She put the rolling pin down, leaned on the table and looked at him. 'What do you want?'

Tears were rolling down his cheeks. Many years ago, one Saturday in Advent, Birgit had baked Christmas biscuits. Then, too, the rolled-out dough had reminded him of France, and he had said so, and she had laughed. He had helped her, had greased the baking tray, cut out the biscuits, put them on the tray and pushed the tray into the oven. He had been happy. He hadn't known that, for Birgit, the baking was just a whim, a one-off, never to be repeated; he had taken it as a promise that in future she would celebrate Christmas, which he loved, with him. The festival meant nothing to her; she didn't want a tree or candles or presents, and she certainly didn't want to go with him to church. That had always pained him, and baking with Birgit had felt good. He had loved her in her apron with the flour on her hands and her bare arms, with her hair pinned up, her flushed face, her concentrated look. She had let him take her in his arms, laughing at the suddenness of the embrace, at the flour that, all at once, was on his face.

Kaspar was embarrassed. 'Sorry. This' – he made a broad gesture that included Svenja, the table with the dough and the oven – 'reminds me of Birgit baking once. In an apron, with flour on her hands.'

'Do I look like her?'

'The dark hair and eyes. Your mouth – when I first saw you, standing in the doorway with your husband, your mouth reminded me of Birgit's. And when you press your lips together . . .'

'Never mind.' He had offended her – he had addressed her using the formal *Sie*. 'If you want to go back to *Sie*, that's up to you. I'm sticking with *Du*. What do you want?'

'I've got a present for Sigrun, and one for you. Is she here?'

'They're out, picking up a spare part. You can leave the things here.' Svenja turned away, picked up a tin, put it on the table, took out a metal star and started cutting out biscuits.

Did she expect him to take the presents out of the bag, put them on a chair and leave? He put the bag down, went over to the table, took a stencil from the tin and joined her in cutting biscuits. He had picked up the first stencil he touched, and it was only now that he noticed it was a swastika, its arms rounded rather than straight, almost a cross in a circle. Svenja said nothing. When Kaspar replaced the swastika and took a cockerel from the tin, she gave a quiet laugh. After a while she switched to another stencil, and he did the same, and a while later they both switched again. Then she took two baking trays, greased them, and, working in harmony, they arranged the stencilled biscuits on them: stars, suns, hearts, cockerels, rabbits and fir trees and the swastika. He sat down and watched as she put the baking trays in the oven, quickly kneaded the offcuts into a ball and rolled out the dough again.

'You're good at baking.'

'You have to not be afraid. Of the ingredients, the dough, the stencils.'

'How did you end up with the swastika?'

'The stencil? The sun wheel came with the others.' She realized he was asking more than that. 'You think I'm ashamed of the swastika?' She straightened up and looked down on Kaspar. 'I drew my first in 1988, on the wall of the cultural association. I'm proud of it. We were the only ones who wouldn't keep up the pretence. The pretence that socialism is all about peace and doesn't exploit anyone and loves the people, and that we all agree on that, the Party and the bourgeois free-thinkers and the Christians and the Churches, all those with good intentions. Oh, how I hated it – all the lies about a common humanist heritage, which was just a lazy excuse for people to find a way to be part of it and feel as if they belonged. Not me.'

'Is that what got you sent to Torgau?'

'My father got me sent to Torgau. He didn't know what was the matter with me. I didn't know myself at first. All he knew was that things with me were not turning out as he had expected.'

'But you didn't have to go on rebelling against all that after the Wall came down. Why . . .'

'Why did I stay with the skins? To break things – to break what had broken me. The punks were spouting all the same stuff by the end; they were part of it. Then the Vietnamese crawled out from under their stones, and the dropouts were everywhere, and then you sent us the Arabs. It was them or us, and if you want to get rid of someone, you've got to scare them, haven't you? Swatting ticks. And burning things down, sometimes.' Her eyes and lips had narrowed; she looked as if she were about to grab someone and punch them. At the same time, though, with the rolling pin in her hand, she reminded Kaspar of the women in cartoons who lie in wait behind a door for their unfaithful husbands, and he couldn't help laughing. 'What's so funny?'

Kaspar pointed to the rolling pin. Svenja saw what Kaspar saw, and now she had to laugh as well. Still laughing, she swung the rolling pin above her head, put it back on the table and sat down opposite him. 'That's what happened.'

'Why aren't you with them any more?'

'The biscuits won't take long. How about fresh biscuits with hot chocolate? I've only got two baking trays; I have to wait until the first batch is ready before I can do the second.' She got up and started to prepare the chocolate. Kaspar said nothing. He didn't want his question to go unanswered. And there was the smell that was starting to fill the kitchen, the smell of baking, of childhood, of comfort, which for Kaspar was not just a nostalgic smell, but also a smell of mourning for the togetherness he and Birgit had had just that once and never again. Why not? He could have baked Christmas biscuits himself, and the smell might have tempted her to join him. Why hadn't he? Again his eyes filled with tears; he wiped them from his cheeks as Svenja returned to the table with the steaming hot chocolate and a plate of biscuits. The swastika sat on top. She pushed the plate towards him. 'Help yourself!'

Did he have to eat it to get her to keep talking about herself? Would she be offended if he didn't, and shut down? He took the swastika and placed it beside his mug. She smiled. Did she understand what he was thinking?

'One day it was all over with the skins. It was obvious even before then that it soon would be. The world looks different when you've got work and you're married with a child. A lot of them had already jumped ship, or were about to, when Björn came along. You couldn't do anything with the ones who hadn't; Björn tried, but it didn't work. It only worked with me.' Svenja looked at Kaspar. 'I was a junkie. I was skinny and ugly and I was falling apart, and I don't know what Björn saw in me. But he saw something. He wanted me, for himself, for a family, for the farm. For a life on our land with our people; for order and community.' She nodded. 'I would have liked to have had lots of children. But once we've got the farm we'll find a man for Sigrun and the farm, and she'll have the children.'

Kaspar doubted that Sigrun would let anyone decide for her. He didn't say anything. Svenja knew Sigrun; she must have the same doubts. Nor did he ask why Svenja had wanted this kind of order and this community; presumably, to her, it had seemed like the logical next step after tick-swatting and burning things down. He was glad that she had opened up to him. He didn't want to scare her off with all the questions he would still have liked to ask. He wanted her to want to see and speak to him again.

They cut out the second batch of biscuits and put them in the oven. He handed over the presents: a package with a little CD player and a few CDs of piano music for Sigrun, and another with a Japanese kitchen knife for Svenja and Björn. Svenja showed him the electric piano in Sigrun's room and told him that she practiced every day.

Then they were standing in the hallway. It was getting dark; Svenja turned on the light, and suddenly they saw each other very clearly. Both were a little embarrassed. They had each revealed more of themselves to the other than they had meant to.

'I don't always cry that much.' Kaspar smiled. 'A German man . . .'

'Safe journey home, German man.' She kissed him goodbye, as she had done after the fete.

Kaspar was walking to the car when he realized that he hadn't spoken to Svenja about either Paula or Raul. He hesitated, looked back at the house, saw the closed door and darkened windows and shook his head. He would write to her. If she didn't answer, it would mean that, as far as Paula and Raul were concerned, there was nothing to say.

27

He wrote a few days later, at Christmas. He didn't want to bother Svenja with a letter so soon after his visit, but the Christmas holidays were quiet, he found it easy to write, and he would have to do the end-of-year stock-take afterwards. He could send it later.

He told Svenja about going to see Raul, and about Raul's interest in her, and about Paula, who had brought her into the world, had attended her Jugendweihe, had sometimes had business in Niesky, had thought about her and looked out for her. She would like to see her again – would Svenja like to go there with him?

He finally posted the letter at the beginning of January. The reply came swiftly, in an email to the bookshop. Svenja didn't want him to give Raul her address. But she did want to see Paula. Could he pick her up next Tuesday at nine and bring her back at four? He should not reply to her email; if he came, she would be ready, and if he didn't come, she would suggest another date at some point. The arrangement was obviously being made behind Björn's back – Kaspar didn't want to read too much into this, but was glad. He explained to Paula that it wasn't easy for Svenja to get away, and Paula took the following Tuesday off. The practice would be busy, she said; he and Svenja should come through the garden to the kitchen.

Kaspar was punctual. Barely had he drawn up outside the house when Svenja came out of the front door and got in the car. She didn't need to say anything; he drove off immediately. Once they had left the village behind, he explained to her where they were going, that the drive would take just under an hour, they would have lunch at Paula's, and he would leave her alone with Paula if she would like him to. Svenja nodded but didn't speak, and when he tried to make conversation, asking if she had a driving licence, if she ever considered a profession, something other than that of wife and mother, if she liked books and music, she remained monosyllabic. They fell silent.

Until she asked, 'Why are you doing all this?'

He wanted to say, 'All what?' But he knew what she wanted to know. No need to play for time; she wouldn't rush him. Finally he answered: 'I wanted to finish what Birgit had started. Or rather, what she wanted to start but didn't dare. She wanted to offer herself to you, and leave it up to you whether to accept the offer or not, and I thought I could do that, too.'

She shook her head. 'But you didn't.' Again she was silent for a long time before speaking again. 'You didn't offer yourself to me; you imposed yourself on me. You barged into our life, Björn's and mine, and Sigrun's — Sigrun's especially. We shouldn't have gone along with it. But you're clever, and Björn is after the money. Not just Björn; we both want the money, for the farm, but Björn's in a hurry. Why didn't you leave us alone? Are you trying to save our souls? Sigrun's soul?'

'What can I say?' That didn't merit an answer, and Svenja didn't give one. 'I couldn't walk away from you. From you, because your voice and your mouth and your dark eyes and dark hair reminded me of Birgit. And Sigrun's attentive face, standing beside you on the step, and then her question: was I her grandfather . . . I wish I had children and grandchildren. I wish I had a daughter who reminded me of Birgit, and a son who might take over the bookshop, and now, at Christmas . . . if they'd all come, and we'd sung and played games and talked . . . Sigrun is a very special girl.' He laughed. 'I'm growing fond of her. Sometimes I think she feels the same.'

'I'll say it again. If you try to turn her against what we believe, it's over. It doesn't matter whether you're fond of her or she's fond of you or if we could still get money from you. It's not about us. Sigrun belongs to Germany, and I will not allow you to take her away from it.'

'Why can't she just get to know the world – yours, mine and all the others there are – and find her place in it? Why—'

'If the world were the right one. If it were a world of volk and family, and community and decency and work. Then she could find her place in it, and she would, because in the right kind of world any place would be the right one. But we're not there yet.'

'When will you get there?' He allowed a little irony to creep into his voice, was immediately annoyed with himself and glad that she didn't notice.

'We won't get to see the new world. We can only fight for it. But it will come.'

Kaspar glanced over at Svenja. How hard her face was; yet her eyes could be so warm, her hair fell so gently. He thought of Birgit's many different faces, how they had alarmed him, confused him. 'Why is it that, when you think about the new world, your face goes so hard? Why can't Sigrun be happy in this world instead of having to fight for the new one?'

'I know. You don't understand that the fight demands that we be hard and also makes us happy. You've forgotten what that's like: the fighting and the big objective and the being victorious. And taking pleasure in the hardness.' Svenja smiled.

'You don't even fight with me. What I'm saying riles you, but you don't argue; you just look understanding, perhaps concerned or sad. If this is how you are with Sigrun as well, that's good.'

Kaspar was angry: at Svenja, and at himself, because he couldn't let his anger out, and suppressed it instead. He drove on without speaking, and was relieved when, twenty minutes later, they arrived. They went up through the garden to the kitchen door and knocked; Paula opened it, and hugged first Svenja, then Kaspar. Still in the doorway, Svenja said, 'I'd like to speak to you alone.' Paula glanced at Kaspar, who nodded. She told him to come for lunch at half past twelve, and he walked back to the car.

28

The pub Zur Deutschen Einheit was open, but it was so cold that, after having a coffee, Kaspar drove back to the parking spot they had passed on the edge of the forest, parked the car and set off for a walk. The sky was grey, many of the pines were diseased and brown, and the cold was such that, although he walked briskly, he couldn't really get warm. But it was better out here than in the pub, and better than in the car.

You don't even fight with me – Kaspar thought it was a mean comment. If he fought with Svenja, he risked her breaking off contact; if he didn't fight, he had to put up with her deriding him as weak. Or was the comment merely stupid? Could Svenja only comprehend resistance as open, noisy contradiction? Fine by him. He wouldn't fight with Sigrun; she wouldn't report back about any fights, and Svenja wouldn't worry. He had tried a different method, and he would keep trying to do things differently. He had to allow Sigrun to experience a different world and have different experiences to the ones her parents offered her. She hadn't responded to his suggestion that they take a trip together in the spring. Should he have suggested some attractive destinations – Venice, Barcelona, Istanbul?

But Svenja's comment was a barbed one; it lodged in him and wouldn't let go. It wasn't only for tactical reasons that he didn't fight with her. He wasn't capable of fighting, of losing his temper, exploding, being aggressive. He could be dogged in pursuit of an objective, stand his ground in the face of opposition and setbacks, and speak sternly to a negligent colleague when necessary. Fighting, though, was something else. Had he forgotten how to do it? Forgotten during the years with Birgit, in which he was afraid of losing her, whereas she could be sure of him, because he took no liberties for himself yet allowed her every liberty, including the liberty to drink; years in which he suppressed his pain and anger? Had his love for her caused him to make himself small and weak?

Had he been different early on? He remembered scraps in the playground, a fight with his mother when he had smashed a plate to bits, and bitter rows with his girlfriend about his behavior at her parents', and at the golf club that was the focus of her family's sporting and social life. He had once got into such a row with his sister's boyfriend that, after being pushed by him, he had knocked him down. What had it been about? He couldn't remember. But it was true that he used to be different.

So what! He was seized with defiant pride in his love for Birgit and his life with her. There was nothing small, nothing weak about it. And not fighting with Svenja and Sigrun was the right tactic, even if it was the only one of which he was capable. He would stick by Sigrun, and he would be successful.

Now he was able to take pleasure in the forest he was walking through, although the pines were no healthier and no greener than before. Some young deciduous trees stood in a clearing, fenced in to protect them from deer. He remembered the two little fir trees his mother had brought out of the forest one day for him and his sister, and had planted in the garden. His sister's grew tall and slender and lovely; his grew mainly outwards, because a deer had eaten the growing tip. Lissom and Pudge, his mother had called them, and they were well suited to his lissom, agile sister and the slow, pudgy boy he had been back then. Were the two fir trees still standing in the garden? How might they look today? He hadn't seen the garden since his parents had moved into the church retirement home. He was surprised his mother hadn't balked at digging up two little fir trees in the forest. Were you allowed to do that, in the early fifties? The way you were allowed to gather firewood in the forest, back then? They had gathered nettles, too, his mother, his aunt, his sister and him, and he remembered them being boiled down to make spinach, but not how they had tasted. There were no nettles here, or blackberries or raspberries; mushrooms, perhaps. And there was enough wood lying around for more than one winter.

He remembered going for a walk in the forest with his grandfather, who had shown him how, in winter, everything is already prepared for spring. He had taken his penknife and cut open a brown bud at the tip of a brown twig, and there were the leaves that would turn the forest bright green in summer, all there already, pale, tiny, folded in on each other. It had seemed to him like a miracle. He was briefly tempted to repeat the miracle, but balked at the cut, the violence, the destruction.

His mother and grandfather were the most important people in his childhood. His father had taken care of his parishioners, not his children. The aunt who lived with them was widowed, childless and a refugee. Since having to flee her home, her mind had been confused; she could help around the house and play rummy with the children and take them for walks, but no more than that. Kaspar's mother left books on the table for him, took him to the theatre and to concerts and the opera, and talked to him about everything that interested him and everything that interested her. As he got older and started to spend most of his time with his friends, they saw less of each other, but remained close until he moved to Berlin. A woman of strong religious and moral convictions, if she didn't share his opinion, she didn't try to convince him; instead, she would inform him of her views, then let him decide whether to argue with her or leave it be, but she would do so with such authority that he couldn't help but argue. His grandfather was different; he robustly defended his nationalistic views, both of history and of the present. Kaspar spent the summer holidays with his grandparents. He loved going on hikes with them, and he loved their stories about German history. He had absorbed enough of his grandfather's views to understand Svenja's and Björn's world. But his mother, in her gentle way, had influenced him more than his vociferous grandfather, and not only because she spent more time with him.

The path led down to a lake. Perhaps Kaspar might have seen it earlier, between the trees; perhaps he had been lost in thought. Suddenly it lay before him, stunningly perfect after the diseased forest. It was as wide as Kaspar remembered the Rhine, and continued in a narrow strip on one side, the end of which Kaspar couldn't see: a tributary, or a connection to another lake and another and another and eventually to the sea. The trees grew right down to the shore, and in one spot there was a small stretch of sandy beach. The water was dull and grey and smooth, ruffled only here and there by the wind. Until suddenly the lake glinted like metal, shimmering and dazzling where the wind stroked it, and Kaspar looked up incredulously at the sky, where the sun had briefly broken through the clouds.

He arrived in a cheerful mood in time for lunch – eggs in mustard sauce, potatoes and salad – where he learned that Paula and her husband were going on holiday for four weeks in the spring, and their son would cover the practice for them; that they wanted to go to South Tyrol and northern Italy; that Svenja had never been abroad and didn't understand why anyone would want to go; that she would rather have been left on the threshold of an orphanage than given to Leo and his wife, but understood why Paula had acted as she did; that she understood Birgit as well, and was glad that she had never met her, and so had never had to decide whether to slap her or hug her or give her the cold shoulder.

'What was it about the Weises? Wasn't your mother a warm, loving woman? Was your father really that bad?' Kaspar asked Svenja on the drive back.

'Maybe. Maybe she was loving and warm. But she was so weak it was painful. As far as she was concerned, Leo was God, and if God gives unto you, fine, and if he hits you, that's fine, too. If she had stood up for me even once . . .' She turned her head away. Kaspar wondered if she was crying; he opened the window and let cold air blow into the car.

After a while, when the window was closed and the car warm again, he asked, 'I assume you wanted to find out more about Birgit from Paula. Why don't you ask me?'

'What would you tell me? That you loved her? That she was a good wife to you? Or that she treated you badly, as well? Am I meant to feel closer to you then? Or am I meant to understand that she was full of contradictions, and struggled with them, so I should forgive her for what she did?' She shook her head. 'There's no point. What I wanted to know from Paula was what happened back then, the facts, the course of events.' She laughed sadly. 'There were times when I could have done with a friend like her.'

'If ever you need her help or advice, she won't turn you away.'

Svenja looked at Kaspar, as if to check whether he was serious, then looked back at the road.

'When we stood and talked at the fete, and when we baked biscuits together, we were getting on. Today you're distant again. As if you don't trust me.'

'Why should I trust you? Because you're my stepfather?' She laughed scornfully. 'The good stepfather, after the bad real one? No. I trust Björn. We have a good partnership; it's give-and-take, as you'd expect, and if I give, I receive. And Björn gives to me, whether I'm able to give or not. He did it before, and he always will. I trust him, and nothing's worth more than that, and I don't need more than that.'

'But . . .' He wanted to say that we can never know what the other is capable of; that people grow and change; that Sigrun certainly would, being a child, but the same was true of her husband, Björn; that trust doesn't mean certainty; that trust always requires an advance. He let it go. To Svenja, who had been let down and hurt by her parents and had finally found security with Björn, it would sound hollow. Know-all, she would think, even if she didn't say it.

They didn't speak again until they reached Lohmen. Svenja asked Kaspar to stop at the sign that marked the entrance to the village, and got out with just a curt goodbye.

A few days later, Kaspar received a postcard from Paula. She thanked him for bringing Svenja to see her. She had thought about Birgit a lot since then. Would he like to spend another evening in the garden with her when summer came? The postcard showed a painting of a girl, not the chocolate girl but a dignified girl in Renaissance dress, seated, head and torso erect, center parting, high forehead, pensive expression. Kaspar had never heard of the artist Joseph Cornell.

29

Again, Björn called in the morning and arrived with Sigrun at five. Again, he walked around the apartment, sat at the table in the kitchen, drank a beer and prohibited television, Internet, cigarettes, lipstick and piercings. He announced that he would collect Sigrun the following Sunday, the Sunday before Easter, and left.

'He forgot cinema and jeans,' Sigrun said reprovingly, as if she missed the prohibition.

'Maybe he meant to allow them. Would you like a pair of jeans? What about the cinema?'

'I want to see Irmtraud. I want to go to Ravensbrück. I want to go to the bookshop. And can I go to the piano teacher again?'

'He's looking forward to it. Every morning at nine.'

Before she even unpacked, Sigrun sat down at the grand piano and played for Kaspar what she wanted to play for the piano teacher in the morning. It was a simple piece from the *Notebook*; she played it slower than it was supposed to be played, but without a single mistake, and Kaspar recalled that after four months he had not got nearly as far as she had. His praise encouraged her to play another piece, a difficult one that she acknowledged she hadn't quite got the hang of yet; twice she had to start again. Kaspar leaned against the door frame, observing the concentration in her face, her frown when she hit the wrong key, the slight smile when she made it through a particularly difficult passage without a mistake. Sigrun's connection with the piano, the way she lost herself in the music, her pinned-up curls, her high-necked blouse – the image reminded Kaspar of paintings from the Romantic or Biedermeier periods. Anyone who feels music this strongly is not someone you need to worry about, thought Kaspar; until he remembered Hans Frank, and then Irma Grese, and then the visit to Ravensbrück, which, if he couldn't avoid it altogether, he was still keen to postpone.

'How would you feel about going on a trip?' he asked Sigrun over dinner. She had asked to go to the Italian restaurant where they had eaten on the first evening of her first visit, and was enjoying the owner's courteous attentions again. No, she didn't want to travel. Certainly not to Istanbul, Barcelona or Venice, because you had to fly there and she was opposed to flying because of the environment. Anyway, she didn't want to miss any of her piano lessons; she wanted to practice, she wanted to get to know Berlin better, they still hadn't done the hike out to Kladow, and what with one day in the bookshop, one day at Ravensbrück and meeting up with Irmtraud, the week would soon be over. 'And maybe we can go to the cinema, too.'

After saying good night, he put on the Adagio from the 'Hammerklavier' Sonata. He thought Sigrun was sure to fall asleep to the long, tranquil movement. But when the Adagio finished, she came running down the stairs. 'What was that? Can I hear it again?' So he played the Adagio again; Sigrun sat on the edge of the sofa with her eyes closed, her left fist pressed into the palm of her right hand, absorbing every note. Sensing that something must follow on from the Adagio, as Kaspar was about to switch it off she put her hand on his arm and listened to the Largo as well, still attentive but relaxed, smiling at Kaspar from time to time. On the stairs, she turned to him. 'Can we go to a concert again?'

Kaspar would have asked her anyway, but it was nicer that she was the one to ask. As he hadn't been sure whether they would in fact go on a trip, he had bought tickets for a concert at the Philharmonie – Mozart and Beethoven – and for the *St Matthew Passion* at the Konzerthaus. He was looking forward to both, and to introducing her to the music the night before. After Brahms's fourth, she wouldn't have any difficulty with the Mozart piano concerto, or Beethoven's seventh symphony. Would the *Notebook* help her with the *St Matthew Passion*? Sigrun had probably never heard a chorale.

30

By the time Kaspar came into the kitchen on Monday morning, Sigrun had made breakfast, listened to the news and the weather report, knew that the weather would be good on Tuesday, and decreed that they would set out for their hike straight after her piano lesson. Before leaving Lohmen, she had arranged to meet Irmtraud on Monday afternoon. She had also called the bookshop, asked to speak to the colleague with the cat, and requested that she bring Lola in on Wednesday. Kaspar nodded in amusement. If he were looking for someone to take over the running of the bookshop, his granddaughter would be a worthy successor.

'Will you come with me to see Irmtraud?'

'Would you like me to?'

'Yes,' said Sigrun. Noticing his surprise, she continued, 'I wrote to her that I've got a grandfather, and she wanted to know what you were like, so I thought I'd just bring you along.'

But that wasn't the only reason she wanted him with her. That afternoon, when they exited the U–Bahn in Kreuzberg and turned off the main road down a little side street, from the side street down a narrow alleyway, and walked past snack bars, a group of young people with beer bottles on a couple of threadbare yellow sofas, second-hand shops, an old woman sitting in an archway with a bottle of schnapps, talking to herself, a man and a woman screaming at each other, Kaspar could see from Sigrun's face that the underbelly of Berlin scared her. The courtyard right at the back, the rubbish and filth, the peeling plaster, the tattered wallpaper in the stairwell made her uncomfortable, too. She was relieved when they reached the fifth floor and found Irmtraud standing in the doorway. But she was also visibly shocked: she had never seen Irmtraud like this, in black jeans, black T-shirt and black baseball cap.

Irmtraud led them into the kitchen, took three bottles of beer out of the fridge, and they all sat down at the table. She asked Sigrun about people whose names meant nothing to Kaspar, about groups and meetings and activities. Sigrun respected Irmtraud; she took pains to give clear, precise answers, and she drank the beer, although she didn't like it. When Irmtraud talked about herself and the group of girls who shared the apartment, Sigrun hung on her every word. The girls had had enough of talking. They went out on the street and fought; they looked for confrontation with the Antifa, and relished tangling with the police. They weren't interested in busts of Hitler and swastika flags, didn't care about the old nationalist authority figures, and wouldn't be told by the men what they should or shouldn't do politically. Yes, the men thought they were a pain in the ass. But Irmtraud reckoned she could still be a German woman and, later, a German mother, even if she and the girls threw bottles and broke through police lines like the boys, and reminded the journalists who wrote shit about them that they knew their names and addresses. 'I'm me, I know what nationalism and socialism and a völkisch community are; I don't need guys to explain the Volksgemeinschaft to me, and I don't need them in order to belong to it.'

'Are you still studying?'

'Yes. And listen – don't even think about running away from home and coming to stay with us. You're going to finish school and go to university. We have to become political partisans. We have to infiltrate the system. The national revolution can only succeed if it comes both from outside and from within.' Suddenly Irmtraud turned to Kaspar. 'What do you think?'

'You're right: Sigrun must finish her schooling.' Kaspar smiled at Sigrun. 'After that – she has plenty of talents, and a strong will, and she'll be successful at whatever she does.' No one said anything. Kaspar supposed Irmtraud was waiting for him to comment on the national revolution. Instead, he said, 'Sigrun was raving about the little silver swastika you wear in your ear – may I see it?'

Irmtraud laughed and lifted her hair away from her ear. 'Are you not allowed, Sigrun? Your parents still won't let you? How about you?' she asked, looking at Kaspar.

'You think I should get my ear pierced?' Kaspar shook his head, laughing; Sigrun laughed as well, and they took their leave.

31

Sigrun brought up their visit to Irmtraud on the hike. They had been sitting for a while in silence on the terrace outside the Church of the Redeemer; Kaspar thought Sigrun was as entranced by the view as he was: the columns that formed the arcades, the lake shimmering silver in the sun, the fresh green of the forest on the opposite shore. But she was preoccupied with her future. 'I understand that I have to finish school. But I don't have to stay in Lohmen to do that. Why can't I live with Irmtraud and go to school here?'

'Because Irmtraud doesn't want you in the shared apartment. Why are you in such a hurry?'

'I don't want to do rope gymnastics and play with hoops and sing songs any more. I want to fight.'

'Against whom?'

'Against the system.'

Kaspar didn't know what to say. Eventually he asked, 'What is the system?'

'Everything. The fact that Germany doesn't belong to Germans any more, that foreigners have it better than our own people, that everything's controlled by the Jews and their money, that there are so many Mussulmen and mosques.'

'Is there a mosque where you live?'

'No, but there was the kebab stall, and Father says that when the Mussulmen stay, they build mosques, and soon there aren't any church bells any more, just the call of the whatsit, the . . .'

'. . . Muezzin?'

'Yes. We don't go to church, but we don't have to be church-goers to love our Western culture and the churches and the bells.'

'Where's the nearest mosque to you?'

'I don't know.'

'Do you know any foreigners who have it better than Germans?'

'There was a man in a Mercedes who would sometimes drive up to see the ones from the kebab stall, a big, brand-new Mercedes – he was a foreigner, too. I know there are Germans with big new cars as well, but you know what I mean.'

'No, Sigrun, I don't know what you mean. I don't see that foreigners have it better than Germans, and you don't see it, either. Where do you see Jews controlling everything with their money?'

'They hide, Father says.'

'There you are again: you don't see them. How do you know they exist?'

'Because there's the Holocaust lie. If there were no Jews to benefit from the lie, the lie wouldn't exist.'

'What do they need the lie for if they already control everything with their money?'

'So we'll feel bad and won't defend ourselves. But we have nothing to feel bad about. Germans don't do things like that. Maybe they pushed the Jews around a bit and locked them up. Maybe a few of them died – people die in wartime. But it was no more than that.'

Kaspar could tell how proud Sigrun was that she was answering all his questions, parrying all his objections. He was tired. This impassioned girl, her ignorance, her arrogance, the impossibility of getting through to her and the impotence he felt in conversation with her exhausted him. What should he say to her? How could he reach her?

'There are some things you have to rely on other people for. When you're ill, the doctor knows more than you; when your car breaks down, the mechanic does. But don't rely on other people for things you can figure out for yourself. Get to know foreigners and Muslims and Jews before you make judgements about them. You already know one, by the way.'

'A Jew?'

'Your piano teacher is from Egypt. His parents were monarchists; they fled the country with him when the king was overthrown.' He laughed softly. 'Maybe he's a Muslim; I've never asked him. You can ask him; if he is, and he goes to mosque, you can ask him if he'll take you with him sometime.'

'To a mosque, you mean?'

'Why not?'

'I don't know.' She spoke hesitantly, as if suddenly there was a lot she didn't know: whether she should ask the piano teacher, whether she should go with him to the mosque, whether she should get to know Muslims and Jews, whether she should re-examine and rethink things she took for granted. She put her water bottle in her rucksack. 'Shall we go on?'

32

Kaspar had imagined that the week with Sigrun in the spring would be much like the week in the autumn. But it wasn't. Sigrun still took over his apartment and his things, made breakfast, cooked, practiced the piano, enjoyed coming to the bookshop and playing with Lola; they still did a lot of things together, and most evenings still ended with him coming to her room to say good night before putting on a piece of music. But Kaspar sensed a tension that he had not sensed in the autumn. It seemed to him that, having engaged with him back then in a fight he hadn't understood, she thought that she was now in a position of power, and wanted to assert it over him. At first, Kaspar saw her insistence on getting her own way in the planning of their days and with the shopping and cooking as an amusing game. After a while, though, he got the impression that, for her, it was more than that: a power game. She also forced him into arguments about history and politics that he found unproductive and would have preferred to avoid.

They enjoyed the concert. Sigrun was overwhelmed by the virtuosity of the pianist who played the Mozart piano concerto; she wanted to be able to play like that, too, and when, after saying good night, Kaspar put on one of Schumann's variations on the theme of the second movement of the symphony for her, she came running back downstairs, wanted to hear all the variations, and sat on the edge of the sofa again with her eyes closed. 'Do you think I'll be able to do that, too, one day?' Kaspar nodded, and she kissed him on the forehead before going back up to bed.

At breakfast the next morning, she said, 'All the great composers were German, weren't they? Bach, Beethoven, Brahms, Mozart, Schumann – all the ones we've heard.'

'Those are the ones we've heard. There are plenty of others, and plenty who weren't German. Why does it matter?'

'I think that's why I love the music. It's my music.'

'Your music?'

'German music. I know you think that all . . .'

Kaspar got annoyed. 'German music for German people?'

'You're making fun of me. But German music . . .'

Kaspar stood up. 'Come with me. Sit on the sofa. I'm going to play you some music, and you're going to tell me whether it's German music or foreign music.' He looked at the clock. 'Yes, I know, you've got a piano lesson at nine. I'll call a taxi; that gives us three-quarters of an hour. First you'll tell me whether or not you like the piece, then whether the composer is a German or a foreigner.'

She had too good an ear not to like Chopin, Dvořák, Grieg and Elgar; Tchaikovsky, along with Bruckner and Wagner, were the only ones she thought were foreigners, and Kaspar was almost mollified when she recognized Bach as the composer of one of the French Suites.

'Your ideas about German and foreign music don't stand up. You couldn't tell which was which, and anyway, that's not how it works. It makes no difference whether music or art or books are German or foreign. The only thing that matters is whether they're good or bad.'

Sigrun didn't reply, and she didn't say anything in the taxi, either. Kaspar didn't know whether she was embarrassed because she could see that he was right, or whether she was just being obstinate. As the taxi was drawing up outside the piano teacher's house, Kaspar said, 'You recognized Bach. You have an ear for music, Sigrun, and a pianist's hands. What you have is something special, something precious – leave politics out of it.'

After the piano lesson she came to the bookshop, and before going to look for Lola she wanted to speak to Kaspar.

'You always want me to think the same as you. With music . . . maybe you're right about music. But now you're going to read what I tell you. I brought *The Truth About the Diary of Anne Frank* with me. I'll give you the book this evening.'

Sigrun had sewn and stuffed something that looked to Kaspar like a little squashed grey ball, but to Lola it looked like a mouse. Sigrun had attached it to a piece of string; she let Lola hunt and catch it, flicked it away from her and let her hunt it again, until Lola grew tired of the game and wanted to wander off; but Sigrun, who was sitting on the floor, grabbed her and made her sit on her lap and be stroked until she resigned herself to her fate and fell asleep. When Kaspar looked over at Sigrun, she smiled up at him happily. That evening, the scratches on her hands itched, and Kaspar soothed them with eau de toilette. When he came to her room to say good night, she gave him *The Truth About the Diary of Anne Frank*.

Kaspar put on Haydn, the slow, boring movement of a piano sonata. He didn't want Sigrun to get excited by the music and come running downstairs again. He opened a bottle of red wine in the kitchen, took a glass and the bottle with him and settled down on the sofa. It was chilly, and he covered himself with the blanket that lay there, folded and close to hand. Birgit always sat here like this, he thought, in this corner of the sofa, with this blanket over her, glass and bottle beside her on the coffee table. How would she have behaved with Sigrun? How would she have reacted to her views?

Not at all. Birgit wouldn't have gotten involved with Sigrun. She was good at that: keeping people at arm's length, distancing herself from people, breaking off contact. She would have offered herself to Svenja and Sigrun as planned, established that they couldn't get along, and withdrawn the offer. Maybe she would have taken her time establishing it, so the novel didn't end too abruptly. She wouldn't have felt obliged to read up on the truth about Anne Frank's diary.

Kaspar sighed, picked up the book and read. He read that the style of the diary was not the style of a young girl, that the manuscript sent to editors was written by Anne Frank's father, that the original, when finally presented, was written in different hands, some in ballpoint pen, which wasn't invented until 1951. The difference in handwriting was immediately apparent; Germany's Federal Criminal Police Office had discovered the ballpoint writing; the father had admitted that he had tampered with the original. The truth was there for all to see. It was suppressed because the diary was big business, part of the Holocaust industry. And because Germans were to be made to look and feel guilty, and be kept small.

No, said Kaspar to himself, he would not go through the book with Sigrun point by point and demonstrate to her yet again that the things she had heard and read and believed were not true. He got up, went to his computer, found an article by the Anne Frank Foundation that addressed the lies about the diary, and printed it out. He left it all on the kitchen table: Sigrun's book, the article by the Foundation, and the diary itself.

33

Sigrun, however, saw this not as considerate, but humiliating.

'You think you're too good to talk to me about the book? You throw this at me' – she waved the printout – 'and I'm supposed to read it and shut up?' She started to attack him as soon as he walked into the kitchen, before he could even say good morning.

Kaspar raised his hands placatingly. 'Look—'

'Don't say "look" – I want you to take me seriously. I want you to listen to me and talk to me. I gave you a book that demonstrates that all the business with the diary is a lie. Do you have anything to say to that? Did you even read the book?'

Kaspar sat down. 'Sigrun, Sigrun. Of course I read the book. I thought you'd prefer to read for yourself about all the things in the book that aren't true, rather than hearing it from me. We can talk after you've read it, or instead of you reading it. We can do it straight after your piano lesson. I don't think I'm too good—'

'Fine, straight after the piano lesson,' she interrupted. She poured coffee for him and for herself and cracked open her egg. She was silent all through breakfast, and Kaspar pitied the man who would one day live with her and be punished with her silence. Before she set off for her piano lesson she said, with her head bowed, as if speaking not to Kaspar, but to the table, or to herself: 'He said that, because I can't come back for a long time, it would be good if I came for two hours on Saturday. If that's all right with you . . .'

'I'm glad to hear it. He believes in you.'

'He wants to make a plan with me so I can practice properly when I'm on my own.'

'Do your parents let you practice as much as you like?'

'Do you think my parents are uneducated? That they don't know the piano is important?'

'It might be too much for you – you might have to help out too much.'

'I've got to go.'

Kaspar realized that Sigrun wasn't playing a power game with him. She felt that she was being called into question – her, her world, her parents and their views – and she wanted to stand her ground. Ideally, she would have convinced him that what she believed was right. That wasn't possible. And so, failing that, she didn't want to lose her belief. Her feelings told her that she was right, even if she didn't have any arguments to back them up. But she was smart, and she knew that arguments were needed.

When she got back from her piano lesson, he explained to her the origins of Anne Frank's manuscript, Otto Frank's interventions and the reasons for them, the reconstruction of the original version, the graphological analysis, the analysis by the German Criminal Police Office, the traces of ballpoint pen, the pages that were found much later, the lawsuits – there was an explanation for everything Sigrun's book denounced, and it all made sense.

'I don't know.' She shook her head. 'I'm going to go and practice.'

She practiced well into the afternoon. Kaspar understood why. When she finished, she was hungry; she went shopping by herself, and cooked by herself as well. At half past four the food was on the table, Königsberg meatballs with potatoes and salad, and as he praised her culinary skills and her piano-playing, she began to talk again. She told him about her school music lessons, and the things she would like to learn about music there, but had to learn from a book the piano teacher had given her instead. Then she asked him if he wanted to play chess after the meal. They both knew that she wanted to beat him – to beat him again at last.

'I've improved. I've been studying a book about chess.'

'Good,' she said, confident that she would beat him any-way, which she did. But he had improved; she had to think for longer, and in the second he made it to the endgame. In the third game he made one stupid mistake after another. 'You're tired,' she said. 'Let's play again when you're properly awake. The first two games were really fun.' She was enjoying her position of superiority, being able to praise him, and he was happy to be praised by her.

'Shall we go on a trip in the summer? If you don't want to fly, we could go by train or car . . .? We could take the overnight sleeper to Italy or France, or a boat to Norway or Sweden or Finland.'

'So I can get to know foreigners and a foreign country?'

'Or we could go to the North Sea coast, or the Baltic, or the mountains.'

'I'll think about it.' She stood up. 'I like that you want to take me travelling. But tomorrow we're going to Ravensbrück.'

34

Sigrun didn't want to talk on the drive there, which was fine by him. She had picked out some CDs of Beethoven's piano sonatas and brought them along, and they listened to them one after another until Sigrun turned off the music after the Fifth, as they were arriving in Fürstenberg, and told Kaspar that they should go their separate ways in Ravensbrück and meet up afterwards. 'I know you'll want to explain it all to me. Or else you'll stand next to me and wait to see what I think and say. I'd rather be on my own.'

They parked, picked up a map at the entrance, and agreed that she would view the SS accommodation first while he went round the command area and the grounds, and then they would swap. He watched her enter the building where some of the female guards had lived and which now housed an exhibition about them; she walked tall, head held high, like Irma Grese in court and on the gallows.

In the command headquarters he went from room to room, read the texts, looked at the few pictures and exhibits, learned how the camp had come into being and how it had developed over time, about the prisoners, daily life in the camp, the SS, the infirmary, the mass deaths, the evacuation and liberation of the camp. Again and again he stopped in front of the information panels that displayed photographs and short biographies of prisoners from Germany and the rest of Europe, and he stood for a long time before the open register, where line after line of new arrivals had been recorded in neat handwriting. Every one of these women was a world, which was born and which died with her: Kaspar recalled the Heine quotation, and could hardly stand the exhibition any longer – the exhibition, the crimes, the destruction, the devastation. Then he came to the room with descriptions of the medical and surgical experiments performed on prisoners, and his horror at what doctors had done was compounded by his dread of what Sigrun would think and say. That they had just been trying to find better ways of treating German soldiers' infected wounds?

He emerged from the headquarters into the large site, where the only structures still standing were a few warehouses on the left and the prison block on the right. The wooden barracks, which had become rotten, unsound and unusable, had been pulled down long ago. But as he walked down what was once the main street of the camp, now lined with tall, old trees, he discerned the ground plan of the barracks marked out in the dark crushed stones, and saw on the map that the barracks had stretched away in neat lines to right and left beyond the trees at the end of the large site. He stopped. Barracks, as far as the eye could see; barracks, and between them the prisoners, the female guards, the dogs.

After a while he realized that he was staring at the ground at his feet. He didn't want to stay here any longer. He went back to the memorial and sat on the steps leading down to the lake. On the opposite shore, the church and houses of Fürstenberg basked in the sunlight. Had it been a comfort or torture to gaze out from the cells of the prison at the lakeside town, where life was simply carrying on? Or did prisoners not think of life in the camp as an abnormal state of constant emergency, but a life that here, too, was simply carrying on? He thought of the drawings and little works of art made by people in the camp: the little rabbit a prisoner had lovingly carved for a victim of medical experimentation; the embroidered handkerchief. How had they managed it? To assert themselves, look after themselves, fight for themselves, without becoming pigs who cared nothing for anyone else? Ravensbrück was a women's camp: is there more solidarity among women than among men?

'Here you are!' She sat down beside him. 'That was interesting. The guards are the baddies and the prisoners are the goodies, as you'd expect. But if you listen and look more closely, you can see that it wasn't like that. The women were criminals; they lived from stealing and cheating and prostitution; they refused to work, they supported the enemy, even went over to the enemy. How were the guards supposed to assert their authority without being harsh and strict? Look at their faces – they're good faces. Some of them were so young!' She shook her head. 'I don't know whether, in three years' time, I . . . Irma Grese was eighteen when she came here.'

Kaspar didn't want to talk about the guards. He didn't want to see the exhibition about them, either. All he really wanted to do was to go on sitting on the steps. Could he take his shoes off and dip his feet in the water? Would it be disrespectful to the women who had suffered and died here? It would help him think clearly again. How was he supposed to talk to Sigrun?

He stood up. 'See you later.'

Sigrun looked at him in surprise. She didn't understand his reticence, or why he was going. 'Is something wrong?'

'The commandant introduced confinement in darkness and beatings as punishment for the women. He had sick and disabled people murdered. He has the face of a friendly postman who makes sure the post is delivered on time.' He shook his head. 'Good faces . . .'

But Sigrun was right. You couldn't read the female guards' cruelty in their faces, and when they had gone on outings, they had been as cheerful and carefree as young women on outings usually are. Many of them were blue-collar workers from impoverished families; they had signed up because of the good wages or the good working conditions, or had been conscripted; prisoners had described how some were friendly at first, but were soon as hard-hearted and pitiless as the others. All this Kaspar could imagine. But there were women who had refused conscription. Where had they found the discernment, the strength, the courage?

An exhibition on the top floor displayed efforts to respond to the camp artistically, with videos and installations in different materials, text and audio. Kaspar went from room to room, then down the stairs and out into the sunny afternoon. In front of him was the car park; the car stood in the shade, and Kaspar got in and just sat there. He didn't know how long he had been sitting like that when Sigrun knocked on the window.

35

Kaspar was too exhausted to talk. Exhausted not by what he had seen, but by what he had not seen, which his mind had supplied and illustrated. The large site, the dark crushed stones, the tall, old trees, the command headquarters and the warehouses, the SS houses – it wasn't actually that bad. It only started to look bad when Kaspar pictured the site with the close-packed barracks, with the weak, tired, emaciated women on the paths, the female guards, their German shepherds, their shouts, their brutality, the triple bunks in the barracks, the close confinement, the stench. Out of the Ravensbrück that was, he had created the Ravensbrück that used to be. It had been hard work, exhausting work, and he drove away exhausted and silent. Naturally he wanted to know what Sigrun had seen and what she had thought. But he wasn't capable yet of asking her and talking to her.

Then she asked, 'Why do you always side with the others?'

'Why do I . . .?'

'You always side with the others. Whether it's foreigners or the Jews or music or Anne Frank or the Holocaust – it's always the others, not us.'

'Oh, Sigrun, it's not about taking sides. It's about facts.

Foreigners don't have it better, and the Jews don't have more money, and with music you—'

'What we've just seen isn't necessarily true. People lie, and photographs can lie, and it's easy to say this happened here, or that happened there. All you have to do is stick a sign on the door. Father was right. The Holocaust is an invention after the fact, and now I know how easy it is to invent something after the fact.'

They passed a few houses, drove across a small lake and back into the forest. The sky had turned dark, the darkness before a storm, and for a moment Kaspar forgot about Sigrun as he eagerly anticipated the first storm of the year, harbinger of summer. Minutes later, drops smacked against the windscreen, and soon it was bucketing down. Kaspar steered the car onto a forest track and stopped. The rain hammered on the roof and flooded the windows, and they couldn't see or hear the road or forest at all. He would have liked to smoke a cigarette, something he hadn't done for decades. He would also have liked to take a swig from a silver hip flask; whiskey or cognac, though he didn't usually drink spirits. He felt the need to spoil himself or, better still, be spoiled. Immediately he was ashamed to be thinking of being spoiled, after Ravensbrück. Beside him, Sigrun sat staring at her hands in her lap.

'There are too many witnesses, victims and perpetrators, too many documents, too much evidence. They kept records of everything: the expropriation of the Jews, their transportation to the camps, their murder in the camps. The Reich railway company kept records of the transports, the factory that produced Zyklon B kept records of the deliveries, and the factory that made the ovens kept records of their construction. The commandant of Auschwitz wrote a memoir and described what happened there. You think these are all inventions, by people who don't like us Germans. Thousands of experts have researched this, both Germans and people from other countries, and if the Germans had found something different and were able to report it, they would. Who would defile themselves and their family and friends by inventing such terrible crimes committed by their own people? I suppose there might be one person like that, but not thousands. I . . . I can't tell you how happy I would be if the Holocaust had never happened. But it did. And you have to learn to live with the fact that it did, as well.'

Sigrun said nothing. She went on staring at her lap, clasping and unclasping her hands. Finally she said, 'But why does there have to be so much remembering and talking about it? It's just not something people should do. The others don't do it about their bad things.'

'The small bad things get forgotten by the others, and we may even forget them, too, and there's no reason to remind people of them and talk about them. The really bad things . . . If you've killed someone, and everyone else knows it, and you act as if nothing happened and you didn't do anything wrong, the others want nothing to do with you any more. You have to own up to what you've done, and show the others that you regret it and that you've learned from it and that you'll never do it again. Then they'll accept you as one of them again.'

'I don't think I can talk to Father about it.'

'What about your mother?'

'She's not interested in all that. She says the Holocaust is a Western thing and we've got other worries: the land, the farm, living the right sort of life. I don't think the Holocaust really matters to the autonomists, either. It's like the swastika flags and busts of Hitler for them.'

'Well then, that's fine. You can still be a good nationalist and a good socialist.'

252

'Are you making fun of me?'

'No, Sigrun. I was thinking that you couldn't have National Socialism without the persecution and extermination of Jews, and I wondered whether you were separating the two too easily. But they can be separated.'

It had got lighter, and the rain was less heavy. 'Shall we go on?' asked Kaspar.

Sigrun shrugged. 'You're driving. Why are you asking me?'

They drove on. By the time they emerged from the forest, the clouds had parted and the sun was casting its rays on a village in the distance.

'But I can be proud that I'm German.'

Again Kaspar turned off onto a track and stopped the car. 'I don't know. I think you can only be proud of something you've actually done. But maybe it can be looked at differently.' He pointed at the landscape, the hills, the fields, the clump of trees, the village in the sunlight, and another in a hollow, with only the church tower and a few roofs visible. The sun was already low over the horizon; there was going to be a beautiful sunset. 'I love my country, I'm glad that I speak its language, that I understand its people, that it's familiar to me. I don't have to be proud that I'm German; it's enough for me that I'm glad of it.' The two of them gazed at the scene in front of them. Kaspar opened the window; he would have liked to hear church bells, they would have gone with the scene, but they weren't ringing. 'Do you still want to know whether you have to like the Jews? You don't have to like anyone. I don't even know how you'd do it – like the Germans, or the Jews, or the French, or whoever. But I don't know what good it does not to like the Germans, or the Jews, or the French, either. There are nice people and nasty people everywhere, and if you don't like the French, you're making it difficult for yourself to find the nice French people.'

He drove off. 'Have I talked too much?' He continued without waiting for her reply. 'I would have liked to have had children, and I would have liked to explain the world to them, or what I know about it. I'd like to explain what I know to you, too. But I promised myself I wouldn't lecture you, and that's how it should be.'

Sigrun assured him that it was fine. All the way home, though, he was preoccupied with the question of when and how he should say something about Sigrun's views, and how much. Better too much than too little? Better too little than too much? When the occasion invited it, or only when she brought it up?

36

He didn't manage to figure it out before Sunday afternoon. On Saturday morning, the piano lesson lasted three hours instead of two; they set off at half past four for the *St Matthew Passion*, and Kaspar told Sigrun the story of the Passion before they left, as she had never heard of it.

He was afraid she would get bored. But she listened attentively, even to the recitatives. 'I've never heard anything like this,' she kept whispering to Kaspar. But also 'I don't understand', as she followed the texts of the arias in the program, and he had a hard job explaining Bach's poetry of faith and love to her on the way home. She was particularly keen on the chorales; she wanted to know what they were, and he explained that Christians sang together the way she and her people had sung together at the festival. When he went up to say good night, he sat down on the edge of her bed.

'I'm going to miss you, Sigrun. You're a lovely granddaughter.'

She smiled at him. 'It's nice here with you. Even if it always has to be your truth, and it's never allowed to be mine.'

'There's only one truth. It doesn't belong to me, and it doesn't belong to you; it's just there. Like the sun and the moon. And, like the moon, sometimes you can only see half of it, yet it is round and bright.'

'Round and bright?'

'It's a verse from a song.

Look at the moon so lonely!
One half is shining only,
Yet she is round and bright;
Thus oft we laugh unknowing
At things that are not showing,
That still are hidden from our sight.

'What should I put on for you? Bach? Mozart? You know what you like by now.'

'Something new, but for piano.'

He put on Satie. Would she come down again and want to hear more? He listened for her footsteps on the stairs. She didn't come down, nor did she call out 'That was nice' or 'What was that?' or 'Good night', and he gently closed the door.

However, when he switched off his electric razor on Sunday morning, he heard music, quiet, at a distance, and as he headed to the kitchen he noticed that Sigrun had put on the Satie. She was sitting at the table with her hands stretched out in front of her, as if she were at the piano.

'Satie was French.'

'Don't make fun of me. I looked him up in your lexicon; he had Norman ancestors. I never said only Germans could compose. There are always exceptions, Papa says, even with the Jews.'

'Even with . . .'

'There are good Jewish musicians and artists and scientists. Papa says it would be stupid to try to deny it. But the Jewish musicians play what others have composed. The Jews always use what others have created. They get rich on it. They don't have any originality.'

'How does your father know this? Does he know that many Jews?'

'I don't know how many he knows. I don't think there are any living near us. But the Poles are different from us, and so are the French and the English, so why should the Jews, of all people, be like us?'

'Does your father know that many English people—'

'You and your "does he know"! You only know what you've seen yourself, as well. Some things you just know. The English are the shopkeepers, the French are more about fashion and food, and the Poles are full of themselves and steal.'

'Oh God.' Kaspar felt helpless. How was he going to chip away at this mountain of prejudice? Sigrun should go to school in England for a year. Nothing he told her about great English people who were not shopkeepers, as with anything he told her about the French and the Poles and the Jews, could stand up against her father. He had thought he'd dealt with German music and German composers, but here they were again – with Satie as an exception. 'Would you like to go to school abroad for a year? In England or Canada or America? There are pro-grams for that sort of thing.'

Sigrun looked at him, bemused. 'I'm no good at English. I've never been that far away. My parents . . .' She faltered. 'What would my parents say? Without me, how would they . . . Would I be all on my own?'

Kaspar explained that she would live with a host family, a family with children, and that, in a world where only English was spoken, she, too, would soon be speaking English. 'Have a think about it. If you'd like to do it, we can talk to your parents.'

'But not today. It's not a good idea to take Father by surprise.' She thought for a moment, then shook her head and stared at Kaspar in disbelief. 'You mean they'd take me? Why should they? I'm not top of the class, and I don't think the teachers like me. I don't think they would write anything good about me. Does it cost money?' Not expecting an answer, she went on thinking, and then her face lit up. 'It would be great. A year out in the world. Everything would be new.' She laughed. 'And so would I.'

She wanted to get away. As long as she wanted to get away, he felt that there was hope. She would come again in the summer, he would take her on a trip and show her a bit of the world and negate some of her prejudices. And as long as she played the piano, he would continue to hope. He wasn't going to think about Hans Frank playing the piano at the castle in Krakow. She had great musical sensitivity; she had realized once that her ideas about German composers and German music were nonsense, and she would realize it again. He went up to her room as she was packing her things and slipped the Satie CD into her suitcase.

37

This time she did leave something behind. Deliberately? By mistake? She had tidied everything up again so neatly that he could only assume she had done it deliberately, and he was glad. On the desk was her silver ring with the braided Celtic design.

They had not agreed a destination for their summer holiday. Sigrun didn't want to fly, but she said she would like to see something of the world, and to play the piano, read and go hiking and swimming. Eventually she had told him, 'You choose somewhere, Grandfather.'

Kaspar asked around in the bookshop. World, piano, reading, hiking, swimming – if these were the prerequisites, where would his colleagues go? To the Mediterranean, but he feared the car journey would be too long for the CO_2-conscious Sigrun. He found a holiday apartment with a piano on Lake Lucerne. It wasn't cheap, but he had got used to having a bank loan, and had already increased the amount to one hundred thousand to cover the second instalment. Björn would bring Sigrun on the last Sunday in July. They would spend the first days of the holiday in Berlin, then three days on the journey, two weeks by the lake, Friday to Friday, and two days travelling back. In Switzerland Sigrun would see something of the world, a place where four different ethnic groups lived together in harmony; perhaps it would make an impression. And he would show her Heidelberg and Strasbourg en route.

Kaspar was calmer than he had been after Sigrun's first visit. He no longer went to the gym because he wanted to keep up with Sigrun on their hikes in the Swiss mountains, but because it had become a habit. He had also got into the habit of cooking dinner two or three times a week, and sometimes re-enacting a game of chess. He was drinking less alcohol, and often made himself a ginger tea.

He read whatever he could find about the far right, about old and neo-Nazis, the NPD and the AfD, autonomous national-ists, identitarians, the Artaman League, the völkisch movement, its settlements and liberated national zones, its women's and youth organizations. It made for depressing reading. He hadn't realized how prevalent they were, how nimbly they adapted to trends, how much support they had among the middle classes, how many members of the youth organizations were the children of doctors and lawyers, teachers and professors. When he went looking for literature by, rather than about, the far right, he discovered to his astonishment that neither the Federal Agency for Civic Education nor the German secret service collected it. The only institution that took an interest was a small anti-fascist initiative in Kreuzberg. The literature it possessed was random and incomplete. Pamphlets written by and for young people contained reports on meetings and trips, often to East Prussia, Pomerania and Silesia, as well as thoughts about the Reich as history and mission, about life as daring adventure, about youth organizations and the organic state, poems about volk and soil, and recommendations for far-right books and far-right films. Again and again they wrote about the experience of community and, at the same time, the re-jection of others, of outsiders who did not belong. Was society failing to provide young people with a positive experience of community? What could he offer Sigrun as a better alternative to her camps, her adventures, her competitions, her responsibility as a group leader? He searched online for scout groups in Güstrow, not because he thought Sigrun would switch to them but because he wanted to know whether they even existed, and found none.

He had wanted to learn how he might broaden and open up Sigrun's ideological horizons, but he was none the wiser. There was no whistle or trick he could use to get through to her. All he could do was talk to her. If she wanted to talk to him. Whenever he thought of their last conversation about music, he felt despondent. She had listened, she had realized she couldn't tell which music was German, they had agreed that with music it wasn't about being German or not German; then a few days later it was German composers who counted again, and Satie was just an exception. He thought of Pavlov's dog, given food repeatedly whenever a bell rang, until it started salivating just at the sound of a bell. It had been possible to decondition it. But when it was given food again at the sound of a bell, just once, the conditioning was as strong as before.

38

'My parents aren't happy that I'm spending three weeks with you.' Sigrun wanted to explain her father's behavior, after Björn had dropped her off and said goodbye: he had not just been curt, as was his wont, but insultingly brusque. 'They don't even like me playing the piano these days. They don't play music, and they don't know anyone who does. If it were the drums or the bagpipes or the lute . . . but the piano? They don't forbid it. If Mother or Father hears that I'm practicing, they come and ask me to help in the garden or with the chickens or with the machinery. I usually practice with headphones on, and then they can't hear me, but sometimes I want to have the music in the room.' She looked at Kaspar, frowning: she understood that, for her parents, she was like a stranger when she played the piano, and she also understood that Kaspar's announcement of their trip had annoyed her father; to him, they were going not just on holiday, but to a strange and different world. 'If you hadn't said that you'd planned the trip by car for me because I don't want to fly, he would have forbidden it. He saw that it made me happy, and he didn't want to disappoint me.'

'Is there anything else?'

'That they don't like? Books I borrowed from the public library in Güstrow; books about the war and the Jews and *The*

Diary of Anne Frank. They think I'm only reading them because of you. And that it was you who gave me the stupid idea of spending a year abroad. Well, it was.' She shook her head. 'They don't like you. You being in my life, I mean; they're not interested in you otherwise. They need the money, but they feel bad about taking it from you. As if they were letting themselves be bought by you.'

'Can I do anything so they'll get on with me better?'

Sigrun smiled sadly. 'You'd have to become one of us.' She took some sheet music out of her suitcase, and, without unpacking anything else, without making herself at home, she went over to the grand piano and played until evening. Before moving on to Bach, she practiced Czerny's Etudes with abandon, pieces Kaspar had also practiced once, with no abandon whatsoever. After half a year, Sigrun was better than he had been after three. She connected with the piano in a way he had not, and he admired it. He hadn't put this music in her suitcase at the end of her last visit; she had got hold of it herself.

She had also asked her piano teacher for his phone number, and had called him herself from Lohmen to arrange a double lesson for the morning after her arrival in Berlin. From this she brought back music to take on holiday. She found books for the holiday on Kaspar's bookshelves and in the bookshop, to which she no longer needed to be invited; she knew she could take whatever she wanted, she just had to tell them at the cash desk. Kaspar was happy to see what she had chosen: Dürrenmatt's detective novels and short stories by Stefan Zweig from his bookshelves; from the bookshop, a history of Switzerland, biographies of Bach and Mozart, and two American novels; he wasn't familiar with them, but his colleague nodded approvingly.

The evening before their departure she confessed that she would like a bathing suit. She had one her mother had bought years ago for her to grow into; too big back then, it was now too small, grey and white with little shorts. She didn't want to be seen in it. They went to the big shopping street, found a green bathing suit that Sigrun liked and, much to her amusement, bought a second one as well, because Kaspar had been taught as a child that you shouldn't sit and lie around in wet bathing clothes after swimming but should change into dry ones.

The summer evening was warm, the street was full of life; they were walking jauntily along, laughing at the confetti raining down on them as part of a marketing promotion. Suddenly they heard a loud 'No!' and saw three men harassing a young woman right in front of them. Kaspar shouted, 'Leave the woman alone,' and they punched him in the stomach. He fell to the ground. The three men ran away, and people just kept walking, circling Kaspar and carrying on as if nothing had happened. All except Sigrun, who accosted the man who had hit him and shouted at him. Kaspar couldn't understand what she was saying. He got to his feet; it hurt. He saw Sigrun, a young girl, scolding the hefty man; he feared for her, and was relieved when the man didn't hit her as well, just pushed her aside and went on his way.

Sigrun wanted to take his arm, but he said, 'I'm all right,' and he was. The pain was subsiding. But his anger grew – that he could be punched and humiliated like that, that he had been unable to defend himself. If the men had directed their aggression against Sigrun, he couldn't have protected her, either. So that's how you feel when you're at someone's mercy, he thought, you and your wife or daughter. Powerless; and your anger doesn't destroy the other person, it only tears you to shreds.

'What did you say to that man?'

'That he should be ashamed of himself. That he wears Thor Steinar, our clothing brand, but he harasses a young woman and hits an old man. Sorry about the old man. I told him we're meant to be better than the others, not worse.'

'You thought he was one of yours? Because of the clothing brand?'

'Yes, I thought so.'

'But?'

'Oh, forget it.'

39

Kaspar had allowed seven hours for the drive to Heidelberg, but what with an accident and a traffic jam on the way there, it ended up being nine. Sigrun slept at first, then they listened to five hours of *The Adventures of Tom Sawyer*, and then she wanted to know whether it was right or wrong to indicate what you believed in through the clothes you wore. He told her about the Amish, and they talked about nuns, monks and soldiers, the kippah worn by Jewish men and Muslim women's hijab. What really interested her was whether your behavior ought to match your clothing: whether the Muslim woman in the hijab had to be a good Muslim, the Jew in the kippah a good Jew. She couldn't stop thinking about the assault by the man in the Thor Steinar T-shirt. She tried to console herself with the thought that the Jews must wear their kippahs, too, when they did all the bad things they did, but it wasn't really much of a consolation.

She wasn't too tired to head out as soon as they arrived in Heidelberg. She was delighted by the city on the river with the old bridge and the big castle, by the narrow streets, the squares, and the steep path up to the terrace in front of the castle where they watched the glowing sun set in the west. It was the same all through their trip. Sigrun took wholehearted, unaffected delight in all that was beautiful, with none of the superciliousness and condescension teenagers like to display, and she didn't hold it against the French that Strasbourg belonged to France now, or against the people of Basel that they had sided with the French in the war of 1870–71 and erected a monument to them. She was captivated by the cathedrals in Strasbourg and Basel, by the ferry across the Rhine, and by the view of Lake Zurich from the Quaibrücke, and Kaspar was happy.

She was also captivated by the apartment he had rented. It was in a building overlooking Lake Lucerne, with six apartments, a big garden and, at the bottom of the garden, a narrow path leading down to the water. Only two of the other apartments were occupied, both by elderly American couples; the rest were for sale, and people sometimes came to view them. Kaspar and Sigrun had the garden and the shore to themselves.

Kaspar had hoped there would be others in the building for Sigrun to play with, and he suggested they went to the public swimming pool in the first few days so she would have company. She didn't want to. She didn't need other children, she said. She saw enough of other children the rest of the time. Playing the piano, lying by the water, reading, swimming, going into Lucerne to go shopping, cooking in the evening, playing chess or Reversi after the meal – she enjoyed all of this, and didn't seem to feel that anything was missing. Whenever Kaspar suggested an outing, she agreed, and she was delighted by the boat trip across the lake, by the Tell Monument and Tell's Chapel and the hike up Mount Rigi. They did a two-day trip, to Lausanne by car, then by boat to Geneva, returning by train and car after spending almost a whole day there, and she absorbed it all with delight, the lake, the vineyards, the towns, the fountains and magnificent buildings, and marvelled at the harmonious coexistence of the German- and French-speaking peoples. But then she was happy to be in the apartment on the lake again, and didn't feel the need to visit any of the places she read about in the history of Switzerland.

The only time Kaspar and Sigrun talked about politics was in Geneva. At the sight of the Palais des Nations she spoke proudly of Hitler's withdrawal from the League of Nations as the beginning of Germany's liberation from the humiliating shackles of the Treaty of Versailles. Step by step he had made Germany strong and great again; she knew about the reintroduction of compulsory military service, how he had marched into the demilitarized Rhineland, and about the Anschluss with Austria. When Kaspar pointed out that Hitler had started a war he couldn't win, that he then went on to lose, she was unperturbed: he had done it for Germany, as a German must always be for Germany; he had played for high stakes and his losses had been high, but every game had another round. When Kaspar asked if she really wanted to go to war again and which territories she wanted back and what she thought should happen to the people there, she began to waver, and Kaspar left it at that. For a while she was silent, and Kaspar didn't know whether she was disappointed in him or in herself: in his refusal to share her point of view, or her own inability to persuade him of it. Soon afterwards, though, she had forgotten Hitler and his great, strong Germany.

It took Kaspar longer than Sigrun to relax into their holiday together. He fretted a lot in the first few days. Was Sigrun happy? Was she lonely? Was it boring for her? Was she playing the piano so much because she enjoyed it, or in desperation, because there was nothing else to do? Was he giving her enough options? Then he remembered the childhood holidays he had spent with his grandparents. He hadn't missed playing with other children, either; he, too, had been happy to have more time to read, and it had made him feel good that his grandparents always paid attention to him whenever their attention was what he needed. They had gone on walks with him, on an outing somewhere, had taken him to a museum, a concert or the opera. That had been enough for him.

In the second week, he finally let go. He didn't have to entertain, distract or amuse Sigrun, and he couldn't educate her politically. If she wanted something, she would ask. In Lucerne they went to the market, visited food shops and a bookshop, walked across the covered wooden bridge, sat outside cafés, ate ice cream and drank espresso and watched the passers-by. One day, when it rained, they stayed in the apartment, and Sigrun played the piano even more than usual. As she was practicing one of the pieces, she asked him what he thought it meant; he didn't understand what she was asking, and realized that her relationship with music was more profound than his. She had got further with the *Notebook for Anna Magdalena Bach* than he ever had. They spent the sunny days in the garden, on the grass or by the lake, and if either of them wanted to be alone, he left, often returning with juice, apples, chocolate. They talked about the books they were reading, the boats on the lake, the mountains and the clouds. Sigrun wanted to hear about Kaspar's and her grandmother's life, and Kaspar told her. The days passed easily.

They got back to Berlin late in the evening. Kaspar had driven for ten hours and was tired; Sigrun, who had woken up just outside Berlin, was wide awake. She made camomile tea, and they sat at the kitchen table. Their surroundings had grown unfamiliar; the tensions between them, their arguments, Björn's carping, all hung around the kitchen like cold tobacco smoke. Hadn't they put them behind them? The next day, though, would be a Berlin day like all the others. Sigrun would spend two hours with the piano teacher, he would go and see to business in the bookshop, she would meet him there, and however she answered the question of whether or not she wanted to go to the cinema with him to see the restored film of *West Side Story*, her parents would inevitably come into it. He smiled sadly at her.

'Are you sad, Grandfather? I'll be back in the autumn.'

He was so touched that he almost wept. He nodded a few times, said that he was dog-tired and had to go to bed; she put on a Chopin Nocturne, and he fell asleep to it. As Björn had no longer expressly forbidden cinema when she visited in the spring, Sigrun went with Kaspar to see *West Side Story* the next day; she was overwhelmed by the music and – unaccustomed as she was to cinema – by the power of the moving image, suffered along with Maria, and didn't seem to care that her skin was dark. On Sunday, she gave Kaspar a goodbye kiss on the cheek in front of Björn.

40

How quickly we become habituated to things! Sigrun had come and gone once, twice, three times; now she was gone again, and soon she would be back. And what happiness there is to be found in habit! When Kaspar and Sigrun spent time together again in the autumn, they enjoyed the things that were the same as ever: the rhythm of the days, the meals in the Italian restaurant, the visits to the bookshop; Sigrun enjoyed her piano lessons and playing the piano and Kaspar enjoyed choosing the music for Sigrun's bedtime. They had shared memories as well as shared routines, and the memories prompted suggestions. Do you remember the Philharmonie last year? Can we go again? Do you remember, last autumn you didn't think you could manage the hike you did in the spring? Shall we go on another one? At her request they returned to the Museum Berggruen; this time she stood in front of the Picassos for a long time, silently, without judgement, positive or negative.

One evening, after supper, Sigrun asked, 'Would you have come to my Jugendleite, if they had invited you?'

'Jugendweihe?'

No, she explained: the Jugendleite was the völkisch ceremony to bid farewell to childhood and mark the entry into adult life. It involved the performance of a task, a big group of family and friends and peers holding torches around a big bonfire, songs and mottoes and, to conclude, a slap in the face, because bidding farewell to childhood was painful, and because people were also slapped when they were knighted.

'Of course I would have come. Was it nice? What was your task?'

'There are some for boys and some for girls. I was telling Father for months that I wanted one of the boys' ones, not sewing or weaving. Well, he took me to the forest and left me there with just a knife and no provisions; not for forty-eight hours, though, like the boys, only thirty-six.'

'And?'

'What do you think? There are plenty of berries and mushrooms in summer; I know where to find the good ones. If it rains you get wet, but it didn't rain.'

'Did you get a motto? When people are confirmed, they're each given a verse from the Bible that's supposed to guide them through life.'

'"Burn, and shine like the sun." Father chose it for me. And he said we're living in a time that requires the whole person. We walked up to the fire, one after another, and we were given the motto and the slap and a sip of mead from a horn, and we sang "A Young Volk Arises". Yes, it was nice. Except the grown-ups drank too much. They'd already been drinking when we got back from performing our tasks, and they carried on during the ceremony, and even more afterwards. Why do they always have to drink so much?'

He wanted to know who the author of her motto was; he looked it up online and found that it was a modified Hitler quotation. He didn't tell her this. She would know that 'A Young Volk Arises' was a Hitler Youth song; it wouldn't bother her. Ought he to habituate himself to this as well? To the fact that she was still the same person she was a year ago? Someone who dove into his world with curiosity, sometimes with enthusiasm, then shook off his world as a dog shakes off water after a dip in the lake, holding fast to her world and the völkisch life as if nothing had happened? Had the summer they spent together, when she had forgotten Hitler as abruptly as she had remembered him, just been an exception for their long holiday?

He had taken her to his heart – on condition that she forswear her world and find her way to his? No: that was not how he wanted to love. And how could he think, even for a moment, that his person, his presence, his influence would correct in the space of a few weeks what had been going awry for fifteen years? How arrogant, how impatient!

They went on another hike, too easy for Sigrun, just right for him, twelve kilometres through the Briese valley. There, in a spot where a few old apple trees stood in a field, he asked Sigrun whether she liked poetry, and, without waiting for an answer, recited happily:

> *An autumn as fine as this I can't recall!*
> *No wandering breath of wind disturbs the air,*
> *Yet still is heard the gentle rustling fall*
> *Of ripest fruit from branches here and there.*
>
> *Disturb it not, this, Nature's sacred rite!*
> *This is the harvest that is self-performed,*
> *The sun alone, with mild and kindly light,*
> *Can lift the fruit from off the trees, soft-warmed.*

'When I first met your grandmother, I recited a spring poem for her. Now it's autumn, so you get an autumn poem. Isn't it beautiful? Don't you think it's perfect?'

They stood there, and the air was indeed undisturbed, and there was a gentle rustling, though not from the trees, whose small, shrunken apples were still clinging to them; the sun's light was mild and kindly, and it was a sacred rite of Nature.

'Yes, it's beautiful,' Sigrun whispered, not wanting to disturb the rite. They walked on, and she asked, 'Do you know a lot of poems? I don't know any. We had one at school, and I didn't like it. I like yours. The one recently was about the moon and things.'

He was annoyed with himself. Why hadn't he recited more poems to her? Although he was a bookseller, he valued music over literature; he would have liked to compose a song at some point in his life rather than write a poem, and had it been possible he would have compiled a yearbook for Birgit containing pieces of music instead of poems. But that was no reason to deprive Sigrun of poems, and if she didn't know any . . . He wasn't annoyed any more; he was looking forward to introducing Sigrun to the world of poetry.

They went to the Philharmonie again: Beethoven's violin concerto and Korngold's Symphony in F-sharp major. Kaspar was as moved as he had been at the age of twelve on hearing the violin concerto for the first time on the radio, sitting at his sick mother's bedside, united with her in their joy in the music. He glanced at Sigrun; she had pressed her hands to her chest. The symphony didn't enrapture her, but she listened intently; it reminded her of *West Side Story*, which, from a musical point of view, Kaspar could understand. She didn't ask what Korngold was, and, as he didn't want to hear again that there were proficient composers even among the Jews, he said nothing.

The last day was cold, and Sigrun lit the tiled stove. The last time Kaspar had done this was for Birgit; without her, he hadn't wanted to light it. There was enough wood and briquette in the cellar, and Sigrun enjoyed showing off her skill as mistress of the fire. Once the tiles were warm, she put cushions on the floor, brought their evening camomile tea, and they sat with their backs to the stove. 'A bit like camping,' she laughed.

Before Björn's arrival the next day, he asked her what she would like for her sixteenth birthday. She didn't want books – she could take any she wanted, anyway – but music, preferably for piano; she had been intimidated at first by the perfection of the piano-playing on the CDs, but now it spurred her on. Then she wanted to know when his birthday was, and what he would like, and he was touched. And he was touched that, once again, she gave him a goodbye kiss on the cheek in front of Björn, and a hug, too, as she did so.

41

However, no sooner had the two of them left than he began to worry Björn might feel slighted, and might take it out on Sigrun. Björn had greeted her by placing his hand on her shoulder, and she had touched his chest with her fist. Maybe that was their custom. But maybe Björn had wondered why, if Sigrun had more to give, she didn't give it to him.

In the next few days he often felt as if she were still there, waiting with breakfast in the kitchen; or that any minute now she would come down the stairs, or start playing the piano, or call 'Grandfather', because she wanted to get going and he was too slow for her. Then, once it was clear to him that she had gone, he worried about her – that her parents would ban her from playing the piano, that they had noticed changes in her and were punishing her, or that Sigrun was finding it hard to cope with living in both her world and his. Then his fears retreated into his dreams. She was in a maze of streets and houses and couldn't find her way in or out; she had to do a piano recital and couldn't move her fingers; and it was her, and at the same time it was him, bringing his old anxiety dreams to his dreams about Sigrun, dreams in which he failed or got lost or was dangling or unable to move.

At the Frankfurt Book Fair he found a volume of *German*

Poems that didn't feel the need to present the world at last with poems that had always been disregarded, but offered what Kaspar knew and loved and was sure Sigrun would love as well. *German Poems* – her parents couldn't object to that, surely. He sent the book to Sigrun for her birthday, along with six CDs, piano from Bach to Glass. He also transferred the next instalment to Björn.

Sigrun called a few days later. Could he come on Sunday afternoon? At five? She didn't sound good: as if she were speaking under duress, was desperate, had been crying.

'What is it, Sigrun? You—'

'Nothing.' She hung up.

It was Thursday. He couldn't do anything, couldn't clarify anything, couldn't make anything any better, could only wait and worry. He left plenty of time for the journey on Sunday; he wanted to be relaxed when he arrived. If there was going to be an argument with Björn and Svenja, he wanted to stay calm. Something was wrong. What could they want? For him not to go on any more trips with Sigrun? Not to go to the cinema any more? Did they not want her to spend three whole weeks with him again? He was open to other arrangements as far as timing was concerned. He would be open to discussing anything.

He parked, walked towards the house, and Sigrun opened the door before he could ring the bell. She didn't greet him, didn't look at him. She had been crying. She went into the kitchen, and he followed.

It was like the first time he had visited: Svenja on the right of the table, Sigrun on the left, Björn at the end. But while the other two sat down – Svenja hard-faced, Sigrun with bowed head – Björn remained standing, his hands resting on a book propped up in front of him whose title Kaspar couldn't see.

'Sit down.'

'What—'

'I trusted you. I knew that you read the lying press and supported the guilt cult and that you're one of the welcome-clappers. You hate Germany. That's self-hatred. That's sick. You don't have an honorable bone in your body. But I thought you did have respect for family. It's a thing that exists between father, mother and children, and you keep out of it, you don't worm your way in and sink your teeth into it.' Björn was still standing with his hands on the book, regarding Kaspar with contempt. 'You people have no respect – no respect for anything. Not for Germany, and not for those who serve Germany, the teachers and officials and soldiers and farmers. You ridicule them. All you're capable of doing is living for yourselves; you smoke hash and snort coke; you breezed through school and university and made sure you got your hands on all the jobs and all the money. Family? Yes, if it's a single-parent family, a patchwork family, a homosexual family; otherwise it's free love. You don't know what healthy families are. You thought, oh, let's see – see if you could poison our family, make a healthy family sick, sick the way you're sick, and you slipped the book into Sigrun's suitcase.' Björn banged the book on the table. 'She should have shown it to me right away when she found it in her suitcase. Not doing so was the first time my Sigrun has ever disappointed me. But it won't happen again. Will it?' Björn looked at Sigrun, a dark, threatening look; she gave him a frightened glance, and nodded. 'Did you think you'd bought me? With the money that belonged to your wife, that slut who abandoned Svenja? Did you think that because I'd taken your money I would keep quiet while you wrecked my family? I don't need your money. You know where you can stick it? Up your ass, that's where. And this' – he held up the book in his right hand – 'you can stick this up your ass as well.' He flung the book across the table, Kaspar didn't know whether at him or for him to catch. 'And don't ever show your face here again. And if you pester Sigrun, I will thrash the living daylights out of you, is that clear? I'll thrash you.'

Now Kaspar saw the cover of the book, with the title, *My Path*, and a picture of a young woman. He didn't recognize it. 'I don't—' he began. And then he saw Sigrun's face. She was afraid. She knew what he was going to say. She was afraid her father would believe Kaspar, and would realize that she had chosen the book herself and brought it back with her, that she wanted to know what was in it. Her father had been angrier with her than she could bear; how could she bear it if he turned the anger he was directing at Kaspar on her as well? All this was written on Sigrun's face, along with a plea for him to go, to say nothing, to just go.

He went. No one said anything; not him, not Björn or Svenja, not Sigrun. He closed the front door quietly behind him, went back to the car, got in, put the book on the seat beside him and took a moment to recover. His hands were trembling. When he felt able to drive, he drove to the timber yard where he had spent the night after the fete, and stopped. The book was a young woman's reckoning with her far-right parents and the far-right milieu she had grown up in and had eventually left behind. The parents didn't come out of it well, and Björn must have seen himself and Svenja in them. He must also have been shocked that the young woman had experienced and written about her departure from the far-right milieu as a great liberation. Kaspar could understand why Björn didn't want this book in Sigrun's hands. When had he found it – before or after she had read it? And had he reacted immediately when he found it, or had he waited for the next instalment of money?

42

Whenever he thought about the meeting with Björn, Svenja and Sigrun, Kaspar felt disgust. The meeting had been filthy, ugly, nasty. He had said nothing, but not only had he felt defiled, he felt he had defiled himself. He should not have sat and listened to the abuse. No – he had had to listen, because he didn't want to lose Sigrun, and didn't know that he had already lost her. He had had to defile himself. And now the filth was in his life. Sigrun was no longer in his life, only the filth.

Over time, he came to judge Björn less harshly. However lamentable the völkisch world was in Kaspar's eyes, it was Björn's world, and he loved Sigrun and wanted to keep her in it. That is what parents do when they love their children. If the parents have created a parallel, alternative world, perhaps they are particularly keen to keep their children in it, so they did not create it in vain. And as for Björn's tirade – perhaps he had been itching to give someone from the other world a piece of his mind for a very long time.

Kaspar wondered how Sigrun was doing at home. Growing up in the parsonage had also been a bit like a parallel, alternative world, and at sixteen he had rebelled against church on Sundays, the Evangelical Church youth group, Bible reading in the evenings and his mother's morality. Was Sigrun asserting her own autonomy over the völkisch world of her parents? She certainly had the courage for it. But what was the relationship between her and her parents like – how close was she to them, and how close were they to her? Kaspar had seen Björn blustering and threatening, and Svenja silent: had they only been like that on one occasion, or were they always so authoritarian that Sigrun wanted and was able to free herself from them?

His parents had been like that; the parents of his acquaintances and colleagues no longer were. They didn't want to exert their authority over their children, but to be their friends; they were supportive of everything the children wanted and did, offered help and advice but didn't make demands or issue orders, and certainly didn't punish them. They backed their children against their teachers and anyone else the children complained about in any context, took an active interest in their children's first relationships, encouraging, sympathizing and comforting, and if their son's girlfriend wanted to stay the night, his parents made her breakfast in the morning. Kaspar often thought that these children must find their parents' constant, loving, protective presence suffocating. But they didn't. The children were happy to be lovingly protected; they expected life to protect them equally lovingly, and they continued to live with their parents for a long time so their expectations would be fulfilled. If Björn and Svenja were like that with Sigrun, she would find it hard to emancipate herself from them. She could flee a blustering, threatening, forbidding, punishing father for a world that was different to his völkisch one, for the piano and books and a first relationship with a very different, sensitive, gentle boy. Kaspar had seen Björn blustering and threatening, and could imagine Svenja being stern and austere. Equally, though, he thought it possible that there were other sides to them, that they did express them, and that they cherished Sigrun; they needed her as much as the left-wing, green, liberal parents he knew needed their children.

He was always thinking of Sigrun. A girl in a skirt was walking in front of him – did Sigrun still not wear jeans? A girl in jeans was walking in front of him – did Sigrun wear jeans now as well? A book for younger readers landed on his desk – might it be something for Sigrun? He couldn't go to a concert or the opera without wondering whether Sigrun would like the music, and he certainly couldn't hear a piece of piano music without hoping that Sigrun was still committed to the piano. He thought of Sigrun when he visited a museum, when he came across Lola in the bookshop because his colleague had had to bring her in again, when he cooked, when he put on a CD in the evening and wondered whether Sigrun would fall asleep to the music.

Time and again he asked himself if there were some way he could intervene. Write to her? Send her books, music, CDs? Wait for her after school? Speak to her teachers? Enquire about piano teachers in Güstrow? Remind her parents of the money that was waiting for them? But if Sigrun wanted him to intervene, she only had to pick up the phone. The fact that she didn't, although it was so easy, robbed him of any hope that she would contact him when her parents' authority over her came to an end.

Paula didn't have any advice for him, either. Kaspar visited her once or twice a year, and if she and her husband came to Berlin for a concert or the opera, Kaspar went with them, and they would have dinner together afterwards. Detlef had taken over the practice, Nina the agricultural business; they hadn't got married, but they were living together. Paula had invited Svenja to visit a few times, but she had never replied. The Luckenbachs' practice didn't have any völkisch patients, but it did have some who lived in Lohmen, and Paula heard from them that more völkisch families had settled in the village, and the Rengers were still saving and waiting to buy a farm. The only things the patients could tell her about Sigrun was that she took the bus to school in the morning and came back in the late afternoon, and went around like the other völkisch girls in a skirt and blouse, or a dirndl on special occasions. They hadn't mentioned hearing piano music from the Renger house, but they wouldn't if Sigrun was playing the electric piano with headphones on.

Once he thought he saw her. He was sitting on the bus; she was walking along the pavement; he saw her from behind, then couldn't see her, because as the bus drew level she turned to look in a shop window, and when she turned back again she was too far away. He jumped up, rang the bell, got off, ran back, saw her some way away, slowed down so he wouldn't be out of breath when they met. They walked towards each other, and past each other. It wasn't Sigrun.

It wasn't a girl at all; it was a woman, not even young, despite her youthful figure and lively walk. Kaspar felt deceived and angry. At the woman who had fooled him, at the bus driver who had let him get off, at himself, unable to stop thinking about Sigrun; and at Sigrun, who had disappeared from his life.

Part Three

I

She had not vanished from his life. Two years later she rang his doorbell. He was about to go to bed, and looked at the clock; it was half past eleven. He slipped a dressing gown on over his nightshirt, went to the door, put on the chain and opened the door a crack. At first he didn't recognize the figure in the black hoodie, with black hair and black jeans.

'Will you let me in?'

He recognized the voice and removed the chain.

They went into the kitchen; Kaspar set water on to boil and put teabags in mugs, camomile tea. 'Have you got something stronger?' she asked. He found whiskey Birgit had bought, put a glass and the bottle on the table in front of Sigrun, and poured the tea. He saw that Sigrun was trembling; she saw his look, poured herself a whiskey, trembling, and drank it, trembling, then stuffed her hands in her pullover pockets and bowed her still-hooded head.

'Can I stay here tonight?' Before he could answer, she added, 'But you have to say you don't know where I am if the pigs turn up.'

'Why would they turn up?'

'The pigs' — she laughed — 'the pigs are a pain. They might

287

be after me. I don't know if they've already been to Irmtraud's and found my things. Your address is in my things.'

'That doesn't answer my question.'

'Your question . . . I just want to stay here tonight. Things went wrong and someone copped it, one of the others. I haven't worked out yet what I'm going to do till the fuss dies down. Can't I just stay here tonight and think about what to do?'

'Fuss?'

'Because of the guy who copped it. What with the pigs and the press and the politicians, of course there's going to be a fuss.'

Kaspar sat down. 'Take off your hood and look at me. Then you're going to tell me exactly what's happened.' He was angry. Not because Sigrun had brought trouble to his door. What had she said? A life had been snuffed out? Why? First the völkisch lunacy, then an insane act of violence – why? Sigrun was smart, quick-witted, musical, she read, she thought about things – why was she throwing her life away?

Sigrun sat up and slowly pushed back the hood. If they had passed each other on the street, he would not have recognized her. Sigrun had dyed her hair and eyebrows black, and she was wearing black eyeshadow and black lipstick.

This was not the girl he remembered. It wasn't that she actually looked hard, wicked and threatening, but she had put on a mask because hard, wicked and threatening was how she wanted to look.

She shrugged. It had probably all gone wrong because they had a rat in the group, a traitor. How else could the others have been forewarned and forearmed? All they'd wanted to do was torch the car of the Left Party district councillor who'd got their pub closed down again. But when they were beside the car, the others came out with baseball bats and chains, and they weren't prepared for that, and when Jörg went down, Axel took out a gun and fired. Sigrun hadn't known that Axel was carrying the gun; she knew he was a gun nut, but they'd never used guns – a stone or a bottle or a firecracker sometimes, but not actual guns, they'd never used actual guns. Then one of the other group was on the ground, and someone shouted, 'A doctor, quick, get a doctor!', and the lights went on in the district councillor's house, and the door opened, and Sigrun and Irmtraud grabbed Jörg and got the hell out of there. The others didn't come after them. They were a couple of blocks away and Jörg was able to walk again unaided when Axel and Helmut caught up with them. Axel was acting like he was drunk: 'I gave them hell, I gave them hell!' Then they heard the sirens.

'Maybe he's just wounded.'

'He's dead. It's already been reported; I saw it on my iPhone. He was dead by the time the doctor got there.'

Sigrun's right, thought Kaspar. This was a serious, nasty event that would preoccupy not just the city but the whole country. For months now there had been repeated attacks on leftist politicians' cars. The police had failed; they hadn't found the culprits. Now a leftist politician had taken matters into his own hands and brought in some leftist thugs; there had been a fight between them and the far-right thugs, and someone had been killed. This was a matter for both the police and the press, and the police could not afford to fail again; they had to find the culprit at all costs. If the victim had a likable, interesting face, the wave of outrage and agitation would be especially high. Kaspar felt sorry for the boy. At the same time, it was all repugnant to him: the attacks, the violence, the fighting. Sigrun was repugnant to him.

Then he saw that she was crying. Tears were coursing down her cheeks, dirty black tears. Occasionally she gave a small, convulsive sob. Kaspar stood up, dragged his chair over to hers and put his arm around her shoulders. She leaned against him. After a while she said, sobbing, 'I didn't want that. For someone to die. I didn't want that.'

'Was it you? Did your group set fire to the other cars?'

'Oh, the cars . . .' She went on crying, loudly, uncontrollably, defenceless. As if she could wash out of her what had happened, what she had done.

Kaspar put his other arm around her as well and held her. She had to go to the police and make a statement. She could speak to a lawyer beforehand; he knew one, and she could take the lawyer to the police with her. But she had to go the next day. Should he say so? No: let her cry herself to sleep first and calm down.

'Why weren't you there?'

'How do you mean?'

'Why did you just vanish from my life? Like Grandmother from Mother's life? Why didn't you help me stand up to my parents, and with the music and the books? You started to, and then you didn't want to any more.'

Kaspar felt . . . no, he didn't feel outraged: he felt a wave of outrage but he controlled it; he didn't stop holding Sigrun, didn't answer her with the coldness he felt, the coldness she deserved. How could she accuse him of disappearing from her life! She had looked at him and her eyes had pleaded with him to go. What else could he have done? And why had she never written a letter or picked up the phone? 'Why . . .?'

But he didn't go on. It wasn't about what had happened or not happened between them, then or since. It wasn't about justified or unjustified accusations. Sigrun had felt abandoned, and she had been alone in her world, a world from which he had partly alienated her without grounding her in another. Whatever her reason for not contacting him – she had been alone. He held her close. 'I'm sorry, Sigrun, I'm sorry. I won't abandon you again.'

He made up the bed in her room and put out one of his nightshirts for her. She washed off the black make-up and lay down on the bed, almost like the young girl she had been two years ago. She fell asleep as he was saying good night.

2

Kaspar couldn't fall asleep. Was she right? Had he been too quick to tell himself that she was able to contact him, and that if she didn't, it meant she didn't want to be in touch? Had it offended him, and was this why he hadn't done more? He hadn't waited for her outside her school; was it because he was too vain to stand there and wait and perhaps be resolutely ignored? Had he been too lazy, too cowardly, to fight Björn and Svenja for Sigrun? Why hadn't he written any letters or sent any parcels, when the worst that could have happened was that they might be thrown away, unread and unopened? Should he have opposed Sigrun's far-right worldview more decisively? When they visited Irmtraud, should he have told her what he thought of the fights with the anti-fascists and the police, instead of getting her to show him the swastika in her ear?

He sat up, leaned against the wall and switched on the bedside lamp. What if Sigrun was not prepared to go to the police? Because her honor was still loyalty, and she didn't want to betray anyone? Would he have to go himself? Not so the police would find out what the group had done — what was done was done — but because Axel was dangerous? Would he hand Sigrun over to the police if she wasn't prepared to turn herself in?

At three in the morning, he gave up. He got out of bed, went to the kitchen, tidied up, laid the table for breakfast, put water and coffee in the machine, doing everything as quietly as possible so as not to wake Sigrun in the room above the kitchen. He tidied the living room, too, although he knew that an orderly kitchen and living room was no substitute for the order that was lacking in his thoughts. He emailed his colleagues to let them know that he wouldn't be coming in to the bookshop that day. He opened the door to the balcony wide, felt the mildness of the spring air, and stepped outside. It would be a while before it got light. Even the birds were still asleep. He heard a rustle in the bushes under the balcony: a rat or rabbit or squirrel. He listened to the other sounds of the night: solitary steps approaching and walking away, a car in the next street, a dog barking.

He fell asleep in an armchair, with the balcony doors open, and was woken by the bin men. It was just before seven. There was nothing in the paper yet; the news was reporting the attempted attack on the district councillor's car, the death of a student from the far-left scene, the collision of far-right and far-left violence. There had not yet been any arrests, which meant either that the traitor had known about the planned attack, but not who would carry it out, or that Irmtraud, Axel, Jörg and Helmut had gone underground. Had one of the group defending the car photographed the attackers? Sigrun had not mentioned seeing a flash. Would she and the others be recognizable in photos taken in the dark? Had they arrived or fled the scene by U-Bahn or S-Bahn – could video footage from the station lead to their identification and arrest?

Kaspar was sitting at the breakfast table with his coffee when Sigrun came quietly downstairs and sat with him. She was despondent. 'I expect you've listened to the news. Did they say who he was?'

'Only that he was a student and from the far-left scene.' Kaspar poured her some coffee. 'Are you going to go to the police?'

'I think I know who the rat was. Timo. All mouth and no trousers: always on about what a great guy he is and all the stuff he's done and how he's not afraid of anything; no one took him seriously. We should have chucked him out. We didn't, because we thought he was harmless. But we hardly ever took him with us. We didn't want him to screw things up.'

'Do you think he'll go to the police?'

'He didn't want the police involved. We were supposed to see that we needed him. That we'd get bloody noses without him. He didn't think it'd mean we'd realize he was a rat.' Sigrun considered. 'But maybe it wasn't him. Maybe they just figured we'd do something after the Left Party guy got our pub closed down again.'

He didn't ask again if she was going to go to the police. He asked what she intended to do. She said she would really like to stay with him for a while. She would have liked to collect her things from Irmtraud's, but what if the police were waiting for her there? It wasn't very likely, but what if they were, and what would Irmtraud say about it all, about Axel and the dead boy, and what should she, Sigrun, say, and how should she behave towards Axel? Her things weren't that important; it was just that Kaspar's address was in her address book, but no one had seen her come to his house, and if the police came and he said she wasn't there, they wouldn't search his apartment right away.

'I think it would be good if you spoke to a lawyer about your situation. It won't go any further. You should find out how things stand.'

'I'm not a rat. I'm not going to the police. They wouldn't betray me, and I won't betray them.'

294

'If Timo did talk to the other side, they'll name him to the police, and from the way you describe him, if the police pick him up, Timo will talk. Listen to what a lawyer has to say. Prepare yourself.'

'Does that mean I can stay with you for now?'

'You've got to get out, Sigrun. You need to think about it, I realize that. But if you want to carry on with them and just hide out here for a while, I want nothing to do with it. You'll have to leave.'

She looked at him, and he thought he saw relief in her face, but there was stubbornness, too. Relief at the reprieve, stubbornness because she didn't want to be a rat? She was biting her lip. When had she started doing that? Did it mean she felt unsure of herself, or that she was turning inwards?

'I'll call the lawyer and invite him for dinner tonight. We're old friends. Then I'll go shopping. You need clothes; what do you want me to get?'

He noted down her size and her requests. She accompanied him to the door of the apartment, put her arms around his neck and gave him a kiss on the cheek. 'Thank you, Grandfather.' He was already halfway down the stairs when she came running after him. 'Hair dye remover – please will you get me some hair dye remover?'

3

Kaspar didn't like buying clothes for himself any more. The shops, the air in them, the music, the bewildering layout, undressing and dressing again, looking at yourself in the mirror, queuing for the till – he detested it, and hoped to get by with the suits and coats he currently owned until he died, with the occasional addition of a pullover, a pair of corduroy trousers, a shirt, a pair of shoes; preferably two of each at a time, four or five of the shirts. Shopping for Sigrun, though, was fun, and he also enjoyed buying the food he guessed she would like to cook. When he got home and unlocked the door of the apartment, he heard the muffled sound of piano music. Sigrun had placed a cloth over the strings of the grand piano.

'I haven't played for six months. I missed it; I realize now how much.' Over a cup of tea in the kitchen, Sigrun told him that in the summer after graduating from school she had gone on another trip with the children, to Gdańsk and Kaliningrad – formerly Danzig and Königsberg – but she had long since tired of it all by then: the customs and the songs and the clothes and the talk of German soil and Reich and honor, and Father, who finally had his farm but was barely managing to get by, and Mother, who both revered and despised him, or was simply afraid of him. Sigrun told them she was leaving, and she left, and moved in with Irmtraud; she worked as a waitress and cleaner, she didn't care how she earned her money as long as she could go out onto the street with the girls, or boys, and fight, and show that Germans aren't just going to sit back and take the crap, not from politicians, not from journalists, not from bloody foreigners and definitely not from the Antifa. They beat up the colored drug dealers, the ones who were messing up our kids, and who didn't go to the police because they knew the police didn't like them, either. Once they threw a Molotov cocktail into a shisha bar; the Arab clan that owned it was supposed to think the other clan had done it, they were supposed to attack and kill each other, but for some reason they didn't. Sigrun knew Kaspar disapproved of what she had done, and she looked a little shamefaced as she told the story. But she was also proud, and when she talked about the cars they had torched, her eyes lit up.

'What did you achieve? Apart from a death?'

'The journalists whose cars we torched were always going on about how they wouldn't be silenced. But when your car's burning outside your house, that's not something you forget, believe me. You should see it.'

'And the boy who died?'

'Yeah, the boy who died . . .' Kaspar was afraid she would say you couldn't make an omelette without breaking eggs, or that anyone who puts themselves in danger risks getting killed. But she bowed her head and said nothing, and although she didn't cry again, she sat there looking as miserable as she had the night before.

'Do you think Axel can be left to roam the streets?'

'I don't know what was wrong with him yesterday.'

'Whatever was wrong with him then can be wrong with him again. He's got to be stopped. You have to stop him.'

'He was trying to protect Jörg.'

'So the world would see that Germans won't take any crap? It's not about politics with you lot. You just want the kick of seeing something go up in flames or crash to the ground, or a fist-fight.' Kaspar was angry. He didn't feel like protecting Sigrun any more; he didn't care if she felt attacked and withdrew from him. 'You've doled it out often enough – what, you can't take getting hit yourselves for once? You shoot a man so Jörg doesn't get beaten up? What spoiled, pampered, pathetic creatures you are! You want to make Germany great again? Fight the Antifa, play your stupid games as much as you like, but games have limits. Axel is dangerous. The danger has to be eliminated: he belongs in prison, and possibly in therapy, not out on the streets. He can't go on walking around with a gun. You said it was like he was drunk; he'll want to feel like that again. The rest of you don't shoot? You just beat up the Nigerian dealer so he'll see that he's not welcome in Germany? Do you think he doesn't know that already? And the journalists – no, they won't forget it; I wouldn't forget it, either, if my car was burning outside my house. So what? Do you think that's going to make the journalist write any differently? Or that they won't dare write anything any more? Do you think if you set fire to my car because I sold the wrong kind of books that I would stop? This is all so stupid, Sigrun. Life is elsewhere. Life is music and work. Study, teach children, or make sick people well again or build houses or give concerts – you're clever, you're strong: do something with it. No one's going to bring East Prussia and Silesia back. Germany's not going to get any bigger, but it isn't too small and it isn't bursting at the seams, even with the foreigners. And they're needed. Who else is prepared to pick asparagus and harvest grapes and slaughter pigs these days? When your father's farm is up and running and he needs a farmhand, and can only find a foreigner, he'll take him. He'll have to learn German and obey the law like everyone else, but if he does that, what's the problem? Whether people live their lives as völkisch Germans, or just as Germans, or as foreign Germans, whether they celebrate a völkisch marriage in the meadow or a Christian marriage in church, or whether Jews stand under a canopy and smash a glass underfoot – who cares? Let people live however they want. Let them live.'

Kaspar was embarrassed by his outburst, but it had done him good. He searched Sigrun's face for agreement or thoughtfulness, but before he could read her expression she lowered her head.

He waited for a reaction – any reaction. *I don't know. It's not like you say. You don't understand. You can't understand. That was a long speech. You've never talked that much before. I have to think about it.* Objections, too, perhaps: that the others had had baseball bats and chains and they hadn't, that her father would never employ a foreigner, that Germany didn't have to be such a rich country. But she just sat there, head bowed and her hands on the table, as if it were a piano and she had simply paused in her playing. Just when he thought he couldn't stand her silence any longer, she raised her head, saw the hair dye remover in the shopping bag, took it, stood up and said, 'I . . . I'll go and do my hair, then.'

4

She emerged from the bathroom with her head wrapped in a towel and sat down at the piano, which was still muffled by the cloth. She must have practiced a lot before she stopped playing for half a year. She was good. After warming up with a few pieces from the *Notebook*, she worked on the variations on Mozart's Sonata No. 11 in A major, not permitting herself a single mistake, concentrating on what she found difficult instead of resorting to what she found easy; she kept pausing, and in the next room Kaspar, who couldn't see what she was doing, imagined that when she did she was following the melody in her head instead of with her fingers.

He used to play the piece himself, but could never master the variations. He knew the melodies by heart; Birgit had loved them, and had practiced them for months until they flowed easily from her hands. They didn't yet flow easily from Sigrun's hands. But she was working not just on fluidity, but also on the delicacy and tenderness of her rendition. Sometimes she permitted herself a minuscule hesitation before succumbing to a shift in the melody; she played the variations with great gentleness, allowing the fourth to lament without pain and the sixth to rejoice without triumph. Kaspar was moved. It reminded him of the way his and Birgit's dog would take a little piece of cheese or sausage from an outstretched hand, gently, carefully, so as not to hurt the hand with its teeth. Sigrun worked on the transitions as well; she didn't just want to line up the variations one after another, but to play them as one piece. She had a clear idea of how the movement should be played, and this gave Kaspar even more pleasure than her technical improvement. He had intended to deal with orders and invoices; instead, he listened to Sigrun, happy to hear her playing, sad to think of how she had gone astray.

They cooked together, and dinner was ready by the time the lawyer arrived, an older gentleman with a shaved head, walrus mustache and paunch, who greeted Kaspar as an old friend and Sigrun as a young lady. She did look like one: her hair was red again, and she was wearing the green shirt dress Kaspar had picked out for her, to go with the red hair. Sigrun had chosen to put it on that evening instead of the jeans and T-shirts he had also brought back for her; he had referred to the T-shirts as *T-Hemden*, and she had given him a pained look.

Kaspar had told the lawyer what he had heard on the news, and the lawyer had done some asking around. The Antifa boys thought they had recognized someone – not the gunman, someone else; the policeman hadn't given the lawyer a name. The man had been questioned, but had claimed he knew nothing about it, and had an alibi. So they didn't have much, the lawyer said; but there were the ballistics, and the CCTV from nearby S-Bahn and U-Bahn stations; neighbors were being interviewed and the alibi checked and informers in the far-right scene were keeping their ears open. Then the lawyer listened to what Sigrun had to tell him.

'If the public prosecutor finds out about this, he'll charge you and the others with murder on the basis of joint enterprise. Will he be able to make it stick? He'll say that in taking Axel with his gun along with you, you accepted that he was going to

301

shoot someone. You'll say you never thought Axel would bring a gun. But will they believe you?' He paused. 'If you report him, because you're horrified that he had a gun with him, that he fired it, that he killed someone, there's a good chance you won't be charged with anything more than attempted arson and that you'll get a suspended sentence. If you don't . . . Or are you afraid? Are you not reporting Axel because, if you did, you'd have to fear for your life? If you can argue that convincingly . . .' He paused again. 'I don't need to tell you what I'd advise you to do. Things like this always come out sooner or later. You don't owe Axel anything. And it'll benefit the others if you make clear right from the start that he had his own agenda.'

Sigrun looked from one to the other, uncertain, defiant, determined to decide for herself, not to need anyone, anyone's advice, anyone's help. Kaspar could see it in her face, and also that she didn't know what her decision should be. She needed advice, but she feared that accepting advice and help meant surrendering her independence. What should she do? Things like this always come out, the lawyer had said. Maybe. But maybe they don't. She didn't want to be a rat! She bit her lip, stood up as if she had made her decision, then sat down again.

After the meal she sat with the two men, drinking red wine and listening. They talked about the past, as old friends do. Birgit had often forgotten to notify the authorities about demonstrations she had organized; she had been put on trial, and the lawyer had defended her. 'She was stubborn,' he said. 'I liked her, but she didn't make things easy for me. She didn't make things easy for anyone.'

'Is that true, Grandfather?'

'She certainly wouldn't have made it easy for you. I don't have the right to parent you; she would have claimed that right.

She'd have felt unsure of herself with your mother, because she'd abandoned her. But not with you.'

Before going to sleep, Sigrun wanted to know if she could read Birgit's notes that he had mentioned some time ago. He promised to think about it. He was sitting on the edge of her bed, thinking that Sigrun could actually go back to the shared apartment if she wanted to, as the police didn't know about Irmtraud. He wondered why she didn't. Was she detaching from Irmtraud's world? Was she finding her way to his? Was she just too lazy to head back to Kreuzberg at this time of night? Was she unsure how to present herself to Irmtraud: with red or black hair, in black clothes or the blue jeans and colorful T-shirts he had bought her?

'When all this is over, what do you want to do with your life?'

'I don't know, Grandfather. You think I don't think about it. I do think about it. It was interesting, what your friend told us about his work. People from our community are always having to go to court. But . . . I know it doesn't sound true, because I haven't played for half a year, but it is: what I'd really like to do is play the piano. I'd like to play and play until I don't feel like playing any more. I've never done that before. At home I always had to stop because there was something I had to do, or I had to help out, and I never dared to with you, because of you and the neighbors. I should have brought my electric piano with me; with the headphones on, I don't disturb anyone.' She smiled sadly. 'All the great pianists started playing when they were four or five. Does Juilliard mean anything to you – the conservatoire in New York? I read about it; that's where I'd want to go. But they only take five per cent of applicants, and you need more than Mozart's Sonata in A major, and it costs fifty thousand dollars a year.'

At four or five . . . Kaspar didn't know, but he could believe it, and he didn't think Mozart's Sonata in A major would be enough to get you in, either. Or was it? People said it was easy, but the Mozart family had counted it as one of the particularly special, difficult sonatas, and the examiners would know that. What if Sigrun played it as it had never been played before? 'Play tomorrow for as long as you like. I have to go to the bookshop, the upstairs neighbors go to work, and they don't hear anything downstairs. Shall I put something on for you to go to sleep to?'

She nodded. He played the first movement of the 'Moonlight' Sonata, called up, 'Good night,' and she responded.

Should he give her Birgit's notes? In the past two years he had read them over and over again, and had sometimes thought about writing the rest of the story. He hadn't known whether he could do it, but he had thought it would make Birgit happy if her novel were completed and printed. Until he had realized that there was nothing to complete. However well he invented and recounted the story of Birgit searching for and finding Svenja, it would never be the novel Birgit had wanted to write. That novel didn't exist. Birgit hadn't really wanted to write it. She hadn't wanted to search for and find herself by searching for and finding her daughter, and writing about the searching and finding. What she had wanted was to accept herself as a person who was not capable of any of this: not of searching, not of finding, not of writing. It was this she had failed at, not the writing. Would Sigrun understand?

5

They breakfasted together, then he went to the bookshop. She was planning to call Irmtraud, then play the piano until she could play no more.

But at eleven she appeared in the bookshop. Kaspar looked up as the door opened and cold air blew in; he saw Sigrun enter, agitated, confused; she didn't greet anyone but came straight over to him, said, 'He shot Timo,' and stood there, as if waiting for some word or gesture from him.

He took her with him to the room where parcel deliveries were stored and unpacked; they sat down, and she told him what had happened. She had called Irmtraud. Timo's girlfriend had found him and had called first the police, then Irmtraud; she was utterly distraught, crying and screaming and accusing everyone and everything: the murderer, Timo's friends who hadn't helped him and hadn't protected him, the whole wicked world. She didn't seem to be aware that the others had mistrusted Timo, perhaps because he hadn't noticed himself, or because he was ashamed and hadn't told her. Irmtraud and Sigrun were in no doubt that Axel had believed Timo was a rat and that he had shot him; they could understand why he had thought of it, but were aghast that he had acted alone. 'He should have talked to us – we would have talked him out of it.' Timo's girlfriend hadn't suspected Axel. But she was outraged that Timo's friends had not protected him; she was sure to have named them, and the police would bring them in for questioning, one by one. And the police would discover that Timo and the Antifa boy had been shot with the same gun.

'Does Timo's girlfriend know you?'

'We've never met. She keeps out of it all, and I've only been here half a year. But she knows Irmtraud and our apartment and the people who've been there a while.'

Kaspar was appalled to realize that he didn't care about the two victims. That shouldn't be the case; the two young men had gone off the rails, but they'd had their whole lives ahead of them, they could have become sensible young men and done sensible things. But Kaspar couldn't help it: their deaths left him unmoved. He was angered by the unpredictable, trigger-happy Axel, and this anger was linked to his anger with Sigrun, who had protected Axel and was about to let him drag her before the courts and thence to prison. Sigrun, locked up for years, even if she were allowed to have an electric piano – it was senseless, it was all so senseless and repellent.

'You can't wait any longer. You have to go to the police, or to the prosecutor's office; we can ask the lawyer which. We'll ask him to go with you, as well. You don't know what else Axel will do if he stays at large.'

Sigrun knew she wouldn't convince Kaspar – she wasn't convinced herself – but she had to say it nonetheless, subdued and defiant: 'As far as Axel's concerned, it's been dealt with. He'll keep quiet now.'

'And what if he doesn't? You'll be responsible for anything else he does that you could have prevented, but didn't. Isn't it enough that you didn't prevent Timo's death?'

She wept. Tears coursed down her cheeks again; again she gave those small, convulsive sobs. This time Kaspar did not put his arm around her shoulder.

'I know, Grandfather, I know. Maybe . . . maybe Timo would still be alive. The rat. I know, I have to go.' But she didn't get up, and she asked Kaspar not to take her to the lawyer. 'Today I'm going to play the piano. Tomorrow I'll be the rat and I'll go and talk. But not today. Today I'm going to play the piano until I can't play any more.' She saw the disapproval in his face. 'You can throw me out of the apartment, then I won't be able to play. But it won't make me go to the police any sooner.'

Kaspar took his phone from his pocket and called the lawyer. Sigrun listened to the call. Yes, he would go with her to the prosecutor's office. Could she come at half past nine? They should talk it all through beforehand.

Sigrun nodded. She remained seated, and Kaspar didn't stand, either.

'You're brave, Sigrun. You're doing the right thing, even though you'd rather not and you might get by without. You're freeing yourself to live your own life. I have no right to be proud of you, but I am.'

'What would my parents say about it all?'

6

Kaspar was preoccupied with this, as well. What would Sigrun's parents say, if not now, then later? How would Sigrun respond? How much power did her parents still have over her – how free of them was she? Did Sigrun's parents see her months with the autonomists as her wild period, just as they had had a wild period – did they expect that after this she would calm down, return to the völkisch life, take over the farm, marry an Aryan man and have lots of children with him? Would Sigrun think this was an option? Not now, but if life were to disappoint her? He would help her: the money he had set aside for her would be enough for two years at Juilliard, certainly enough to train at another conservatoire. But what if nothing came of it?

Kaspar didn't walk Sigrun home. He wanted her to have the piano to herself. But he couldn't stay in the bookshop, either. He went to the park. Spring was conjuring the first pale green on trees and bushes; children were romping in the playgrounds, dogs chasing each other across the lawns, and old people were sitting on benches. All was right with the world. It would get warmer and greener from week to week; here and there flowers would bloom, and on his morning and evening walks he would smell the earth and the trees and the blossom again.

Why shouldn't Sigrun go to the conservatoire here in Berlin? The piano teacher would know what she needed to prepare. With her love of the piano and commitment to practicing, Kaspar couldn't believe she wouldn't pass the entrance exam, if not this summer, then the next. She could live with him. Sometimes they would have breakfast together, or dinner; sometimes they would go to a concert together; apart from that, she would live her own life, and he would leave her in peace. He wouldn't find it difficult. Birgit had lived a life of her own alongside his.

He sat down next to a couple on a bench. The two old people sat there without speaking; her hand was in his. Would he ever experience that again: sitting on a bench with a woman, hand in hand, with or without words? If he tried to imagine it, it was Birgit who sat beside him; Birgit, whom he still missed: when he got up early and didn't have to be quiet, when he came home and couldn't tell her about his day, when he stared at the empty place in front of him as he ate, when his arm stretched out to search for her in his sleep and didn't find her. Sometimes, though, before falling asleep, he realized that he hadn't thought of her all day. Sometimes it even happened that she only came to mind the following morning. He wanted to keep her in his life. She was retreating from it.

He tried to imagine another woman on the bench beside him. Two years ago he had taken on an apprentice, a cheerful, hard-working girl with an unselfconscious manner; unselfconscious, too, about hugging, touching, leaning against him. He found her attractive; her full lips and slender body were a temptation, and she was setting her cap at him. But he didn't want this youthful beauty as a trophy; nor, as her boss, did he want to be the trophy of an apprentice. He found it inconceivable that Laura was genuinely interested in him, that she could genuinely love him. Was he wrong? Was she no longer a girl but a young woman, and isn't a young woman a woman above all? He didn't know. In any case, he did not reciprocate.

A year ago he had gone to the doctor for a check-up and had had a vascular screening done at the same time. The neurologist was younger, but not too young for him, just as he was not too old for her, and he thought he could tell from her expression that she liked him. She was blonde, with blue eyes, a generous mouth, straight white teeth, and her figure beneath the white coat was clearly an attractive one. Were it not for the wrinkles on her forehead and the laughter lines around her mouth and eyes, Kaspar would have found her beauty intimidating. But she did have those lines; she approached him with a smile, and his impression was of a person who was warm-hearted and worldly-wise.

She placed the equipment on his neck; he heard the blood in his veins, a throbbing, rushing sound, his beating heart. She explained to him what the rushing sound had told her before even looking at what the needle had recorded on the paper. When she finished, she briefly put a hand on his shoulder before he got to his feet.

Words started pouring out of him. 'Could we see each other? Go for dinner one evening? I apologize – I didn't even look to see if you were wearing a ring. I don't often do this – proposition women, that is – in fact, I've never done it.' Under the calmness of her gaze, he, too, became calm. 'I see now that you're wearing two wedding rings. I'm sorry you lost your husband. You clearly loved him, or you wouldn't be wearing both rings. I . . . But I'm talking too much. I just wanted to say that it would make me happy if I could invite you out one evening.'

That was how it started; and it started well, he thought, even though he was awkward, or perhaps because he was awkward and that was her first impression of him, and still she accepted his invitation. But over the weeks that followed it never went beyond the liveliness and intimacy of the first evening. Neither of them had the patience to empathize with all the life the other had accumulated. They would have had to work at it, and neither of them suffered so from being alone that they were prepared to do the work.

What more could he hope for? More than what he would get from living with Sigrun? More than occasional company at breakfast or dinner? More than going to the occasional concert together? That would be enough for him. And she would play the piano, and the music would fill the apartment.

7

Sigrun had cooked and set the table. She was relaxed and cheerful, as if in making the decision a burden had fallen from her shoulders; as if she had freed herself. She didn't talk about what had happened, or about the visit to the prosecutor's office the following morning. She was open to his proposals. Talking to the piano teacher, studying with him again, preparing for the entrance exam, living with Kaspar – yes, that would be good.

'You know I'd let you come and go and do as you please.'

'Yes, Grandfather, I know. We'd be sharing the apartment. I'd like that, and I'd go with you to every concert and every opera you go to. I'd like to get to know a lot more music.'

'You were wondering what your parents—'

'My parents . . .' she interrupted. 'Father will never forgive me for not wanting the farm. I have to want what he wants, that's the only way. But he'll find a völkisch man to take it over, and that'll do for him. As long as the völkisch settlers keep coming. It'll be harder for Mother. She worked her fingers to the bone for that farm, and I think she has this dream: her retiring to their part of the property, me on the farm with a husband and plenty of children for her to spoil as she would have liked to have been spoiled herself.'

Kaspar tried to clear the table and do the washing-up, but Sigrun wouldn't even let him help with that. This evening she wanted to do it all herself.

As they sipped their espressos, Kaspar turned the conversation to money. 'I think you should have the money I didn't pay to your parents these last two years, and in any case you'll get what you've been entitled to since your eighteenth birthday. That's one hundred and twenty-five thousand euros. Shall I transfer it to your account? Or do you want the money in instalments?'

She shook her head. 'I know from Mother that you only said it as a way to get to us, to her and me. I'm not entitled to the money.'

'When we say something, for whatever reason, we put it in the world. I said you were entitled to the money, so you're entitled to it.'

'Oh, Grandfather,' she smiled. 'I don't even have a bank account. I'll come to you if I need anything, and it's great that there's enough for Juilliard, even if I don't get into Juilliard – but maybe somewhere else that'll also cost a lot.' She debated for a moment whether or not to tell him what else was on her mind, then took the plunge. 'At the fete that summer, the fete with the rope and the bonfire, I saw you standing together, you and Mother. You looked as if the two of you could get on. Do you think you could talk to her now and then?'

He didn't know what to make of the suggestion. 'She doesn't trust me.'

'I told her it wasn't you who put the book in my suitcase. I didn't tell Father. I could tell her; not then, but a year later. And she was glad that I wasn't seeing you any more, but she was glad as well that you hadn't betrayed her.'

'Isn't it more important that you talk to her now and then?'

'She'd be pleased if you did. She wouldn't show it to begin with. But she'd be pleased about it. Another thing. What your wife wrote about her and Mother – you said you'd think about letting me read it. Can I? Tonight? I think Mother would like to read it, too.'

Why tonight? Because she had made a decision that would mean turning her back on her old life and starting a new one, and she wanted to know how her grandmother had transitioned from her old life to the new? Did she want tonight to mean she had finally, definitively become an adult? Sitting there opposite him, serious and self-assured, she already was: her suggestion that he talk to Svenja, her request for Birgit's notes, had been so assertive, as if he couldn't deny them. She had pinned up her red hair, which always made her look a bit severe, and her mouth reminded him of Birgit's when she was very sure of herself. Did she have a right to see Birgit's notes? No, but he had promised he wouldn't abandon her again, and he felt he would be abandoning her if he didn't give them to her.

They stood up, and he kept her company while she washed up; he put out Birgit's notes for her, and stood for a long time in front of the CDs, unable to decide. She came over, took out Bach's Piano Concerto No. 7 in G minor and handed it to him. 'Please will you play the whole thing?' She gave him a kiss on the cheek. 'You don't need to come up again.'

8

At ten o'clock the lawyer called the bookshop. Where was Sigrun? The appointment with the public prosecutor was at eleven thirty, and they absolutely must co-ordinate beforehand. Kaspar went home, growing more worried and uneasy with every step. He had got up early, had drunk his coffee standing up and left the house. He had been a little surprised not to see Sigrun; she was usually up before him. But she did have a hard day ahead of her.

He went along the street instead of through the park; he kept breaking into a run, but couldn't keep it up for long; he ran fast, panting, pain stabbing at his chest. Had something happened to Sigrun? The steep stairs to her room? A fall in front of the U-Bahn? A careless or drunk driver? His footsteps, so loud on the paving stones, were inaudible on the stairwell carpet, and when he reached his apartment and stopped panting and could no longer feel his heart pounding, there was total silence. He had briefly hoped he would find her sitting at the piano, that she was immersed in playing and had forgotten everything, but he had known that this hope was a delusion. Just as, when he called out 'Sigrun', he knew she would not reply.

Coming home, looking for her, going from room to room, not finding her, then finding her, dead – the evening of Birgit's death came rushing back, and he couldn't take another step. He stood in the corridor, afraid to go into the kitchen or the living room or the dining room or her bedroom, afraid to go anywhere. Keep still. Don't move.

The telephone wrenched him out of his reverie. The lawyer wanted to know whether he had found Sigrun. No, stammered Kaspar, he was still looking, he would call back in a minute. Now he did go from room to room, and finally up to Sigrun's bedroom. Her letter was on the table. No envelope; a single sheet of paper with writing on both sides. Kaspar picked it up and sat down on the bed.

Dear Grandfather,

I can't do it. I know Axel has to be taken off the streets and that he has to stand trial. But Irmtraud and Helmut and Jörg and Axel were my people, and I can't betray them. I'm not a rat. I don't want anything to do with them any more, but I can't let the public prosecutor come between us. I'm leaving.

You know I know where everything is in your apartment. There's money and the note with your PIN number in the little wooden box on your desk. Tonight, while you were asleep, I took money out of the wooden box and your credit card out of your wallet. You can block the card. But I won't use it to buy anything stupid, and I'll find a job. The card runs out in September, anyway.

I meant what I said yesterday. I would like to live with you and play the piano and go to the conservatoire in a year's time. But, for better or worse, my people wouldn't leave me alone, and my parents wouldn't leave us alone, either. You would help me as best you could. But how well could you? Perhaps you think I ought to face up to it all, with my people and with my parents. But why should I? When I read Grandmother's notes this evening, I understood her. Sometimes you have to admit to

316

yourself what you are or are not capable of. Sometimes you have to run away.

I love you, Grandfather. Thank you so much for the piano. I mean, the piano in general. Thank you for the electric piano, too; I shouldn't have left it in Lohmen, then I could have taken it with me now. I'll buy a new one soon, with your card. I don't need an expensive one; I just need to be able to carry it in a case, like a violinist does his violin.

Oh yes – I took your suitcase as well, the little black one with the wheels. I don't have much; it's just big enough. I took three books for the journey, as well; you'll see which ones.

I did understand all the things you said to me. When I was here on my own yesterday, I listened to Chopin, Dvořák and Rachmaninoff. I'd like to play the Piano Concerto No. 3 one day. But I'd rather play the Sonata in A major as no one has ever played it before. I know how. But I can't do it yet; I'm not up to it.

Wish me luck, Grandfather. Big hug,
Sigrun

9

Kaspar called the lawyer, who asked him to come to the office. What should he tell the public prosecutor? Kaspar wasn't much help. He was struggling to come to terms with what Sigrun had done; with the fact that she had vanished from his life and his life was now lonely again, that she had only done what she had to do, that he had wanted her to be grown up and free and now she was both, that his sadness was well founded and would take time to get over, but his sorrow was for himself alone; he didn't need to feel sad for Sigrun.

The lawyer didn't want to hear about Kaspar's problems. He wanted to know what Kaspar knew, and he learned what Sigrun had reported about Timo. He promised not to mention Sigrun to the prosecutor. Axel would have come to the attention of the police by now, along with the others in Timo's circle. The lawyer would confine himself to tipping them off that if they searched the place where Axel was living, they would find the gun that had been used to kill two people. How he knew this was something he could keep to himself.

And that was what happened. The following evening, the lawyer informed Kaspar that the search of Axel's apartment had been successful. Kaspar was relieved. Axel was no longer a danger to anyone; Sigrun would not have to bear responsibility for another murder. If her name hadn't come up so far, it wouldn't come up in future, meaning that if she wanted to return, she could; she had nothing to fear from the public prosecutor. Kaspar was relieved about that, too. But his relief was like a seal on the fact that she had gone.

Before he had a chance to decide that he would comply with Sigrun's request and talk to Svenja, Svenja came to him. Irmtraud had told her that Sigrun wasn't living with her any more, but with Kaspar, and, after failing to find him at home, Svenja appeared in the bookshop early one afternoon.

He took her with him to the apartment. She kept insisting, as they walked through the park, that he should talk to her there and then. 'Where is she? What's she doing? How is she?' When he replied that he didn't know, she got nasty. 'Why did you drive her away? What did you do to her?' Her questions angered him, and he had to restrain himself from snapping. He sat down with her on the nearest bench and told her what had happened.

She listened, twisting her handkerchief in her hands. 'That's what we were afraid of. That she'd get involved in violence with the autonomists. Björn says violence is needed if Germany is to awaken, but as revolution, not this childish nonsense. He says we have to be patient. That's what he taught Sigrun.'

'Why didn't Sigrun want to stay with you any more? Why did she come to Berlin?'

'When she was little, she and Björn were like this' – Svenja wrapped her middle finger around her forefinger – 'and when she started to go her own way, he couldn't stand it.' She laughed. 'If things had worked out as we'd imagined, and she'd met someone and got married and they'd taken over the farm, I think he would've gone mad with jealousy.' She gestured helplessly. 'How could I have done things any differently?'

'Sigrun said you both revered and despised Björn. Or that you were just afraid of him.'

'Sigrun despised us. You taught her that. That we're uneducated and don't have many books, or any music. The piano – you'll say it was just a piano, but it didn't come from us, it came from you, from outside, and it ruined everything.'

Kaspar wanted to contradict her. But perhaps she was right. So he didn't mention Hans Frank in the castle in Krakow, or how Sigrun had only spent a few weeks with him. With the piano, Sigrun had had a world of her own that had nothing in common with the völkisch world of her parents.

'No, I don't despise Björn. I don't revere him, either. And I'm not afraid of him.' She laughed. 'So what is it, I suppose you want to know? Without him, I would be . . . I would be homeless and an alcoholic and a junkie, and how I'd get money is not something I want to describe to you. No – it's what I would have been. I'd be dead by now. I owe Björn my life. And as I told you before, I can rely on him, I can trust him. You're thinking I owe my life to Weise and his wife as well, but I don't want anything to do with them. With birth and parents and children, it's different. But I needn't tell you that. Your wife – my mother – knew it better than anyone.'

'Did Sigrun feel you sided with Björn instead of with her?'

'I don't know.'

Kaspar found that hard to believe. Perhaps she didn't want to know. Irma Weise had sided with her husband instead of Svenja, and she didn't want to be like her. Nor did she want to lay herself open to the accusation implicit in his question. He shouldn't have asked.

'The night before she left, Sigrun talked about you. She wants you to be happy.' He glanced at Svenja, but couldn't tell from her expression whether she was glad to hear this or not. 'Shall we call each other if either of us hears from Sigrun?'

She shook her head. 'I don't think I'll hear from her.'

'But if you do . . .' He wondered whether to tell her that Sigrun had thought they could talk to each other. Since meeting Svenja, he had known her to be cautious and unapproachable on some occasions, and almost trusting on others. He didn't know where he was with her, how to get through to her, how to talk to her. He was nervous around her. But he plucked up courage.

'I'd like to see you again. We both love Sigrun, you and I; we both miss her. Do you have a photo of her, by the way? One you could send me? I haven't got one; I don't take photos.'

Svenja opened her handbag and found a photo in her wallet. It was of Sigrun, the age she was when Kaspar had first seen her, standing on a rock in the dirndl-like dress she wore on special occasions; her hair and dress were fluttering in the wind, and she was laughing.

'You can keep it.' Svenja stood. 'Right, I'm off.'

IO

Kaspar thought Sigrun had vanished into thin air, and that if he didn't hear from her, he would never find out where she was.

But at the beginning of the following month, his credit card statement arrived. Sigrun had flown to Australia; she had taken out money in Sydney, stayed in a hostel, eaten a lot of cheap meals in a Chinese restaurant and bought an electric piano. Then she had taken a bus to Brisbane. Had she made friends there with whom she could stay? She hadn't paid for a hostel in Brisbane, and hadn't taken out any money that looked as if it might be to pay rent. Occasionally there was a meal in a restaurant, clearly for more than one person. She hadn't used the card at all in the last week of the month.

And so he accompanied Sigrun month by month until September. She stayed in Brisbane, bought second-hand furniture from a charitable organization, a mattress, a food processor, books, sheet music, and there were regular food purchases from the supermarket. She took out money so seldom that she had to have a job; it was only in September that the withdrawals became more frequent, presumably because she wanted to provide for the period after the card ran out. He had received the new card some time earlier but didn't activate it until the end of September, as late as possible.

Svenja also accompanied Sigrun during her first months in Australia. Whenever a new statement arrived, Kaspar called Svenja and told her the latest. She came to Berlin again as well, just so he could tell her again what had happened before Sigrun left. From her, Kaspar learned that Sigrun had got her passport, without which she would not have been able to fly to Australia, for the youth group trip to Kaliningrad. It was supposed to connect her to the German soil, and had estranged her from it instead. Svenja laughed bitterly. She talked about how much work they had with the new farm, and about Björn, who felt betrayed by Sigrun, didn't even want to hear her name any more, and blamed her, Svenja, for Birgit and for Kaspar and for Sigrun's betrayal. Kaspar offered to let Svenja read Birgit's notes, but she declined: she could imagine what was in them, she said, she didn't need to read them.

They sat on the bench in the park again. Svenja didn't want to go up to the apartment with Kaspar, or to a restaurant. She didn't want to stay long. She was distant, showing neither sadness that Sigrun was gone, nor happiness that she was not wholly lost but had arrived in Australia and was doing all right. She was tired and bitter. Kaspar felt sorry for her. For both their sakes, he wished they could be close, as Sigrun had hoped they would be. He put his arm around her. She didn't pull away, but she didn't accept the gesture, either. She stood, and said again, 'Right, I'm off.' She smiled as she spoke, but the smile did not contain a promise.

Kaspar read. He read about the history of Australia, about Australian society, about Australian literature and painting. That there was an Australian impressionism and expressionism and an Australian Nobel Prize–winner for literature; that lots of actors and musicians were from Australia; that Australia was one of the richest countries in the world. He found all of it interesting. What beautiful paintings the impressionist

Heidelberg School had produced in Melbourne! What lively, original contemporary novels there were! Kaspar enjoyed that sunny October, spending long lunchtimes sitting on his balcony with an Australian book, and it seemed to him that the distance between Berlin and Brisbane grew ever smaller.

From the Internet he learned that there were two conservatoires in Brisbane, the Queensland Conservatorium and the School of Music of the University of Queensland. Sigrun would apply next year, he was sure of it, and he would fly to Australia and find her in one of the two conservatoires. If not in Brisbane, then a conservatoire elsewhere in Australia. There were twelve others; it was manageable, it was doable. When the students gave a concert, as they did in Berlin, he would go and sit in the audience. Or he would simply ask where her classes were and say he would like to listen for a while. The porter would say that wasn't possible, he could be anyone. And he would say he was her grandfather, and the porter would smile and take him to his granddaughter.

A Note from the Translator

In April 2024, shortly after completing my translation of *The Granddaughter*, I traveled to Berlin, where I met Bernhard Schlink for the first time. We had worked together on this book and a previous novel, *Olga*. Bernhard's English is excellent, so once the translations were finished, I would email them to him, he would edit them and send them back, and we discussed any outstanding issues over Zoom in meticulous detail, with various entertaining conversational detours along the way.

Until April, though, we hadn't met in person. Bernhard was slightly surprised when I suggested we visit some of the locations he had written about in the book, but he readily agreed, and we took a taxi to Bebelplatz, the square in front of the Humboldt University where Kaspar and Birgit first meet. It was a crisp spring day, and the buildings glowed in the sun beneath a wide blue Berlin sky. We strolled across the square, past the Staatsoper, and on to the Neue Wache memorial to the victims of war and tyranny, where—as Kaspar shows Sigrun—Käthe Kollwitz's powerful sculpture of the *Mother with her Dead Son* sits alone beneath the oculus, exposed to the elements.

I asked Bernhard about his personal experience of Berlin in the early 1960s. He recounted that he, like Kaspar, had come to Berlin as a student, had been keen to visit the GDR, had attended the Pentecost Meeting of the German Youth in May 1964, and had met a girl, whom he then helped escape to the West. Kaspar's and Birgit's story is not theirs; the beginning of that relationship, the description of the Berlin of that time, the details of Birgit's escape, are based on the author's own experience.

It describes a world, a time, even a country, that no longer exist. Thirty-five years have passed since the fall of the Wall. East Germany, the GDR, is gone; Berlin is a completely different city. The first time I saw the Brandenburg Gate, in 1991, it was surrounded by empty space. This time, I found myself trying, and failing, to map those memories onto the busy roads and tall buildings that occupy the space today.

Yet history seldom confines itself to the past. It reverberates down the years, across generations; it reaches into, shapes, and colors our present, both personally and politically. How we deal with—come to terms with—the past is fundamental to how we live now, and will live in the future. This is a question to which Bernhard Schlink returns, again and again, in his fiction.

Charlotte Collins

BERNHARD SCHLINK was born in Germany in 1944. A professor emeritus of law at Humboldt University, Berlin, and Cardozo Law School, New York, he is the author of the internationally bestselling novels *The Reader*, which became an Oscar-winning film starring Kate Winslet and Ralph Fiennes, and *The Woman on the Stairs*. His latest novel, *Olga*, was a #1 international bestseller. He lives in Berlin and New York.

CHARLOTTE COLLINS studied English Literature at Cambridge University, and was an actor and radio journalist in Germany and the UK before becoming a literary translator. She was awarded the Goethe-Institut's Helen & Kurt Wolff Prize in 2017 for her translation of Robert Seethaler's *A Whole Life*. Other translations include Bernhard Schlink's *Olga*, *The Eighth Life* by Nino Haratischvili and *Darkenbloom* by Eva Menasse.

Here ends Bernhard Schlink's
The Granddaughter.

The first edition of this book was printed
and bound at Lakeside Book Company
in Harrisonburg, Virginia, in December 2024.

A NOTE ON THE TYPE

This novel was set in Bembo, a typeface originally
cut by Francisco Griffo in 1495 and revived by
Stanley Morison in 1929. Named after the Venetian
poet Pietro Bembo (1470-1547), Griffo's original
punch-cut design was a departure from the popular
calligraphic style of the day. Its warm, human touch
would inspire later roman typefaces like Garamond
and Times Roman. Morison, one of the twentieth
century's most influential typographers, reworked
the typeface for typesetting and machine composition. Bembo is noted for its attractiveness on the
page and high legibility, making it a popular choice
for printed matter.

HARPERVIA

An imprint dedicated to publishing international voices,
offering readers a chance to encounter other lives and ⌐
points of view via the language of the imagina